SUNDOWN GIRLS

Also by L.S. Stratton

Not So Perfect Strangers

Do What Godmother Says

SUNDOWN GIRLS

L.S. STRATTON

 Nancy Paulsen Books

NANCY PAULSEN BOOKS
An imprint of Penguin Random House LLC
1745 Broadway, New York, NY 10019
penguinrandomhouse.com

Edited by Stacey Barney
Design by Suki Boynton • Text set in Columbus MT Pro

Library of Congress Cataloging-in-Publication Data
Names: Stratton, L.S. author
Title: Sundown girls / L.S. Stratton.
Description: New York: Nancy Paulsen Books, [2025] | Summary:
Sixteen-year-old Naomi Ward's family vacation in a Virginia town with a violent past turns into a terrifying ordeal when a ghost appears at her window pleading for help, starting Naomi on a chilling search for two missing girls that forces her to confront both local dangers and her own haunting memories.
Identifiers: LCCN 2025037350 (print) | LCCN 2025037351 (ebook) |
ISBN 9798217004942 hardcover | ISBN 9798217004959 ebook
Subjects: CYAC: Missing persons—Fiction | Ghosts—Fiction | Racism—Fiction |
African Americans—Fiction | Mystery and detective stories |
LCGFT: Thrillers (Fiction) | Novels
Classification: LCC PZ7.1.S7755 Su 2025 (print) | LCC PZ7.1.S7755 (ebook)
LC record available at https://lccn.loc.gov/2025037350
LC ebook record available at https://lccn.loc.gov/2025037351

First published in the United States of America by Nancy Paulsen Books, 2026

Manufactured in the United States of America
BVG

ISBN 9798217004942
1st Printing

The authorized representative in the EU for product safety and compliance is Penguin Random House Ireland, Morrison Chambers, 32 Nassau Street, Dublin D02 YH68, Ireland, https://eu-contact.penguin.ie.

To Dad, for spurring my love of all things that go bump in the night.

To Great-grandma, for teaching me that there is nothing to fear from the dead.

–NOTE TO THE READER–

This book includes mentions of murder, racism, kidnapping, and lynching.

When the sun goes down in a sundown town
Be wise and beware.
When the sun goes down in a sundown town
Make sure you are scarce.
For when the sun goes down in a sundown town,
Only the foolhardy stay there.

—From the Introduction of *Sparksburg: A Dark History of a Sundown Town* by Joshua Ellington

THEY'D SAT IN THE DARK FOR SO LONG THAT NAOMI lost track of how long it had been. It was pitch-black down here, so black that she couldn't even see her own hand inches from her face. She couldn't see the other girls either, though she knew they were here. The two girls that were living—and the silent girl who was always watching.

Naomi could hear the others. A soft whimper. Shuffling footsteps and the clink of metal. The chanting whisper of "I wanna go home. I wanna go home. I just want to go home."

"Shut up! Shut up!" one whispered. "No one's going anywhere. We're *never* leaving. Don't you get it?"

Naomi could smell the others, too. It was an overwhelming stench that permeated the hot basement . . . or cellar . . . whatever *room* this was, which seemed both stiflingly claustrophobic and mind-numbingly vast. The smell was an acrid mix of armpits that had gone way too long without antiperspirant, sweat, a used, overflowed toilet, menstrual blood—and desperation. She hadn't known before that desperation had a smell, but it radiated off her skin in invisible waves.

Then suddenly there was the bang of a door opening and a shaft of light. It came from above, through floorboards. Naomi winced at its brightness and held up her hand again. This time to shield her eyes. She could finally see a little. One of the girls was a year or so younger than herself. She was partially illuminated by the tiny spotlight now. It showed her matted dark hair, a dirty, swollen pale cheek, and terrified brown eyes.

Naomi instantly recognized her, though she looked different down here. She was relieved to finally spot a familiar face.

Naomi opened her mouth to call out to her, but stopped short when they heard thudding footsteps over their heads and the slight groan of wood under heavy weight.

The girl started to whimper, "No, no, no, no, no," before letting out a sob.

This time no one told her to shut up.

He'd been gone for so long, but now he was back. The Big Bad Wolf had returned home to feast on his little pigs. He was coming for one of them, and Naomi suspected it was her.

So this was how it would end. Naomi had lived most of her life as a missing girl without even realizing it. As fate would have it, she would die as a missing girl, too.

The shaft of light flickered as the thudding footsteps finally stopped. Naomi held her breath. The muscles in her body tensed as they waited. She could feel bile rising in the back of her throat.

"No, no, no, no! No! No! Nooooo!" the brown-eyed girl screamed over and over again as the trapdoor overhead was thrown open.

THREE WEEKS EARLIER . . .

2

"CAM."

"Cam!"

"Camryn!"

Naomi felt one of her headphones being tugged from her ear. She looked up to find Dawn standing at her side, waving and gazing down at her.

She quickly shut her notebook.

Dawn hadn't seen what she was writing, had she? Naomi certainly hoped not.

She tossed her pen aside, took her headphones off, and dropped them onto her lap. "Huh?"

"Sorry," Dawn said with a slight smile. "Didn't mean to startle you, honey, but you didn't hear me when I was calling you."

No, you weren't calling me, Naomi thought, *because that's not my name.*

But she didn't want to start another argument, to see that hurt look in Dawn's eyes yet again, so she shook her head instead.

"Yeah, sorry. I was . . . listening to music."

She could feel the thump of the bass through her headphones on her thigh like the buzz of a bumblebee's wings.

She was always listening to music nowadays. In the Stoakes

family household, Naomi was subjected to a constant barrage of sounds: the bouncing of a basketball on the court outside her bedroom window, the bark of their dog, the thumping of feet up and down wooden stairs, video game explosions on television speakers, and loud phone conversations. It made her miss the days when she could simply read, write, or sketch in that two-bedroom apartment on Berwyn Street with nothing but the faint sound of street traffic outside her window or her mom's jazz playing through her bedroom door.

Naomi figured if she could no longer control where she lived or whom she lived with, she could at least attempt to control the noises that reached her ears.

"Okay, well. We're leaving in the next fifteen minutes." Dawn pointed to the gray suitcase now sitting open at the foot of Naomi's four-poster bed. "Make sure you've packed everything. Where we're going, there won't be a lot of stores around. It's about a thirty-minute drive to the nearest mall."

"Uh, yeah." Naomi shot to her feet and padded barefoot to her suitcase. "Yeah. I've got it. I'm good."

If there was one thing she did well, it was pack thoroughly and quickly. She'd done it enough times in her life that she was a champion at it.

Dawn inclined her head. "That top looks really cute on you. I guess I got it in the right size. I wasn't sure since it looked a little small."

Naomi looked down at herself. It was a pale yellow tank top with silver beading on the seams. It wasn't her style at all, but she had to admit it complemented her sun-kissed skin that was already deepening to a burnt umber in early summer. She'd worn the shirt as a peace offering, to show she was making an effort—like her therapist had encouraged.

It seemed to make Dawn happy to see her wearing it. She

wore a proud grin, revealing the slight gap between her two front teeth—a gap identical to Naomi's.

It always unnerved Naomi how much they looked alike: both petite and curvy with big, curly hair that Dawn usually flat-ironed but Naomi tamed with enough conditioner and brushing that she could put it into a single braid down her back.

"It fits fine," Naomi said.

"You know, I saw a shirt just like it in another color," Dawn continued. "In blue. I could get you that one, too, if . . . if you'd like, sweetheart."

"Oh, yeah, umm, sure," she said, shifting around the pile of socks on top of the clothes in her suitcase. "Thanks, Dawn."

She zipped the suitcase closed and turned to find Dawn's grin had faded. That hurt look was in her brown eyes again.

"Okay, well," Dawn said, blinking, "just make sure you're down in fifteen."

She backed out of Naomi's bedroom, leaving Naomi to stare blankly after her.

What'd I do now?

As if on cue, Naomi heard the sound of plastic wheels rolling over hardwood. Naomi soon spotted Maya, Dawn's oldest kid and soon-to-be Spelman freshman, standing in her doorway, dragging an oversize bubblegum-pink suitcase behind her with one hand. A matching carry-on bag dangled from her other elbow. Gold-rimmed aviator sunglasses were perched atop her long bohemian braids. She wore a spaghetti-strapped white eyelet mini-sundress and canvas platform sandals, showing off her long, coltish legs.

The Stoakes family and Naomi were headed to a secluded cabin in the Shenandoah Valley and Maya was decked out like they were about to take a cruise liner to Cabo.

She glared at Naomi from the doorway.

"What?" Naomi snapped, flapping her arms and glaring right back at her.

It wasn't like the two of them usually spoke anyway. Maya barely had anything to say to her nowadays that wasn't accompanied by a droll eye roll.

When Naomi moved in, everything had been awkward and stilted between them, like roommates at summer camp assigned the same bunk. Maya had tried a little at first to make Naomi feel at home, like one of them. She'd offer to do Naomi's makeup or invited her to hang out with her and her friends after school, but when Maya saw that Naomi wasn't warming up to her or the rest of the family like they'd hoped, she gave up.

Now Maya's aloofness had morphed into full-on loathing.

And the feeling's mutual, Naomi thought.

"Why do you keep calling Mom that?" Maya asked.

"Calling her what? I don't know what you're talking about."

"*Dawn!* You called her Dawn. It's so disrespectful. We're all going on this stupid trip to butthole Virginia because of *you,* and you can't even call her Mom, Camryn? Because she is your real mother . . . *our* mother, or did you forget again?" Maya sucked her teeth and slowly shook her head. "You're so fucked up."

She stomped away with the squeak of suitcase wheels. After a few seconds, Naomi fell back onto her bed. She sighed.

Maya was right. She was fucked up. But it wasn't her fault.

3

"ALL ABOARD!" ANDRE CALLED CHEERFULLY OVER the roof of the Range Rover. Like Maya, he was tall and lanky, funding his undergrad education decades ago on a basketball scholarship.

Andre climbed into the front seat just as Naomi hopped inside, taking her place in the back seat next to nine-year-old Blake. She slammed the car door closed behind her.

"Are you guys ready to go?" Andre asked.

It certainly seemed like it. Blake was already engrossed with his handheld. His thumbs flew at warp speed, zapping zombies on-screen. Maya was near the passenger window on the other side of the SUV, taking pouty-lipped videos of herself that she would later post.

She'd become a bit of an influencer in the past year, capitalizing on the public's fascination with the Stoakes family and Naomi, "their long-lost missing daughter," according to the piece a *Newsweek* reporter had written about them. Maya saw her small following spike to more than eighty thousand when the family's story became national news. She'd even gotten a few five-figure offers for makeup and clothing sponsorships, but Andre and Dawn had drawn the line at that.

"If we're rejecting movie and book deals," Andre had argued, "our kids damn sure aren't gonna make money off of it. I refuse to be the dancing clown in this circus. We're going to get back to *normal* lives."

Maybe the Stoakeses could, but Naomi couldn't.

She wished every day she could get back to her old life. That the police hadn't come knocking at her door a year and a half ago and put her mom in handcuffs and Naomi in the back of a police cruiser. If she could have one superpower, it would be the ability to rewind the clock and erase that moment when the cops told her the truth: that her "mother" had kidnapped her and she was the missing baby girl that Dawn and Andre had spent more than a decade searching for and had given up for dead.

But Naomi couldn't turn back time or delete the past, which was why she was stuck here watching Andre in full dad mode as the family navigator.

He'd put air in the tires that morning and checked the first aid emergency kit—*twice.* Naomi now watched as Andre tapped on the car's dashboard screen to adjust the temperature and map out the route to the cabin. He probably had a preloaded playlist as well. Maybe he had even planned the list of activities that would help them finally bond as a family, though Naomi wasn't very optimistic.

Three weeks of hiking, kayaking, and toasting marshmallows couldn't erase the past—*her* past, in particular.

"I can't get a yes or no, guys?" Andre chided playfully. His blithe attitude was starting to grate on Naomi's nerves. "Huh? Y'all just gonna leave me hanging?"

"They're ready, Dre," Dawn said before adjusting her sunglasses. "We're all ready. Let's just go, honey, okay?"

Unlike her husband, Dawn looked resigned, not cheerful. Naomi wondered if she was the reason for that.

Mom.

It's Mom, not Dawn.

She's my mom, she silently practiced as Andre adjusted the rearview mirror, where an air freshener with the symbols of his college fraternity, Omega Psi Phi, dangled. He backed out their driveway.

But after more than a year and a half of living with the Stoakeses . . . *scratch that* . . . living with her *real* family, Naomi still had a hard time thinking of Dawn as Mom, Andre as Dad, Maya as her sister, and Blake as her brother—even if it were all true. And she still had a hard time accepting her name as Camryn. Not after she'd lived as Naomi Ward for so long. Almost fifteen years. Calling herself "Camryn Stoakes" and Dawn "Mom," felt like a betrayal to her mother, the woman who had raised her.

But Mom isn't really my mother. She never was.

"So where are we going again, Dad?" Maya asked, lowering her phone and slumping back into her seat. "I know it's some run-down cabin in Virginia, but where in Virginia exactly?"

"It is *not* a run-down cabin. Your mama and I paid a pretty penny for a nice vacation rental that was built only two years ago, baby. The town is called Sparksburg."

"Sparksburg?" Maya snorted. "Sounds like redneck country."

For once, Naomi had to agree with her.

"Maybe it was a long time ago, but it's going through renewal," Andre said. "From what I understand it's trying to become a hot new tourist spot in the Blue Ridge Mountains."

"Is there a TV where I can set up my games, Dad?" Blake asked.

"We're going all the way to the mountains of Virginia, and you want to play your stupid video games?" Maya replied with a lip curl.

"They're not stupid!" Blake yelled. "You're stupid!"

"You guys, please don't start." Dawn groaned. "This is going to be a very long trip if you're fighting the entire time."

Their dog, Teddy Bear, or Bear for short, a Chow Chow mix, started to bark and pant in his crate.

"Bear, quiet down," Andre said. "Great. Now y'all got the dog riled up, too."

"How is Bear barking my fault?" Maya lamented, pointing at her chest.

"This is gonna be fun," Naomi whispered before grabbing her noise-cancellation headphones and tugging them onto her ears again, resigning herself to the long three weeks ahead.

NAOMI CLOSED THE HARDBACK SHE WAS READING and put it in her satchel next to her notebook. She rested her elbow on the doorframe and pressed her forehead against the cool glass of the passenger window. They'd been driving for more than an hour and were finally in the mountains.

She looked at the scenery—what little scenery there was. Naomi had expected giant rock faces or deep, murky hollows. Instead, the highway was lined on both sides by a constant march of 10-foot-tall concrete barriers and trees. Rows upon rows of trees.

Naomi stared at the canopy above. They'd left the sunshine back in Maryland. There were now nothing but gray skies overhead. She wondered if it would be raining by the time they arrived at the cabin.

Great way to start a vacation, she thought before cracking open her novel again.

"Hey, Cam," Andre said, glancing at her in the rearview mirror, "I don't mind you reading for fun, but I hope you brought those geometry and chemistry textbooks and study guides Mom got you. It'll help you when you head back to school in a couple of months. Gotta bring up those grades, kid. No more C minuses and D pluses."

Naomi stiffened. "I don't need help."

"Dad was just making the suggestion, honey," Dawn said, nudging her husband's knee. "We're on vacation. You don't have to do homework out here. The point is to chill. Relax. We'll worry about grades in September."

"But I don't need help," Naomi repeated, feeling her neck grow hot and not just because it was sweltering in the back seat. "I told you guys, I don't need those workbooks."

When she was homeschooled, Naomi had been a straight-A student and scored high on PSATs, but her grades tanked when she moved in with the Stoakeses. It wasn't just the fact that she was now in a new place with brand-new people—or that this was the first time in her life that she'd ever gone to a real school with teachers, classrooms, and crowded hallways, but because she couldn't fade into the background and be like all the other students, even if she tried. Not a day went by at her locker or in the lunchroom when she didn't notice someone staring and pointing at her, or kids would just walk up to her, wanting to know her life's story.

"What was it like to be kidnapped? Were you scared?"

Who could possibly focus on calculating the hypotenuse or memorizing the periodic table when you had that to deal with?

Naomi opened her mouth to say as much, to defend herself, but winced when she felt a knobby elbow jab her in the ribs.

"Oww! Could you move over, please?" Naomi asked Blake, who was staring at his handheld again and squirming in the seat beside her.

"Nope. Stay right where you are, Blake," Maya ordered, before eyeing Naomi over Blake's curly head. "You're not sending him over here. He's been leaning on me for the past twenty minutes. Let him lean on you for once."

"There's nowhere to go!" Blake whined, squirming even

more. Naomi cried out as one of his Air Jordans landed on her exposed toes. She knew she shouldn't have worn sandals. "I'm stuck in the middle between you guys."

"Just a little more patience, kids. We're going to reach a rest stop soon," Dawn said, turning to look at them from the front seat. "Then everyone can get out and stretch."

"*And* use the bathroom," Andre muttered. "It was a mistake to have all that damn coffee."

Five minutes later, Naomi spotted a roadway sign announcing that a rest stop exit would be coming up in a half mile. Soon after, they took a bumpy ramp that led them to a smog-filled parking lot that overflowed with cars, RVs, several tour buses, and tractor trailers. As soon as Andre pulled into one of the empty parking spaces sandwiched between a battered Jeep and a cherry-red Ford Mustang, they all scrambled to unbuckle their seat belts and throw open their car doors.

"Use the restroom and get some snacks, but I want everyone back here in twenty minutes. You hear me? *Twenty minutes!*" Andre shouted over the roadway noise as the kids hopped out of the car. "Not twenty-five or twenty-three or twenty-two. *Twenty!* If you aren't back by then, we're leavin' without you."

"No, we are not," Dawn said firmly. "But if you're not back by then, we *will* come looking for you."

Naomi didn't know if it was her imagination, but she swore Dawn had given her a pointed look over the rims of her sunglasses when she said that. Dawn then opened the hatchback to take Bear for a walk and his own bathroom break.

Meanwhile, Andre and Blake raced toward the rest stop facility while Maya whipped out her phone, which was already beeping insistently. She tapped a green button on-screen and leaned back against one of the SUV's doors.

"Hey, Troy," she gushed to her boyfriend, who was now

grinning on her screen. "I'm *so* bored, babe. What are you doing now? Are you headed to Shawn's house?"

Naomi tossed the strap of her satchel over her head and shoved her hands into the pockets of her hoodie. She was in search of a ladies' room. It was probably too hot outside to wear a hoodie but the gray skies from earlier were giving way to a blanket of angry, dark clouds. She didn't want to get caught in a downpour with nothing to cover her head when she walked back to the car.

Naomi trailed after Andre and Blake to the large, one-story building several feet away but paused when she caught the faint whiff of something foul. It made her cringe.

She checked the bottom of her sandals to make sure she hadn't accidentally stepped in any dog poop. Except for a few scuffs and a wad of gum, her sandal bottoms were clean. She glanced at the grass and sidewalks around her but didn't see anything there either.

Besides, the odor didn't seem like it came from what you'd find in a toilet. Naomi had smelled something similar years ago one summer. For more than a week, her mom had tried to figure out the source of the awful stench, searching the bushes in their yard, digging through closets and cabinets, and even checking the space behind the refrigerator in search of rotting food or a dead mouse. Finally, she found a cat had died while trapped in a sewer drain behind the basement apartment they were renting.

When their neighbor pulled it out, they could see the cat's matted fur was covered with fruit flies and maggots. The flesh underneath had gone purple and green in some spots like rotted fruit. Naomi had turned away and fled indoors from the sight of it. But Naomi could still smell it in their apartment. She had an object to match with the smell, making it even more vivid and the rankness was almost unbearable.

Naomi now stared over her shoulder at the rest stop parking lot. Something was dead and rotting out here. Maybe along the highway or in the neighboring woods. She thought again of the dead cat, of its discolored flesh being feasted on by maggots, and she shivered in revulsion.

She stepped through the glass doors into the freezing, air-conditioned interior to escape the odor, pushing the dead cat to the back of her mind.

After zigzagging her way through other travelers who were buying pizza and burgers at the fast food counters or browsing through the gift shop filled with *Virginia Is for Lovers* T-shirts, Naomi found the bathrooms. Luckily, the line to the ladies' room was short. Naomi quickly relieved her bladder, washed her hands, and saw she still had fifteen minutes to spare before Andre would do a family roll call back at the car.

She wandered into the gift shop to look around. Her eyes landed on the bookshelves first. She had about four novels in her satchel and suitcase and two downloaded on her iPad. They were mostly fantasies set in Africa and Asia—more books than she could ever read in three weeks.

But it won't hurt to get another if it sounds good, she thought as she examined the book covers and flipped a few over to read the blurbs on the back.

Unable to find a novel in the gift shop that wasn't about the Civil War or famous Virginia landmarks, Naomi wandered to the jewelry display case that showed earrings, bracelets, and necklaces made with pieces of stalactites from nearby caverns. She was holding up one of the necklaces, marveling at how it twinkled in the overhead lights, when through the windows a bolt of lightning etched its way across the dark sky. Naomi flinched as a booming crack of thunder followed soon after.

The few trees dotting the parking lot all bent in unison with the blast of the wind, as if they were spectators at a stadium doing the wave. Within seconds, buckets and buckets of rain were falling, sending everyone in the rest stop parking lot racing to get to their cars, like a starting gun had been fired. She jumped at the second boom of thunder.

She'd been terrified of thunderstorms as a little girl. She had envisioned lightning as a predator searching for her, waiting to strike. She imagined thunder as its angry roar.

Naomi remembered crying out one night when she was five or six years old and her mom rushing into her bedroom.

"You don't have to be scared, honey," her mom had assured her, holding her close. "It'll pass. Count to ten with me. And as you count, the gaps between the thunder will get longer and longer. That means it's getting farther and farther away. Count with me, NayNay," she'd said, squeezing her tighter. "One . . . two . . ."

"Three," Naomi had whispered with her. "Four . . ." She'd squeezed her eyes shut when she heard the boom.

Of course, thanks to high school science classes, she now knew that lightning was never stalking her. It wasn't a supernatural creature that growled and roared in the dark. Lightning was the product of electrical charges that built up in clouds during a storm. Thunder was simply the sound of the thermal expansion of plasma as it slices its way through the air. But that didn't stop her from flinching with each crack of thunder, or the hairs from standing up on the back of her neck.

Naomi closed her eyes and began to silently count. "One . . . two . . . three . . ."

"Whoa, it's mad crazy out there," a deep voice said from over her shoulder with a laugh, making her eyes flutter open. "Look at all those people running!"

She turned to see a guy her age, maybe a couple of years older, peering out the windows at the downpour.

Abruptly, all thoughts of thunder and lightning disappeared.

The guy was cute. *Really* cute. And at least a foot taller than her. He had deep brown skin, broad shoulders, a goatee, and the longest lashes she'd ever seen on a boy. When he smiled, she saw he had dimples, too.

"Yeah, it's . . . it's crazy," Naomi mumbled, feeling tongue-tied. She always did when she talked to guys, particularly cuties like this one.

She'd never had a real boyfriend; her mom hadn't allowed her to go on dates, saying that she was still too young. And Naomi had barely kissed anyone—unless you counted Darren Marple, who she'd kissed at the neighborhood playground back when she was ten years old, and it had been so awkward Naomi wished she could forget it.

The guy tilted his head. "I know this probably sounds like I'm lying just so I could have a reason to talk to you but . . . do I know you? I feel like I've seen you somewhere before. You don't go to Charles Duvall High School in Harrisonburg, do you?"

No, Naomi most certainly did not go to Charles Duvall High.

He'd probably seen a story about her on the news or the web. He'd inevitably ask her all the invasive and inappropriate questions she was used to strangers asking when they realized she was the infamous Naomi Ward / Camryn Stoakes, the girl who went missing for fifteen years.

"No, I don't. I don't even know where that is. Sorry," she said, glancing at the entrance, prepared to make her hasty exit before he recognized her.

"Nah, that's cool." He shrugged and leaned against a case where Virginia state–shaped key chains were displayed. "I guess you just look like somebody I know. You're probably not even from around here if you don't know where Harrisonburg is."

"No, I'm from Maryland. We're just passing through. We're headed to Sparksburg for a family vacation."

"Yo, my nana lives near Sparksburg! We're headed there to visit her, too."

"This is the first summer for us. My . . . my dad," Naomi said, forcing herself to say the word, "is renting a cabin in a new community up there."

"I think I know what you're talking about. I remember when those cabins were being built. My uncle's a carpenter and worked over there. He said they're really nice." He looked her up and down. "Your family must be hella rich to get one of those cabins."

"Not really," she mumbled, lowering her eyes and fidgeting with the zipper on her satchel.

Though the truth was the Stoakeses had more money than most families.

Andre was an orthodontist. Dawn was a lawyer. They'd gone to good schools and came from nice families. They were the kind of Black people that the guy W. E. B. Du Bois would have called the "Talented Tenth" a hundred years ago. The Stoakeses lived in a five-bedroom colonial in Silver Spring, Maryland, drove nice cars, and gave their kids almost anything they wanted. It had been yet another adjustment for Naomi, who had grown up in small apartments with a single mom who lived on such a tight budget that, some months, it meant choosing between buying groceries or paying the electric bill.

"My name is Khalil, by the way," he said. "I probably should've told you that by now."

"It's okay. I didn't introduce myself either. I'm . . . I'm Naomi."

She waited for his expression to change, for his mouth to fall open and his eyes to grow big. Would he finally make out who she was? Would he be fascinated to meet a real-life celebrity or pity her for her sad life story? But he did neither; his smile stayed in place.

"Cool, cool, cool." Khalil gave another nod. "Nice to meet you, Naomi. Look, uh"—he started to gnaw his bottom lip—"I don't know how long you'll be in Sparksburg, but you know, I could show you around sometime if you want."

Was he asking her out? She tucked a stray lock of hair behind her ear. Her cheeks went warm. "That . . . uh . . . that could be nice."

"Can you give me your number so we can set something up?" he asked, handing her his cell.

"My . . . my number?"

"Yeah, your number." He squinted. "You have one, don't you?"

She looked down at his screen, struggling to remember her own cell phone number for a few seconds. She was so nervous. After a few tries, she typed it in and handed his phone back to him.

"I'll text you in a couple days," he said. "I know this—"

His words were cut short when they both heard someone scream, "Camryn! Camryn!" at the top of their lungs outside the gift shop in the rest area's main concourse. It sounded like Dawn. "Camryn, where are you?"

Naomi grimaced as her phone buzzed. She already knew who was calling her. *Twenty minutes.* She was supposed to return to the car in twenty minutes.

If you don't, we'll come looking for you. It looked like Dawn was making good on that promise.

"I'm sorry, Khalil, but I have to go," Naomi said, rushing past him out of the store, following the sound of Dawn's voice.

5

"CAMRYN!" DAWN YELLED INTO HER PHONE. "Camryn, where the hell are you?"

Several of the people in the concourse were staring at Dawn as she whipped around in circles. She looked frantic, almost in tears. Her long hair was wet and pasted to her forehead. Her clothes were drenched, like she had been running in the rain.

"H-h-have you seen my daughter?" Dawn said, rushing to a couple who walked by, heading toward the double doors leading outside. "She looks a lot like me. Sh-she . . . she's sixteen and was wearing a . . . a yellow top and jean shorts. She's about five foot two and . . . and—"

"Dawn, I'm right here," Naomi said, jogging across the concourse. "I'm right here!"

Dawn whipped around again. When she saw Naomi, she exhaled. Her face . . . her entire body sank with relief. Dawn reached out and abruptly tugged Naomi against her. She squeezed her tight.

People were staring at them both now. Naomi stood awkwardly in Dawn's arms, aware of their gazes and grimacing at the fierceness of Dawn's hug and the clammy wetness now pressed against her.

"Oh my God! We waited for you, and you—you didn't come

back," Dawn whispered against her ear. "I thought you were . . . I thought you had . . ."

Her words drifted off. Naomi knew what Dawn wanted to say, but couldn't.

I thought you were gone.

We thought you had run away again.

She'd only done it once before, five months ago, after her mom was sentenced to twenty years in prison for kidnapping, and Dawn and Andre had been relieved—no, *elated* by the news.

"She's going away for a very long time, honey," Dawn had told her when they arrived home from the sentencing hearing, like Naomi should be elated as well.

"Not long enough, if you ask me! That piece of sh—I mean garbage should be in jail even longer after what she did to us," Andre had said. "She took our daughter away from us. We'll never get those years and sleepless nights back. Never!"

It had all felt so heartless, listening to them talk about her mom that way. She was stuck with these people. The life she once knew was over. Things could never go back to the way they'd been.

A few days later, Naomi took a metro to Union Station in Washington, DC, after stealing sixty-four dollars from Andre's wallet. She didn't know where she would go from there.

Back to her old apartment three states away? There was nothing for her there anymore.

Take the train, then hitchhike to the federal prison where her mom now sat in a jail cell? They would never let her inside for a visit even if she managed to make it there.

Naomi considered other cities, other places where she could start over, but none seemed practical. Where would she live? How would she take care of herself?

In the past, her mom had always been the one with the plan,

who knew where they would go next and how they would live. Now she had to make those decisions all on her own and in no way did she feel prepared to do it.

Naomi wandered the train station for hours. After ignoring Dawn's and Andre's frantic texts and phone calls, she finally texted them back when the train station and metro closed and she saw she didn't have enough for a cab ride to their house. She told them where she was.

They drove into the city to get her. They drove back to Maryland in silence. In the days following, neither Dawn nor Andre asked her why she'd gone to Union Station. She assumed they already knew the answer.

"I'm sorry. I was in the gift shop talking to someone. I just . . . I just lost track of time," Naomi now explained. "You didn't have to worry."

Just as abruptly as Dawn pulled her into a hug, she shoved Naomi away, glaring at her.

"*Didn't have to worry?* We didn't have to worry?" Dawn asked, looking furious. "You know what we've been through! Do you know the toll it's taken on us? We said to be back at the car in twenty minutes and you didn't come back! Why would you do something like this, Camryn?"

"I'm sorry," Naomi said feebly.

Dawn closed her eyes. She took a slow, deep breath, making her nostrils flare. She finally hung up her phone. "Just . . . let's just get to the car. Everyone is waiting."

Dawn headed back toward the doors.

Naomi glanced over her shoulder to find Khalil standing in the doorway of the gift shop. She gave him an awkward wave goodbye before pulling her hood over her head, and following Dawn into the rain.

"YOU FOUND HER!" ANDRE SAID AS DAWN AND NAOMI climbed inside the SUV. "I knew she was in there somewhere. Where'd you go, kid? Got stuck in the pretzel-dog line?" He turned to face his wife. "Where'd you find her, honey?"

Dawn didn't respond. Instead, she stared at the pouring rain and rhythmic swish of the windshield wipers.

"Ooookay," Andre said before backing out of the parking space and pointing them toward the highway. He turned on his R&B playlist instead of asking any more questions.

Good decision, Dre, Naomi thought as a saxophone, drums, and a soul singer's falsetto filled her ears.

No one talked, with the exception of Blake, who ranted nonstop about a new video game that was coming out later that summer that he would die, just *literally die,* if Dawn and Andre didn't buy it for him.

Naomi was getting used to these types of family car rides with heavy silences between her, Dawn, and Andre. The weight of the words they didn't dare say would hang in the air like an oppressive fog. But Blake and Maya seemed oblivious to the tension between Naomi and their parents.

Or maybe not, Naomi thought as she looked up from the fantasy novel she was trying to read despite the knot tightening in her belly. She found Maya glowering at her across the back seat.

Naomi shifted and tried to focus on her book, but it was hard now that she felt like she was under the hot spotlight of Maya's glare.

Maya knew their mother was upset, and once again, Naomi was the reason.

Naomi suspected that if that day at Union Station she'd settled on a city, paid the ticket, boarded a train, and disappeared from the Stoakeses' lives forever, Maya wouldn't have minded at all. In fact, she would have been thrilled.

They took an exit off the main highway and found themselves on a deserted road. Deserted except for a large pickup truck that took the exit with them.

Was the truck headed to the cabins, too?

"Dre, slow down, please," Dawn said several minutes later, making Naomi look up from her book again just as the warrior's quest into the cursed forest was about to begin. "It's raining and you're driving way too fast."

"I would, baby, but it's a one-lane road and whoever is behind us is riding my ass right now." Andre's eyes flickered to the rearview mirror.

Naomi looked through the rear window. She couldn't see well through the downpour and Bear's crate, but she could see it was the same black pickup truck still following them. The truck was so close that most of the details of the car and even the face of the driver was lost in the glare of its headlights reflecting off the glass.

Andre had his headlights on too because of the low visibility in the rain.

"Why are you going *faster*?" Dawn asked. "Slow down, Dre."

"I told you why," Andre said. There was a tighter edge to his voice this time. "They're pushing me down the road and there's no room to pull over."

"This is what happens in redneck country," Maya muttered,

crossing her arms over her chest. "We're about to get killed."

"Maya," Dawn said, giving her a death stare, "you're not helping."

"Just take the shoulder and go around us if you're in such a damn hurry!" Andre shouted at his rearview mirror.

But the driver behind them didn't. Instead, they started to lay on their horn. Bear began barking then. The cacophony drowned out the sound of Andre's music, making Naomi clap her hands over her ears.

"Dad," Blake whimpered, slumping low in the seat. He squeezed his eyes shut.

The beeping was getting more insistent now as the driver in the truck drew even closer. Naomi swore she could feel the vibrations of the truck's engine through the rear of the car. The vehicles were so close that their bumpers were practically kissing.

"Andre, *you* take the shoulder!" Dawn yelled. "Just let them through. Get out of their way!"

Andre whipped the wheel, pulling them suddenly to the right, making Maya and Blake slam into Naomi as she collided with the passenger door. They all cried out with a chorus of screams and squeals. Even Bear let out a scared yip.

The car skidded to a stop. Naomi winced, terrified that they would hydroplane, that they'd go off the road entirely and end up somewhere in the trees or even flip over. But the tires connected with gravel and twigs and regained traction. She opened her eyes to see that they were still upright and the pickup truck had sailed past them. It continued down the road with its angry red lights receding behind a sheet of rain.

"Jesus." Dawn exhaled. She held her hand against her chest.

Naomi wondered if Dawn's heart was racing as fast as her own.

Andre turned to gaze at them. "Y'all okay?"

"Barely," Maya murmured before shifting back to her side of the car.

"Yeah," Blake said.

Naomi gave a shaky nod.

He turned to his wife. "I'm gonna check on Bear."

Naomi watched as Andre hopped out into the rain and opened the hatchback. All the while, she kept her eyes fixed on the road where the truck had disappeared.

Would the pickup truck return? Why had the driver done that? Were they trying to make them crash?

"Sorry for the drama, everybody," Andre said about a minute later after he climbed back into the driver's seat. "It'll be smooth sailing from this point on. I promise." He buckled his seat belt and started driving again.

Naomi clutched her book against her like it was a shield.

She hoped Andre could make good on his promise.

"WE'RE HERE," ANDRE ANNOUNCED OVER THE crunch of gravel.

It was just after one o'clock, though it felt a lot later.

They'd left the paved road miles back and taken a series of mud and dirt roads for the past ten minutes, bringing them to a small hilltop where Naomi saw a wooden sign with the words CABIN 18 along the roadside.

"Told you guys the cabin was nice," he said.

"Where is it?" Blake asked, pushing himself up in the leather seat so that he could see over Maya's shoulder.

"What do you mean, 'Where is it?' It's down there!" Andre said with a laugh, pointing. "It's a two-story, two-thousand-square-foot building. How could you miss it?"

Naomi looked in the direction that everyone else was now gazing. She squinted. The cabin did look big—what little of it she could see at this vantage point through the rain and the mist.

The cabin sat nestled in a clearing surrounded by trees and what looked like acres of forest land. It was a real log cabin with an intersecting gabled roof, a wide wraparound porch, and lots and lots of windows. As they drew closer, Naomi saw the rear of the house was almost entirely made of glass—floor-to-ceiling windows on the first floor, arched windows perched above, on the second. Now, with all the lights out, the interior of the cabin was as black as slate. The top windows looked like two big black eyes peering at them through the fog.

Taking it all in, *nice* wasn't quite the word Naomi would use to describe the cabin. *Off-putting* would better describe it; the cabin didn't look like a welcoming haven at all. Andre brought the car to a stop near the porch stairs.

"All right, crew. Let's head inside," Andre said, clapping his hands. "We can unload later when the rain stops. For now, pick out your rooms. Maya, Cam, and Blake, y'all are upstairs. Mom and I are in the master bedroom on the first floor."

"I call dibs on the biggest room!" Blake shouted as he practically climbed into Naomi's lap to get to the passenger door.

"No, you don't!" Maya yelled back, flinging her door open.

Naomi grimaced and shifted out of the way to let Blake through. She watched as he raced his sister up the stairs. Naomi choked back a laugh as Maya wobbled on her platforms, almost twisting an ankle in an effort to beat her brother.

"Wait! You don't even have a key to get inside," Dawn cried with exasperation, opening her umbrella and trudging through the mud after them.

Naomi lingered in the car, halfway in and halfway out, gazing at the woods around the cabin.

She raised her hand to cover her nose.

There was that stench again. It was more powerful here than it'd been at the rest stop. She could practically taste it on her tongue, like curdled milk.

"Ugh! What is that smell?"

"What smell?" Andre asked.

Naomi blinked at him. He stood under the hatchback door, watching her.

"You really can't smell that?" she exclaimed. "It's disgusting! It's like . . . like roadkill."

He shook his head. "No. Definitely don't smell roadkill. I don't smell anything but wet grass and Bear back here." He shrugged. "Maybe you're picking up the smell of someone's garbage or a septic tank from one of the neighbors' cabins."

What neighbors?

She thought Andre had said that other families had rented time-shares around here. Why couldn't she see anyone else? Hear anyone else? All she saw was pines, oaks, and shadows. All she heard was the pelting of raindrops on the car roof and crickets chirping.

Where the hell is *everybody?*

"Go ahead inside, Cam," he urged as he unloaded Bear from his crate. "Don't let your brother and sister get all the good rooms. You leave it up to those two, and you'll end up sleeping in the broom closet." He chuckled.

Naomi nodded before hopping out of the car and heading up the porch stairs to the front door, which now stood open.

Dawn had turned on all the lights, revealing the cabin's interior. It was fully furnished with leather sofas and chairs, faux calfskin rugs, a dining room table, and two gargantuan bronze chandeliers that hung from the two-story ceiling in the great room. It had a stone fireplace and a modern eat-in kitchen. A metal spiral staircase near the dining area led to the second floor, where she could already hear Blake and Maya arguing.

Naomi turned to the windows that seemed even bigger from the inside. She saw Andre walking Bear through the rain.

Though the isolation of the property was eerie, at least it afforded them some privacy. The trees kept Naomi from feeling completely exposed, like a goldfish in a fishbowl with nowhere to hide. But who would she need to hide from?

Naomi's thoughts hearkened back to the pickup truck and

those angry red lights. Maybe this wasn't exactly "redneck country" like Maya kept saying, but obviously not everyone out here was friendly.

She walked toward the spiral staircase but paused when she passed the master bedroom. Dawn stood with her hands on her hips, staring off into space. Suddenly Dawn closed her eyes, as if she was overwhelmed. She sat down on the bed, dropped her head into her hands, and stayed that way, not moving.

Did she have a headache? Was something wrong?

Naomi considered calling out to her, asking if she needed anything. Should she get Andre? But she hesitated.

We're all going on this stupid trip to butthole Virginia because of you.

You know what we've been through! Do you know the toll it's taken on us?

The only thing that equaled the longing Naomi had for her mother and her old life was the constant guilt she felt for disappointing Dawn and Andre, for not being the daughter they'd hoped and expected her to be. It was like she was a goblin in one of her novels, left behind by an evil sorcerer to replace the baby Dawn and Andre had lost more than a decade ago. But even if Naomi looked identical, she couldn't fool them; she could never, ever be that girl they'd lost.

Naomi climbed the stairs to the second floor. She quietly walked down the hall, passing the bedrooms that Maya and Blake had already claimed. Blake had chosen the south-facing one and was bouncing up and down on the bed, making the springs squeak. He looked like a leaping cricket.

"There's a deer head on the wall, Camryn?" He pointed at the taxidermy animal hanging two feet above his headboard. His afro billowed around him like a cartoon bubble as he jumped. "Isn't it cool? I'm gonna call it Bambi."

She nodded, trying not to wince at the deer's vacant staring eyes. "Yeah, it's . . . uh . . . cool, Blake."

She saw Maya was talking on her cell to Troy again.

"We're finally here," Maya said to the screen. "It's been raining the whole time and some insane hillbilly tried to drive us off the road, but we made it. At least my room doesn't suck. Let me flip my screen so you can see it." She held her phone aloft. "It's so crazy. It's like something out of a movie."

As Naomi walked by, her eyes met Maya's. Maya paused.

"Wait just sec, Troy," Maya said before marching to the door and shutting it in Naomi's face.

"Sorry," her muffled voice said on the other side. "Where was I? Yeah, the room. I mean, look at the walls! They're made of like . . . *real* logs. It's so wild, babe."

Naomi walked into the last room, and looked around. It was the smallest, but nowhere near a broom closet, like Andre had warned. There also weren't any dead animals on the wall—another plus. In fact, the size and simple furniture kind of reminded her of her old bedroom back on Berwyn Street.

She walked around the bed, pulled back the linen curtains, and was surprised to find sliding glass doors that led to a small balcony. If she could tolerate the smell outside, it would be a perfect place to write or read—or to break out of this place if it all got to be too much. An improvised rope made from bedsheets looped around the deck banister could do the trick. She could shimmy down and—

No, Naomi thought, turning away from the balcony. *No more running away.*

Besides, there was nowhere else to go. She'd already established that. This was her family. Her home was with them now, and she'd better get used to it.

8

Friday, June 21

Dear Mom,

Well, we're officially on our family vacation. We're staying in a ritzy cabin in the Shenandoah Valley in the middle of nowhere. I knew I shouldn't have told my therapist how you and I used to go on nature walks together. But she asked me to remember the last time I was happy, so I told her about when we took that walk in the park the day before everything fell apart, before they took you away. I was moody that morning, and you thought a walk outside would cheer me up because it usually did. The sound of the birds in the trees and babbling of that little creek under the old wooden bridge. The warm sun on my face. We played that game where I would point out plants and animals and quiz you on the names.

"That's an autumn blaze maple," you said without even hesitating. "That's a northern cardinal."

I still don't know how you always knew the answers.

My therapist said I may have to start taking antidepressants when I get back to Silver Spring, but in the meantime, she said a few weeks in the forest away from our neighborhood and my school might do me good. It could help me smile again. I don't really smile anymore. I don't crack jokes. I don't feel anything most days, and when I do feel, it's only frustration or anger. Otherwise, I'm dead inside.

My therapist said with time, I'll be that happy girl I used to be, but I don't know if I believe her. I don't think I'll find that girl again, especially out here. Not in these woods. The forest around our cabin is so different from the one back home. It even smells different. It feels strange, Mom.

I can't quite—

Naomi stopped writing when she heard a knock at her bedroom door. She closed her notebook and shoved it into one of her night table drawers.

"Yeah? Come in," Naomi said.

Since they began their sessions, her therapist had encouraged her to write down her thoughts in a journal, to express the things she struggled to say aloud. But her therapist hadn't said who Naomi should address her journal entries to, so she wrote them to the one person who she'd told her secrets to for so many years, the person she would talk to now, if she could. Naomi knew she had to keep her imaginary letters secret from the Stoakeses. She could only imagine the nuclear-size fallout that would happen if Andre or Dawn discovered she'd been writing her innermost feelings to someone they despised, to the person they believed had ruined all their lives.

Naomi shut the drawer and rose to her feet to finish putting away the clothes just as her door swung open. She found Blake staring down at his ever-present handheld.

"Dad's been calling you, Cam. He said to come downstairs," Blake relayed in monotone, never raising his eyes from the glowing screen. "Dinner's ready. He made pizza."

Naomi shook her head. "I'm skipping dinner tonight. Tell Mom and Dad I'm not hungry. I filled up on snacks." She gestured to an opened box of cheese crackers and an abandoned granola bar wrapper on her bedspread as evidence.

But the truth was she wasn't full. She wouldn't mind eating one or two slices of pizza. She just didn't have the energy to put up a facade tonight, to attempt to be a big happy family—even for Dawn's sake.

"You gotta come down for dessert though," Blake insisted, pressing pause and tearing his gaze away from his game. "We're roasting marshmallows!"

Naomi was still getting to know the Stoakeses, but she was certain that there were two things Blake Stoakes loved more than anything else in this world: his video games and his desserts. Cookies. Cake. Ice Cream. Donuts. The kid adored anything that was thirty percent sugar, though Naomi wasn't sure where all those calories went. He barely weighed seventy pounds soaking wet and most of it was probably his hair.

"Mom said there's a firepit outside," Blake continued.

Naomi shook her head again. She tossed a stack of T-shirts into one of her dresser drawers. "No, thanks. Besides, there's no way I could stomach eating in all that funk."

"Huh?" Blake wrinkled his button nose. "What funk?"

"What do you mean, 'What funk?'" She frowned at him. "You really can't smell that stank out there?"

When the rain had stopped and the sun came out, Naomi had opened her sliding glass door and tried to read one of her books on her little balcony. But she'd only made it a couple of pages, reaching the part when the river deity Oyá was granting the power to control lightning to the heroine, before she closed her book and went back inside.

She couldn't take the smell, even while holding her T-shirt

over her nose. Once she closed the door, she hosed down her bedroom in lilac body spray to keep the nastiness from seeping inside.

She now watched as the same bewildered expression that had passed over Andre's face when she mentioned the foul odor permeating the property appeared on Blake's face, too. "No, I don't smell anything," he said.

"Blake, where are you?" Dawn called upstairs. "Where's your sister?"

"Coming, Mom!" he called back, now racing down the hall. "Cam says she's not hungry!"

Naomi wondered why she seemed to be the only one who could smell the stench outside. Was her nose really that sensitive? Or was she going crazy?

She opened the door again and winced, recoiling from the odor. The rancid smell was thick and unmistakable. Its molecules clung to the air like an invisible haze that you could almost touch with your fingertips. Decaying flesh. That's what it smelled like.

Did depression cause phantom smells? Naomi didn't remember her therapist listing it as one of the symptoms. Or maybe she'd developed a brain tumor and it was messing with her senses.

She started to head back inside but paused when she thought she saw something moving in the trees in the distance. Naomi squinted against the flaming sunset to see more closely. There it was—a figure drifting among the tree trunks and dense leaves. It wasn't a deer though. From the shape, she could tell it was a person. Not tall like a man or small like a child either. A girl, maybe.

Naomi stepped onto the balcony and saw that the person was wearing white. It looked like a rain poncho.

No, she thought, leaning over the railing. That's not a poncho.

It was a robe or a long nightgown.

They seemed to notice Naomi watching them and stopped. She wished she could see them better. In the dying light, without recognizable eyes, ears, or mouth, it was like staring at a faceless ghost.

Goosebumps erupted on her arms. A cold chill went down her back. Naomi forced herself to breathe in even though she didn't want the rotten taste of the air on her tongue.

Finally, the person began to walk away, unhurried, deeper into the woods. The whiteness of their gown was eventually obscured by branches and foliage.

Naomi stepped back inside and closed the door, locking it behind her. Her pounding heartbeat slowly began to decelerate.

Who was that? A lost hiker? Or maybe it was one of the mysterious neighbors that Andre had mentioned.

But why would a hiker or one of the neighbors be wandering around in a nightgown? She shrugged, grabbing a purple aerosol can on her dresser and spraying her room again.

9

NAOMI OPENED HER EYES WHEN SHE HEARD A knock.

She slowly sat up and looked around the darkened room. For a few seconds, she thought she was back in her old bedroom, that her mom was the one knocking at her door, telling her to wake up because her oatmeal was getting cold, or because she'd missed the squirrels playing by their neighbor's bird feeder.

"There's four of them this time, NayNay, and they're frisky. Hurry up!" Her mom would giggle before knocking again. "You're going to miss it."

But the voice she heard wasn't her mom's. It was Dawn's.

"Camryn? Camryn?" Dawn called through the door. "Are you awake?"

She wasn't in her old bedroom. She was in the cabin in Virginia.

Naomi rubbed her eyes with the heels of her hands. "Yeah, I'm up," she croaked just as Dawn pushed the door open. She saw that Dawn was already dressed, wearing khaki shorts, a white T-shirt, and green Crocs.

"Everyone is downstairs. We're about to eat breakfast," Dawn said. "Dre's making pancakes and eggs."

Naomi wrapped her arms around her knees and shook her head. "No thanks. I'll just grab a granola bar later."

Dawn heaved a heavy sigh. "Honey, you didn't eat any dinner last night. You *have* to be hungry. You have to eat something besides crackers and granola bars."

She leaned against the doorframe. "Look, Cam, I know yesterday wasn't . . . well . . . it wasn't the best start to our vacation. But let's resolve to start fresh. I think we really can have a good time here, sweetheart. *All* of us can. It'll just take some effort. So will you come downstairs and have breakfast with us? Please?"

Naomi's stomach answered before she could make up another excuse. It growled so loudly that Dawn's eyes went wide.

"Whoa, is something trying to crawl out of there?" Dawn asked, making Naomi laugh.

"I guess I could eat something," Naomi admitted.

"Good. We'll save you a spot at the table and three pancakes. See you downstairs." Dawn stepped back into the hall and closed the door behind her.

Five minutes later, Naomi walked down the spiral staircase in her pj's, scratching at the curly hair beneath her silk bonnet.

Andre was at the stove, doing a little shimmy and humming to himself as he flipped pancakes over a skillet. Dawn was beside him, opening the stainless steel fridge and taking out a bottle of OJ. Maya was putting plates on the dining room table, sporting another mini sundress—this time in bright pink—and Blake was holding up a treat for Bear.

"Sit, Bear," he ordered. "Sit! *Siiiiiiit.*"

The dog only stared up at him blankly, panting and drooling.

"Bear's still not sitting, Mom," Blake called over his shoulder. "We spent all that money on obedience school and he failed twice. I've given up," Dawn said with a shrug.

Andre quickly stacked pancakes on a plate. "I'm convinced he just speaks another language," he said, turning off the burner. "We don't know what family had him before we adopted him. For all we know, he might be able to do cartwheels if we gave him commands in Spanish or French."

"Does anyone know how to say 'sit' in Spanish?" Blake asked with a frown.

Dawn snorted. "Daddy's kidding with you, Blake. Just give Bear the treat, honey."

Blake tossed Bear his treat, which he gobbled up in less than a second. Blake sat down for breakfast.

"Umm, can I . . . can I help with anything?" Naomi asked timidly.

"You can help Maya finish setting the table," Dawn said.

"I've got it covered, Mom! I don't need any help," Maya snapped.

Then Maya gave Naomi a tight smile she knew was more for Dawn and Andre's benefit than her own. "Thanks though, Camryn."

Just then there was a knock at the cabin door. Bear began to bark. Everyone turned to look at the door as whoever it was on the other side knocked again.

"I wonder who it is," Dawn said.

"I guess I'll go check," Naomi said, jogging out of the kitchen. She looked through the stained glass. On the front porch stood two middle-aged white women—a tall blonde and a petite, gray-haired woman with a pixie cut—along with a dark-haired Asian girl Naomi's age dressed in black jeans and a long-sleeved T-shirt. Naomi tugged off her bonnet before opening the door to greet them.

"Hi, can I help you?" she asked.

"Hey!" the blonde said with a perky wave. "Good morning! We're your neighbors down the road. Cabin nineteen. We were driving by and saw your car parked out front and wanted to say hi."

So, Andre was right after all. *We do have neighbors,* Naomi thought. She also noticed that the awful odor was slightly fainter now. Was she growing used to it or was it starting to fade?

"Oh, umm." Naomi turned back to face the kitchen. "Dawn . . . I mean Mom! It's our neighbors down the road," she called over her shoulder. "They wanna say hi!"

Dawn strolled toward the door and smiled. "Hello. Good morning."

"Hey," Pixie Cut said. "We're sorry if we interrupted anything." She leaned to the side and peered through the doorway. "I told Cheryl you guys might not be up yet."

Dawn batted away her apology. "Oh, it's fine. We're all awake and were just about to eat breakfast. Hi, I'm Dawn, by the way," she said, reaching for a handshake. "And this is my daughter Camryn. The rest of the fam is back there."

"Krissa Jamison," Pixie Cut said, giving Dawn's hand two quick pumps. She gestured over her shoulder. "This is my wife, Cheryl, and the one over there dressed in all black like she's at a funeral is our daughter, Elly."

"Moooooom!" Elly groaned.

Krissa laughed. "Anyway, we've been here for almost a week and were wondering if another family was going to rent a cabin nearby. We're about a half mile down the road. We hadn't seen anyone out here all week except for a few campers walking through the woods."

"If you need any tips on the best places to go canoeing or

hiking, don't hesitate to ask us. We can also tell you the best places to eat in town," Cheryl volunteered.

Krissa cocked a finely arched eyebrow. "Honey, there's only like three places to eat around here. There's not much to choose from."

"Well, some are better than others," Cheryl countered before pursing her lips. "I swear my wife is *such* a city girl. She forgets that not every place has a different restaurant or bistro on each street corner. I'm shocked I managed to talk her into coming out here."

"I'm shocked, too," Krissa said with a snort.

"We were thinking of heading to town today just to look around," Dawn interjected. "We were going to plug the directions into Siri."

"Oh, you don't need directions. You can't miss it!" Krissa assured her. "Just go back to the main road you took to get to the cabin and follow it south. You'll hit downtown Sparksburg in five to ten minutes, depending on how fast you drive."

Dawn nodded. "Good to know."

"Well, we'll let you guys get back to your breakfast. Enjoy the rest of your day," Cheryl said with another perky wave.

"Thanks for stopping by! It was nice meeting you," Dawn said, shutting the front door and heading to the kitchen.

Naomi lingered at the door, watching curiously through the stained glass as Cheryl and Krissa linked arms and walked down the stairs. Their daughter, Elly, stared back at Naomi.

Why was she just standing there? Had she recognized them as the famous Stoakes family with the kidnapped daughter?

Naomi's gaze locked with Elly's, whose eyes still didn't waver. Elly opened her mouth, as if to say something.

"Elly . . . sweet pea, let's go, hon!" Cheryl called.

Elly's head snapped in their direction. She gave Naomi one

last lingering look before making her way down the stairs to her moms, waiting at their SUV, which had a bumper covered with marathon stickers.

That was weird, Naomi thought. Seconds later they drove off.

She shrugged and walked back to the kitchen where everyone else was already eating breakfast.

10

KRISSA HAD BEEN RIGHT. "DOWNTOWN" SPARKSBURG was hard to miss. Naomi knew they'd reached it when they saw the big stone chapel and the sign nearby that said SPEED LIMIT 15 MPH, STRICTLY ENFORCED.

She took off her headphones and squinted to make sure she was reading the sign correctly.

"Fifteen miles per hour?" Andre raised his brows and sucked his teeth. "Damn, I go faster on my bike at home. We might as well get out and walk."

"Either way, slow down, please," Dawn said, patting her husband's knee. "We don't want to get a ticket when we've been in town for all of sixty seconds."

Andre dropped the speedometer from thirty to fifteen.

As they stared at downtown Sparksburg, Naomi felt as if she had just been dropped into a Technicolor movie. It had a small-town atmosphere that some would describe as charming, but she just saw it as so saccharine sweet she almost winced as if she had a toothache.

Main Street, which stretched for about five blocks, was lined on one side with two-story brick buildings and one-story glass storefronts. Pete's Hardware. Fashionable Florals and Designs. Heritage Bistro. She saw not a single brand name she recognized. Doors were flanked by oversize flower pots filled with marigolds, zinnias, and sunflowers. Doorways were adorned with American flags. The sidewalks were made with brick, not concrete, and were sparkling clean. Scrollworked lampposts sat next to wooden benches.

On the other side of Main Street was a park with a pond and a white gazebo topped with a large cast-iron bell patinated by time. A few feet in front of the gazebo was a bronze statue of a bespectacled guy in an old-fashioned suit with a vest and high collar, staring off into the distance. Naomi wondered who he was. She squinted, but she couldn't read the inscription on the plaque below the statue.

Andre spotted an open space and parked.

"All right, hop out, y'all. Time to go exploring."

Naomi took a deep breath as she climbed out the SUV, happy the vaseline and perfume concoction she came up with and rubbed inside her nostrils was working. She inhaled mostly roses, cinnamon, and vanilla and only caught a faint whiff of the underlying stench she knew that only she could smell. Naomi kept a container of the salve in her purse just in case she needed to apply it again later.

"Where should we go first?" Andre asked.

"Do they have a game store around here?" Blake asked hopefully, turning in a circle.

"Does it look like a place that would have a game store?" Maya replied in a mocking voice. She crossed her arms over her chest, now in full sulk mode.

"Maya, enough already. You hear me?" Dawn said, punctuated by a "mom stare." She turned her attention to Andre. "Let's try the grocery store. I want to make some shish kebabs on the grill tonight and I'm missing some ingredients."

The Stoakeses walked down the sidewalk with Naomi pulling up the rear, snapping pics with her phone along the way.

“This place is unreal,” she whispered, taking another photo. She did it almost to prove to herself that they hadn’t been transported back in time.

“Good morning!” Dawn said to a woman as they walked by.

“Hey! How you doin’?” Andre said with a wave to an older guy wearing sandals and sports socks.

They got curious stares or polite nods in response.

“Good morning, folks!” a man said as he waved and strode toward them.

He wore aviator sunglasses, a red polo shirt, khakis, and a navy-blue dress coat with an American flag pin on the lapel. A cross hung around his throat. His dark hair was combed and gelled into submission so that he resembled a slightly overweight human Ken doll.

“Hey, I’m Robert J. Bartz, mayor of Sparksburg,” he said, whipping off his sunglasses and offering his hand to Andre. “I take it that you’re visitors to our beautiful hamlet?”

How could you tell? Naomi thought sardonically, noticing that, so far, they were the only brown faces she’d spotted since they’d driven into Sparksburg.

“Yes, we’re here for the next three weeks,” Andre volunteered as he shook the mayor’s hand. “We’re on our family vacation.”

“Is that right?” Mayor Bartz said, narrowing his eyes. “You know, I could swear I’ve seen you somewhere before.” His blue eyes slowly scanned their faces like they had tattoos on their skin. “Your family as well. Are you a famous actor? Or maybe you were on reality TV? Do you have one of those home improvement shows? My wife, Jessica, just *loves* them! I swear she comes up with a new project just about every week after watching those things.”

Naomi tried not to flinch. *Here it comes,* she thought, holding her breath. They were bound to be recognized eventually.

But Andre's confident smile beneath his goatee didn't waver. He shook his head. "No, I'm not an actor and we've never been on reality TV. I guess we just have those kinds of faces."

Mayor Bartz laughed.

Naomi slowly exhaled.

"Well, anyway," the mayor went on, "I want to *personally* welcome you all to town. If you ever need anything . . . and I mean *anything*, don't hesitate to reach out to me *personally*." The mayor reached into his shirt pocket and pulled out a business card and handed it to Andre. "You can also find me at city hall. It's at the end of the next block."

He pointed into the distance and Naomi followed the path of his finger to a brick building with white double doors down the street.

"We certainly will. Thank you," Andre assured him, taking the card.

"Enjoy your day," the mayor said before continuing down the block.

"Nice guy. Nice town, to be honest." Andre tucked the card into the pocket of his shorts, gave a thoughtful nod, and turned around to eye Maya. "It's like people aren't so bad if you actually keep an open mind and give them a chance," he said loudly.

Maya tossed her braids over her shoulder and rolled her eyes.

Naomi hung back and watched the mayor as he walked away. She noticed he slowed near a lamppost where a flyer was taped. On it was a photo of a young dirty-blond woman winking and blowing a sultry kiss to the camera. The word MISSING was written in a large red font above her image.

The mayor let out a gruff sigh. His face darkened as he ripped down the flyer, before crushing it into a tight ball.

Mayor Bartz glanced over his shoulder and saw Naomi was still watching him. His dark expression immediately disappeared. He gave another smile and a wave before shoving the balled-up flyer into his jacket pocket and walking away.

"Camryn, you coming?" Dawn called to her.

Naomi slowly nodded, running to catch up.

11

WHEN THEY PUSHED OPEN THE DOOR TO SUNNY Market a minute later, a bell jingled overhead. A man behind the counter wearing a green apron with the grocery store's emblem waved in greeting. A bright smile broke from behind his thick gray beard. "Good morning, folks! Welcome to Sunny Market."

"Good morning," Dawn and Andre replied. Naomi, Maya, and Blake gave limp waves.

"I'm Nelson. This here is my little shop," he said, stepping from behind the counter as Dawn picked up a plastic basket. "Are y'all new in town or just passing through?"

This was the second time someone had asked that. Andre had said Sparksburg was trying to become the new tourist hot spot of the Shenandoah Valley, but Naomi wondered if the town got a lot of visitors.

Andre nodded. "Actually, we're vacationing here for the next few weeks. Might make it a yearly thing if the kids have a good time. I'm Andre, by the way. This is my wife, Dawn. And these are our kids, Maya, Camryn, and Blake."

"Nice meeting y'all," Nelson drawled. He gestured toward the aisles. "If you're lookin' around and can't find anything, just give a holler. If you can't find it out here, it's probably stored in the back. We don't get a lot of visitors here in Sparksburg except in summer months. I try to stock up on what most people want, but every now and then, I get a curveball. Had two ladies come in here a couple of days ago, and one of them asked for oat milk. I told her that we don't carry that here, and she looked at me like I'd spit in her face."

Naomi stifled a laugh. She wondered if he was talking about Cheryl and Krissa. She could imagine their neighbor Krissa, "the city girl," being annoyed by something like that.

"We don't need any oat milk," Dawn said. "Just garden-variety fruits and vegetables are fine."

"Well, you can check over there. That's where we keep our veggies and fruits," Nelson said, pointing toward a sign on the left side of the store. "Oh, and if you need any help loading your groceries, that big guy over there—Liam, my son—can take care of that for you," he said, nodding to a tall man with dark hair who was pushing a hand truck loaded with crates.

Liam lifted the bill of his cap, gave a quick nod, and continued on his way.

"We even started a home delivery service online like those grocery stores two towns over," Nelson said. "Liam handles the deliveries for that, too."

"Well, that's convenient," Dawn said.

Just then, a phone began to buzz. Maya reached inside her purse and tugged out her cell. "It's Troy," she said with a grin.

"Take the call outside," Andre said. "The entire store doesn't need to hear you two get all lovey-dovey."

Maya didn't argue. "Hi, baby!" she crooned into her phone just as the bell over the door jingled.

Naomi's gaze lingered on the door as it closed. She didn't have a boyfriend she was eager to talk to but she didn't want to spend the rest of the morning trailing after Dawn and Andre as they grocery shopped.

"Hey, uh, is it okay if I go exploring on my own?" she asked. They both turned to look at her.

"I don't see why . . ." Andre began, but his voice trailed off as he glanced at Dawn whose brow furrowed at Naomi's question. "Uh, ask your mother," he said.

It always amused Naomi that despite Andre being twice Dawn's size and having all this "take charge" manly swagger, it was obvious Dawn was the true head of family, and she knew how to wield her power. More than once, Naomi had witnessed Dawn make Andre go silent with just one look.

"So can I go, Mom?" Naomi asked.

Dawn lowered the basket in her arms. She pursed her lips.

She's gonna say no, Naomi realized. Dawn had insisted that they were going to start anew today and pretend like the events of yesterday hadn't happened, but she didn't trust Naomi to walk around town by herself. She didn't trust her not to disappear.

"Blake can come with me if he wants," Naomi blurted.

They wouldn't think she would run away if she had Blake in tow. She turned to him. "What do you say, Blake? Want to go look around town with me while Mom and Dad pick up stuff for dinner?"

Blake nodded eagerly. "Yeah, can we go, Dad? Mom?"

Dawn hesitated. She gazed at Naomi a beat longer. Gradually, she nodded. "Sure."

"We'll meet you guys by the bench in front of the store in thirty minutes," Andre said. "*Thirty* minutes. Three. Zero."

"Got it. Thirty minutes," Naomi said, giving Andre and Dawn a thumbs-up. "Come on, Blake," she nudged his shoulder and headed toward the door.

She didn't want to give Dawn the chance to change her mind.

12

"WHERE SHOULD WE GO NEXT?" BLAKE ASKED twenty minutes later.

They'd already gone to most of the stores along Main Street. There wasn't much to see.

Naomi and Blake had gotten the same curious stares as they'd gotten earlier while they were walking with the rest of the family. At one point, a curious stare had turned to an outright hostile glower when Blake held up a handmade gingham-and-straw doll at an antique store and began to laugh.

"Oh, man! This is butt ugly!" He'd clutched his stomach. "Look, Camryn! Do-do-da-doo-da-dooo!" he'd sang as he made the straw doll dance.

The elderly shopkeeper had pursed her wrinkled lips and squinted her watery eyes at him. "Are you buying that?" she snapped.

"Dude, put it down," Naomi whispered, mortified by her brother's antics. "No, sorry," she muttered, then placed the doll back on the shelf before quickly ushering Blake out of the store.

Now Naomi looked around her, letting her gaze linger on the signs and storefronts to her right and left. She'd noticed while exploring that they hadn't run into Maya at any point. Where had Maya gotten off to? Was she still talking to Troy? Or maybe Maya was somewhere around town taking videos and selfies and posting them online since her followers were undoubtedly starving for content after not hearing from her for a *whole* day.

"How about the park?" Naomi said to Blake, pointing across the street.

"Yeah! Race you!" Blake laughed before barreling across the two-lane street, pumping his gangly legs.

"Blake!" she shouted after him. "Didn't anyone ever teach you to look both ways before you cross the street? Do you have a death wish?" she muttered under her breath.

That was just what she needed—for Blake to get hit by a car and for her to be blamed for exacting *yet another* trauma on the Stoakes family, but there were no cars. Naomi followed Blake to the gazebo. He stood at the center and stared into the roof.

"Hey!" He pointed at the ceiling beams. "There's a big bell. You think I can climb up and ring it?"

"No!" Naomi groaned. "Don't even think about it."

Instead of joining Blake in the gazebo, she drew near the bronze statue that she'd noticed when they first drove into town. She scanned the plaque embedded in stone at its base.

"'The Honorable Reverend Charles Davis Meacham, mayor of Sparksburg from 1920 to 1953,'" she read. She took a picture, zooming in on the statue's face.

The dude was practically scowling. Naomi looked at the plaque again.

"'The beloved mayor and defender of the town of Sparksburg, protecting its citizens and the integrity of its borders for more than thirty years.'" Naomi frowned.

"Protecting its borders from what?" She took a picture of the plaque, too. She glanced up to find Blake leaping off the gazebo's stairs to the grass below.

At least he wasn't climbing onto the roof.

Naomi was taking more photos—this time of the gazebo and its aging iron bell—when a text popped up on-screen.

Hey! Remember me? It's Khalil. The guy from the gift shop, the text said, followed by a waving emoji. **How y'all like Sparksburg so far?**

Naomi gaped at the message, wondering if she was really seeing what she was seeing. She closed her eyes, then opened them. Yep, the text was still there.

Khalil had texted her like he promised, even though he'd seen that humiliating exchange between her and Dawn outside the gift shop. Despite how awkward she'd been that day. She thought she'd never hear from him again. Naomi hesitated, unsure what to text back. Should she say something flirty? Should she crack a joke?

"I'm so, so bad at this," she mumbled.

It's OK, she finally wrote. **The town is kinda like a 1950s TV show.**

She saw three little bubbles, then a laughing emoji. He wrote: **Not everything around here is like that. Wanna meet up tomorrow night? How about seven? I'll show you we're not all corny down here.**

She broke into a grin and started to type back an emphatic *yes*, but stopped herself.

She doubted that a month ago Dawn and Andre would have objected to her going out on a date, but after that rough episode at the rest stop, Naomi wondered if Dawn trusted her being out of her sight. And why did Khalil want to go on a date with her anyway?

"Camryn! Mom and Dad are done shopping. Mom! Dad! We're over here!" Blake called. She didn't have a chance to respond before Blake went sprinting past her.

She watched as he neared the sidewalk and waved at Andre and Dawn, who had just stepped out of the grocer's carrying paper bags brimming over with a lot more than fixings for shish kebabs.

Out of the corner of her eye, Naomi saw a black pickup truck driving down Main Street much faster than fifteen miles per hour. Blake stepped into the street, heading toward Dawn and Andre. Naomi sprinted after him.

"Blake, watch out!" Dawn screeched.

Naomi lunged forward, yanking the back of Blake's T-shirt so hard that the momentum sent them both careening to the sidewalk just as the truck swerved and came to a tire-squealing halt.

Blake landed sprawled on top of Naomi, knocking the wind out of her.

"Oww," Blake moaned, gripping his throat. "That hurt!"

Probably not as much as she did right now. Naomi shoved Blake off her, touched her left shoulder, and winced.

"Watch where the hell you're goin'!" a voice shouted.

Naomi looked up, dazed, to find the passenger-side window of the pickup was now lowered. A man glared at them from the driver's seat. Matted, greasy hair hung limply around his reddened, gaunt face. His gray beard was so scraggly that his pockmarked cheeks showed through.

"You people come here and think you own the goddamn place! Do somethin' like that again and I might not stop next time! That'll teach you!" He spat out a brown stream of chewing tobacco onto the asphalt. He shifted in the driver's seat, gunned the engine, and drove away at the same speed as before—maybe faster—leaving a plume of exhaust in his wake.

"Are you guys all right?" Dawn asked as she and Andre rushed toward them.

Naomi nodded and grabbed her cell phone. It had taken the fall better than she had; at least the screen wasn't cracked. Andre helped her to her feet.

Naomi's gaze lingered on the receding pickup truck. She wondered if it was the same black pickup truck that had driven them off the road yesterday.

"Blake, honey, don't ever run into the street like that again," Dawn admonished. She showered him with kisses and squeezed him in a tight hug. "You know better! You scared us half to death! What if that truck had hit you?"

"You're lucky your sister was looking out for you, son," Andre said.

"He *is* lucky she was looking out for him, isn't he?" Dawn whispered.

She looked up at Naomi. For once, her big dark eyes didn't hold sadness or disappointment. She actually looked proud of her.

"Is everything okay? You two took quite a spill there."

Naomi shifted slightly to find a tall woman in a police uniform striding toward them. The woman adjusted the bill of her cap as she approached.

"Is anyone hurt?" the officer asked.

"That man almost hit my son and he just . . . he just drove off!" Dawn sputtered.

"Blake did run into the street, honey," Andre reminded her.

"Yes, but the speed limit is fifteen miles per hour and he was driving nowhere near that! He could've hit any pedestrian at that speed, Dre. He's dangerous—whoever he is!"

"Travis Meacham," the officer said, staring into the distance where the truck had disappeared. "That's who was driving. We've written him enough tickets to plaster a bedroom wall, but that doesn't seem to slow him down, let alone stop him.

The DMV is probably gonna have to revoke his license to get him off the road."

"Meacham," Naomi said. "Like the guy who used to be mayor? That guy?" She pointed in the direction of the bronze statue but winced at the pain in her shoulder as she did.

"Yep, they're related. But just about everybody's related around here." She smiled. "I'm Sheriff Turner, by the way. Pleased to meet you folks." She glanced at one of the grocery bags Dawn and Andre had been carrying. It now sat on its side in the middle of the street, abandoned. "Let me get that for you. Don't want any more roadway mishaps."

Naomi watched as Sheriff Turner stepped into the street, holding up her hand to a sedan as it approached. She grabbed the bag and waved at the driver, who gave her two quick beeps. She handed Andre the grocery bag.

"You shouldn't have any more troubles. The rest of us folks in town are much better drivers," the sheriff assured them with a chuckle.

THEY FINALLY TRACKED down Maya and piled back into the SUV. As they drove out of downtown, Naomi gazed at storefronts and houses, at the wooden and brick exteriors and Victorian terraced roofs. More than once she noticed a shopkeeper peering through the glass or someone pulling back a curtain to look at the Stoakeses' passing SUV.

It wasn't until Andre made it past the SPEED LIMIT 15 MPH, STRICTLY ENFORCED sign and back on the main road leading to the cabins that Naomi lost the unnerving feeling that unseen eyes were following them.

That they were being watched.

13

HOURS LATER, NAOMI SANK LOW IN AN ADIRONDACK chair, adjusting the ice pack on her left shoulder.

The sun was starting to set, leaving red, orange, and purple streaks across the evening sky. They'd set up the chairs around the firepit in the backyard to eat dinner. Andre was still hovering over the grill, cleaning up the char, last bits of food, and aluminum foil. Maya and Dawn were assembling graham crackers, marshmallows, and chocolate bars on a foldout table for the s'mores they'd make over the pit in a few minutes. Blake was chowing down on the last of his shish kebabs, smacking his lips and licking the grease from his fingers.

He didn't look like a kid who'd almost gotten hit by a car a few hours ago; he looked as if he barely had a care in the world.

But Naomi kept replaying the scene in her head as she stared into the firepit's orange and blue flames. She kept seeing herself reaching out to yank Blake back to safety. She remembered the angry old man, Travis Meacham, shouting at them and then watching him spit tobacco onto the ground.

What if she'd been a second slower, or hadn't managed to grab Blake's shirt and had only locked onto air? And Naomi couldn't let go of the worrying thought that Meacham, who'd almost hit Blake today, might have been the same driver who had tailgated them yesterday. The man was a menace.

Sheriff Turner had assured them they shouldn't have any more problems while in Sparksburg, though Naomi couldn't help but wonder if that were true, especially with guys like Meacham driving around town.

She looked at the surrounding trees, again sensing unseen eyes watching their family gathering. *Was* someone out there? Could it be Meacham?

"You barely touched your food, Cam," Dawn said.

Naomi looked up. Dawn was staring at her. She glanced down at the paper plate that sat in her lap.

She'd only nibbled at the grilled beef, chicken, and veggies. She'd finished half of her hamburger and was absently stabbing at it with one of the wooden skewers.

"I guess I'm not that hungry." Naomi sat forward in her chair. "I think I'm going to head inside. I'm feeling kinda tired."

"It's only eight thirty. How can you be tired?" Maya said, like she was personally offended.

"She had a rough day," Andre volunteered from the deck.

Naomi looked over her shoulder to find Andre raising a beer bottle to his lips. He nodded before taking a quick sip. "Go ahead, Cam. Get some rest."

"I'll save you some s'mores and you can have them tomorrow if you want, sweetheart," Dawn said.

"Thanks."

As Naomi pushed herself to her feet, Bear came galloping toward her. He had been running around, chasing something in the grass—maybe a rabbit or a squirrel—but now he came to a stop in front of her and gazed up at her with pleading eyes. Threads of slobber hung from the side of his mouth as he panted.

Naomi sighed before removing the skewer and holding out her hamburger. Bear took it right out of her hands and began to eat it, dropping bits onto the ground and gobbling and licking the crumbs, too.

Naomi carried her ice pack and what was left of her plate of food up the deck stairs and into the kitchen, tossing her plate into the trash and her ice pack into the sink. She trudged up the spiral staircase.

Almost a half hour later, after she'd brushed her teeth and changed into her pj's, Naomi heard a knock at her bedroom door. She opened it to find Dawn standing in the hall, smiling at her timidly and holding a small green canister.

"I found this in my suitcase," Dawn said, holding out the canister to her. "It's a mint and eucalyptus soothing gel. If you rub it on your shoulder, it should help with the soreness."

"Thanks," Naomi said, taking it from her.

"You know . . . uh . . . Blake may not appreciate what you did for him today. He's nine. Kids all think they're invincible at that age. But your dad and I do, Cam. We appreciate it deeply."

"It's okay. You already told me." Naomi shrugged and looked down at her feet, no longer able to hold Dawn's intense gaze. "It really wasn't that big of a deal."

"No, it was! You belong here *with us*, and today was another reminder of that. I hope you realize it, Cam."

No, I belong with my mom, Naomi wanted to argue, but she didn't have the heart to do it. Not when it seemed like there was a chance for the look of heartache and disappointment to finally lift from Dawn's eyes.

"We've been so long without you, honey, but your dad and I never forgot how important you are to us . . . to our family. It was not the same without you. We know that it hasn't been easy . . . well . . . adjusting. Leaving behind your old life. After all the brainwashing I'm sure you were put through all those years, I know—"

"Can I go on a date?" Naomi blurted out. Dawn blinked in surprise.

"What?"

"Can I . . . umm . . . go on a date tomorrow?" Naomi repeated, slowly raising her eyes.

She knew it was an abrupt subject change, but she didn't like where the conversation was headed.

Her therapist had used that word during one of their sessions: *brainwashing*. She said that was essentially what Naomi's mom had done to her for years, and what Naomi was going through now while living with the Stoakes family was deprogramming, like she'd escaped from a cult.

But Naomi thought the whole idea was bullshit. Her mom hadn't "brainwashed" her. She never abused her physically or verbally. She'd loved, nurtured, and protected her like any mother would. No one had the right to talk about her mom that way, and she wanted to say as much to Dawn right now, but she didn't want to start a fight.

"I was texting this guy who I met at the rest stop on our way to Sparksburg," Naomi continued. "I gave him my number because he seemed nice . . . and . . . well, cute. His grandmother lives around here. Anyway, he texted me and asked me out just when Blake ran past me and all that stuff happened after. I still haven't replied because I didn't know what to say. I don't know how you and . . . uh . . . Dad would feel about it."

Dawn pursed her lips. "Does this guy have a name?"

"Khalil. His name is Khalil."

"Is he your age?"

"Yeah! Of course he is. He's still in high school."

. . . *I think,* Naomi thought, but didn't say aloud.

Dawn inclined her head. "Well, if he seems okay, I don't see why not. But he has to pick you up here. Dad and I would like to meet him, too."

"Sure, that shouldn't be a problem!" Naomi said, relieved that she'd said yes.

"And if we ask you to check in with us during your date, you have to respond ASAP, Cam. I mean it. Either with a call or a text."

"I will." She gave Dawn a hug and, on impulse, gave Dawn a kiss on the cheek, making Dawn's smile return. "I'm going to text him right now. 'Night!" She stepped back into her bedroom and shut the door.

Naomi ran to get her cell off her night table and quickly typed a message to Khalil.

Sorry it took me so long to get back to you, she typed. **Had some family drama. Anyways, let's meet up! Can you pick me up here at the cabin?**

She set down her cell, gnawing her lip, anxious to see Khalil's reply. She hoped he still wanted to go out with her. But something outside the window drew her attention. She peered into the darkness.

In the grassy field, in the hazy moonlight, several yards beyond the trees, she saw a skinny Black girl who looked to be her age wearing a long-sleeved white cotton nightgown that stood out sharply against her dark skin.

The girl was standing barefoot in the grass. On one side of her head was a fat braid that snaked like a vine down her chest. It was tied off with a ribbon. On the other side, her hair was loose, large, and buoyant. It fluttered gently around her face like a dark cloud in the breeze. The girl's wide dark eyes and angelic, heart-shaped face almost glowed in the moonlight. Her eyes were fixed on Naomi's balcony window. She was watching her.

Naomi's breath caught in her throat. She stared back at the girl. What was she doing out there all alone? Was she the person Naomi spotted walking in the trees yesterday? Naomi had thought Cheryl and Krissa said no one else was staying around here, that their family and the Stoakeses were the only people who were renting any of the cabins right now. But maybe a new family had moved in today.

Naomi started to unlock the sliding glass door to ask her if she needed help, but stopped short when she heard her phone buzz. She turned around to glance at the screen. There was a message from Khalil.

Hey! I was wondering what happened to you, Khalil wrote. **Yeah, I can pick you up tomorrow. Which cabin number are you?**

Naomi quickly typed **18**, then tossed her phone onto her bed. She rushed back to the balcony door, but the girl was gone.

14

"HEY, UH, DAD," NAOMI SAID AS SHE STROLLED DOWN the porch stairs the next morning. "Can we . . . uh . . . can we talk?"

Andre was standing in the driveway in front of the SUV, holding a water hose. He was spraying one of the front tires and the bumper, trying his best to remove the bloody debris from a squirrel they'd unwittingly hit on the way back from town yesterday. He glanced over his shoulder at Naomi and nodded. "If you don't mind talking while I do this . . . Sure," he said, blinking sweat out of his eyes. "Shoot, kid."

Naomi shoved her hands into her shorts pockets and gnawed her bottom lip, unsure of where to begin.

She'd wanted to tell Andre and Dawn at breakfast that morning about the girl she'd seen outside last night, but had held off for so many reasons. It seemed like an awkward thing to bring up over blueberry waffles while Blake raved about his new video game high score, Maya complained about the Wi-Fi service in the cabin, and Dawn asked where Khalil was taking Naomi for their date tonight. Naomi didn't know how to segue to the strange girl who seemed to be wandering around their vacation property at night and hiding in the nearby woods.

Maya would likely say she made it all up, that she was attention seeking. A panicked Dawn would want more details about the girl that Naomi didn't have so they could contact police. Naomi thought her best move was to speak to Andre alone. He would have the most calm, practical reaction.

"So, last night . . . last night," she began, "I think I saw someone near the cabin, looking at my balcony window."

Andre whipped around to face her. His entire body was tense and alert now.

"What do you mean someone was looking at your window last night, Camryn? Why are you just telling me this now?" he nearly shouted.

Okay, Naomi thought, taking a step back, *maybe Andre isn't as chill as I thought.*

"It was a girl my age," she said, hoping to make him less freaked out. "A Black girl in a nightgown."

"A Black girl in a nightgown?" Andre repeated, now frowning.

"She looked lost or . . . or confused. She was just standing in the field. I was going to ask her why she was out there. I turned away for less than a minute because my phone buzzed, and when I looked up again, she was gone. I guess she ran back into the woods while I wasn't looking. Do you think she might be homeless? Maybe she's camping out there and looking for food."

"Maybe," he answered slowly. "But are you sure you saw someone out there? She would have to be running pretty fast to make it across the grass back from the cabin to the woods, Cam. That's a long distance to pull off in a matter of seconds."

"Yes, I saw her! It was hard not to notice her in that white nightgown."

"Yeah, that part sounds even stranger. Why would a girl be standing in the middle of the field at night in her pj's, honey? You really think someone could walk through the woods like that? And to be honest, if anyone was out there, Bear would've let us know. He barks at everything."

Naomi opened her mouth, then closed it.

Andre was right. Bear usually barked his head off whenever a delivery guy even came within twenty feet of the house. He did the same when Cheryl, Krissa, and Elly showed up at the cabin yesterday. Wouldn't he have smelled or heard the girl, too?

"I don't know. Maybe you're right," Naomi said.

"Look, kid, yesterday was crazy." Andre placed a warm hand on her shoulder. "You were tired . . . damn near exhausted after dinner, and it was dark outside. You thought you saw a girl, but you probably saw something else. It was a trick of the eye. Happens all the time. Okay?"

He returned his attention to washing off the car, muttering to himself about stubborn blood stains.

Naomi watched Andre for a few seconds longer, considering his words. It could've been a trick of the eye, but what if it wasn't? What else could she have mistaken for a girl in a field? Naomi vividly remembered the details of the cotton gown's tattered lace, of the loosely tied ribbon around her braid. What if a girl was lost and needed their help?

Naomi turned away and headed up the cabin stairs, resolving that if the girl came back, she would take a pic of her and talk to her. But she would have to let the issue go for now.

15

Dear Mom,

Guess what? I'm going on my first EVER date tonight! His name is Khalil Crowley, and he's tall and has the cutest, deepest dimples. And he seems nice. Yes, I know you never liked the idea of me dating, but I'm sixteen now. I had to date eventually.

Dawn and Andre want to meet him. I'm worried that someone will say something to scare him off. (Maya can be such a bitch sometimes that I wouldn't put it past her to try to sabotage my date.) I'm hoping Khalil doesn't recognize us when he sees us all together either. For once, it would be nice for a guy to see me as normal. I've always found it hard to talk to them . . . to boys, I mean, and now I feel even more awkward. Like if they look hard enough, they'll see I'm a weirdo, Mom. A freak. I'm the girl who didn't know who she really was until she was 15 years old.

Part of me keeps wondering why such a cute, nice guy wants to go out with me in the first place. When we met, I was so flustered. I couldn't even remember my own phone number. He was so smooth. Maybe too smooth. Maybe he already knows who I am but he's pretending he doesn't. I hope he didn't ask me out just so he can date someone famous.

Ugh, I'm getting in my head now. I want to stay excited! This date is the one good thing that's come out of this stupid vacation so far. I'm not vibing with Sparksburg, Mom. There doesn't seem to be any other Black people that live here, which is kind of what I expected, it being "redneck country" and all. And everything about the town just seems . . . off. Weird stuff keeps happening.

It's too much to explain right now. I'll go into more detail another day, but in the meantime, I should probably settle on an outfit for my date tonight. Khalil will be here in an hour and I'm still torn between a green jumper and a white sundress. Or maybe I should go more casual and wear jeans. Arrrgghh! I wish you were here to help me.

I guess I'll have to figure this one out on my own.

Love you and miss you.

Your "Ride or Die,"

NayNay

NAOMI HAD JUST tightened the buckle of her sandal when the bell rang.

"I got it!" she heard Blake shout, followed by the slap of bare feet against hardwood.

She hopped to her feet and quickly applied her perfumed petroleum jelly inside and along the rim of her nose.

"Dad!" she heard Blake shout less than a minute later. "Dad, come quick! Some guy is here, asking for Naomi! I think he's a reporter."

Naomi's eyes widened. She had completely forgotten that "Naomi" not "Camryn" was the name she'd given Khalil.

She hopped off her bed and grabbed her satchel, wincing

slightly at the lingering pain in her shoulder. She raced downstairs. Naomi had just reached the bottom step when Andre came strolling out of the kitchen toward the front door, where a very confused-looking Khalil stood in a black T-shirt and ripped skinny jeans.

"*Reporter?* I'm not a reporter," Khalil said, his frown deepening. "I'm here to pick up Naomi . . . for our . . . our date."

"Hey!" she said, skidding to a stop beside Blake. "Hey! I'm . . . I'm here. I'm here! Hey, Khalil!" She then turned to Andre and Blake. "Dad . . . Blake, this is Khalil. Khalil, this is my dad and my brother, Blake."

They gazed at Khalil warily for a few seconds longer before Andre finally gestured for Khalil to come inside. "Pleased to meet you, son." Andre offered Khalil a handshake.

"Pleased to meet you, too, sir," Khalil said.

His questioning stare shifted to Naomi. She could only imagine what conversation they would have later in his car.

"Hi! You must be Khalil," Naomi heard Dawn call from behind them, all smiles. "I'm Dawn, Camryn's mom. Pleased to meet you!"

"He thought her name was Naomi," Blake piped, making Naomi flinch.

"Oh." Dawn's smile faded.

"Wait. She told him her name was Naomi?" Maya asked as she strolled down the stairs.

Great, Naomi thought. The last thing she needed was salty commentary from Maya. Naomi grabbed Khalil's hand.

"Well, we better get going," she said, tugging Khalil through the door.

"Be back by eleven," Andre called after them.

When she and Khalil pulled away, she saw the Stoakeses were still standing in the doorway watching.

16

NAOMI WAITED FOR KHALIL TO BRING UP THE awkward conversation about her name with her family back at the cabin, but he didn't. Instead, he asked her about downtown Sparksburg.

"It really hasn't changed since the 1950s?" he asked as he drove to an outlet mall that was thirty-five minutes outside of Sparksburg.

"Seemed like it. It was old-fashioned. It had this *Leave It to Beaver* vibe. Wait . . . haven't you been there?" she asked. "I thought you said your family is from around here. That they lived near Sparksburg."

"Yeah, my dad, uncles, and my grandma grew up here, but they don't ever go into town unless they have to. We do all our shopping at the mall."

"You guys drive this far all the time just to get groceries?" She shifted in her seat to squint at him. "To buy socks? *Why?*"

He'd shrugged. "I don't know. We just do because . . ."

"Because of the smell in town," she finished for him.

"Smell?" He did a double take. "What do you mean?"

So he didn't smell the offending odor either. Of course he didn't. She felt foolish for saying it out loud. "Never mind. It's all in my head," she mumbled. "You were saying?"

"Uh, yeah, well, I always assumed it was because there were

more stores out here. Sounds like there isn't a lot in Sparksburg anyway."

Khalil had a point. Later as they walked around the mall, blending into the sea of shoppers, Naomi was relieved to finally spot names of stores she recognized. Honestly, she'd much rather shop here than at any of the small, hokey shops she'd seen during her brief tour of downtown Sparksburg.

As they passed a bookstore, one of the displays caught her eye. It advertised local history, showing a map of Virginia along with the Virginia state flag, a model-size Monticello with its octagonal dome and white Doric columns, and a small battlefield of Union and Confederate soldiers with cannons, horses, and bayonets at the ready. There was also a tiered arrangement of hardbacks and paperbacks. Naomi slowed her steps when she saw a familiar face on one of the book covers.

"Hey, I know that guy," she said, peering through the glass.

Khalil eyed the display. "What guy?"

"The one on that book cover." She pointed at the glossy hardback toward the left, aggravating the slight pain in her shoulder. She leaned in closer to read the book's title.

Naomi had instantly recognized the round spectacles and high collar. He was even wearing his hair the same way when she last saw him: parted down the center.

"It's Mayor Meacham," Naomi explained. "I saw his statue in the park."

"Who?" Khalil asked.

"One of the mayors of Sparksburg," she said, already walking into the bookstore. She went straight to the cashier counter, asking for the book in the shop window. After paying twenty-five dollars, she had a copy in her hands.

"*Sparksburg: A Dark History of a Sundown Town,*" Khalil said, reading the book's title. "Damn. That sounds creepy."

Naomi had to agree. She flipped the book over to read the blurb on the back.

> Founded by German immigrants, Sparksburg, Virginia, was a thriving township known for its tobacco plantations, wheat fields, and dairy farms for more than a hundred years. The inhabitants believed it to be the epitome of pastoral tranquility. But when the Shenandoah Valley became the site of numerous Civil War battles and skirmishes, the town witnessed a sharp change in fortune or, as one historian put it, was "devastated by the hell of war." When many of the formerly enslaved left with the Union Army to seek their freedom elsewhere, the white citizens of Sparksburg were all too happy to see them go, blaming them for the dire plight that had befallen this once-great town. After Reconstruction, matters only got worse for the African Americans who stayed. The white citizens made a concerted effort to drive them away. The most horrific period took place under Mayor Charles Davis Meacham, the "King of Sparksburg," who guaranteed through a de facto policy of intimidation and outright terror that the African Americans who returned to Sparksburg in the years to come wouldn't want to stay for very long.

"What . . . the . . . hell," Naomi murmured. "Read this."

She handed the book to Khalil and watched as he mouthed the words as he read. She also watched as his eyes gradually grew bigger and bigger. Finally, he handed the book back to her.

"Did you know about this stuff?" she asked.

He shook his head. "No. I hadn't heard any of it."

"Not even that Sparksburg used to be a sundown town? You know what that means, right? What a sundown town is?"

He shook his head again.

"I learned about it in a Black history book I read a few years ago," she said. Her mom had given it to her as one of her eighth grade assignments. "That means Black people weren't allowed to live there, Khalil. That's what a sundown town is. You have to get out of town before dark."

"Well, damn. I knew we didn't usually go there unless we had to, but like I said . . . I didn't know why. I just thought it was a boring small town. My dad and my uncles never talked about it. There's plenty of other places to go around here instead. I mean, my nana's said some stuff about Sparksburg, but she's always saying the wildest stuff anyway. That's just how she is."

Naomi stared at Mayor Meacham's photo. "They gave this guy . . . this racist, a statue, Khalil," Naomi said. "He has a monument in the middle of town."

She remembered the plaque at the base of the statue, how it said he was a defender of Sparksburg and had protected its citizens and "the integrity of its borders for more than thirty years." Was this what they meant? This "de facto policy of intimidation and outright terror" was protecting the town's borders?

"It's probably an old statue, like the ones of Confederate generals you can find anywhere around the South, Naomi. And it's not a sundown town anymore. I told you, one of my uncles worked there building stuff in the cabins, late into the night sometimes. And *you* guys are there now. It's the past. A messed-up past, but still . . ." His words drifted off. "Look, let's grab something to eat. Forget about all this stuff. How does pizza sound?"

Naomi looked at the book a few seconds longer before putting it into her satchel. "Sure. Pizza is fine," she said. "Let's eat."

As THEY SAT down at the pizzeria—Naomi with her slice of pepperoni pizza and Khalil with his ham and pineapple calzone—Naomi tried not to think about the book or the disturbing story of Mayor Meacham.

"Oh my God, this is good!" Khalil said after slurping a string of mozzarella from his calzone. He ripped off a piece and held it out to her. "You should try some."

She considered his offer, charmed that he was willing to share his food with her, but she declined. "There's no way I could eat that. Pineapple on pizza is gross."

"What? How dare you!" he cried, eyes wide in mock outrage, making her laugh.

The laughter caught her off guard. Naomi hadn't done it in so long. "Pineapple on pizza is not gross. One and a half million Hawaiians would agree with me," he said before taking another bite. "Besides, this is a calzone, not a pizza. And it's not a crazy combo like pickles and ice cream or banana and mayo sandwiches."

"Or butter burgers." She nodded thoughtfully. "They're hamburgers with a big spoonful of fresh butter on top. I had those all the time when we lived back in Wisconsin. They're gross in concept but taste so, so good."

"You're from Wisconsin? I thought you said you were from Maryland."

"I live there now, but I'm really from all over. Before I moved to Maryland a few years ago, I lived in Brockton, Mass. And before that, Reading, Pennsylvania. And before that, Madison, Wisconsin."

"Whoa, y'all do move around a lot. Is your dad or mom in the military or something?"

"Nope," she said. She lowered her eyes to her plate, not offering any more information.

Naomi shouldn't have mentioned the constant moving during her childhood. She'd wanted to avoid talking about her family and her past.

"So do you miss your friends from Brockton?" he asked. "You miss your school?"

"I didn't have a lot of friends. And I've been homeschooled most of my life."

"Well, I went to regular public schools. I graduated in June. I got an academic scholarship to Marymount University in Virginia. I start there officially in the fall, but I've taken about a semester's worth of college classes at community college so I can get my degree early. I wanna study psychology and maybe get my PhD before I'm thirty."

"Wow, you must be smart," she said, gazing at him with even more appreciation.

So, he was cute and intelligent. Once again, Naomi was trying to figure out what he saw in her.

"I do okay." Khalil dipped his head and shrugged off her compliment.

Her phone buzzed. She checked the screen and saw it was a text from Dawn.

How's the date going? Everything OK?

Naomi rolled her eyes and quickly typed back.

I'm OK. He hasn't kidnapped me.

She saw three blinking dots, then a frown face. **Not funny, Cam,** Dawn typed.

I'M FINE! We're having fun. I'll see you at 11.

She set down her phone.

They chewed their food in silence, hitting their first lull in the conversation.

She'd been so busy trying not to stumble over any chitchat landmines that she hadn't realized he'd been the one asking most of the questions. Naomi didn't want him to think she wasn't interested in getting to know him, that she only wanted to talk about herself. She scoured her brain for a question to ask.

Come up with something. Anything!

"So, why psychology?" she began just as he blurted out, "Why did you say your name was Naomi?"

She blinked. "What?"

"You told me your name was Naomi. Is it like a nickname or somethin'?"

Damn it.

She'd hoped they'd managed to avoid this topic.

Naomi gulped down her soda to buy time, feeling the cold lump travel down her throat and almost lodge itself in her chest.

"No," Naomi said, and coughed. "Umm . . . it's . . . it's my name."

"So why did your mom call you Camryn? And why did they think I was a reporter?" He laughed. "That was . . . weird."

"My name *is* Camryn . . . and Naomi, too. My parents, Dawn and Andre, gave me the name Camryn but . . ." She hesitated. "But my mom called me Naomi. It's the name I've gotten used to. It's . . . it's just hard to let it go."

Khalil leaned forward, bracing his elbows on the sticky tabletop. "*Your mom?* So you're adopted?"

"No, not really."

"I don't get it. How do you have two moms who gave you different names? Was she, like, a surrogate or something?"

Naomi hesitated again.

She hadn't wanted to do this. Not *this* soon. She didn't want to give her whole sordid life story over pizza slices and cola. Even though she'd told it more than three dozen times in almost two years, it was exhausting to say the words, to watch the myriad of emotions flash across the listener's face as she spoke. So instead, Naomi took out her phone and did a quick search for herself online. One of the most recent articles that included a photo of her with the Stoakeses and even one of her mom in her orange jumpsuit, being led away by bailiffs after her sentencing came up.

Her mom had always been plump, but she had lost a lot of weight at the time the photo was taken. Her wheat-colored face looked tired and haggard. Naomi's heart broke every time she saw the photo.

The article shared testimony from the trial that detailed the kidnapping. There was even footage from the grocery store where it had happened, of her mom watching Dawn as she shopped. Dawn juggling her attention between a crying ten-month-old and a rambunctious toddler. When Maya broke free and Dawn went running after her, Naomi's mom seized her opportunity, grabbing Naomi, kissing her cheek, and gently rocking and shushing her before taking her out of the store and away from the Stoakeses for the next fourteen and a half years.

Naomi set her phone back on the table and slid it across for Khalil to see.

"It's easier to read it yourself," she said.

He slowly picked up her cell phone and began to read.

She continued to eat her dinner, keeping her eyes focused on the motion of pulling the long, greasy string of mozzarella before taking a bite, of stirring her straw around and around in her plastic cup, because she didn't want to look at his face. She didn't want to see his pity or his fascination. For once, she'd just wanted to be an average girl on a first date, but Naomi guessed that was nearly impossible, considering everything that had happened to her.

"Whoa," Khalil said a few minutes later. He gazed at her

like he was seeing her for the first time. "I thought you looked familiar. I didn't know . . . I mean, I had no idea that was why."

She didn't respond.

"Man, I can't even imagine what it's like to . . ." His words drifted off. "How are you . . . I mean . . . how do you even deal with all this stuff? How do you seem so . . ."

"So what?"

"So normal."

She laughed. "You think I'm normal?"

"Yeah, when I saw you, I thought, 'Man, that is a cute girl right there. She's a baddie.' "

She closed her eyes and giggled, feeling her cheeks and neck go red.

She always thought Dawn was beautiful and she knew she resembled her. The same big brown eyes, long curly hair, and curves, but Naomi wasn't used to being described that way.

"Then we sat here and started talking and I realized you aren't just a cute girl."

Naomi opened her eyes again.

"You seem pretty cool, too."

That wasn't what she'd expected him to say. It was so disarming that Naomi could feel the restraints she had put around herself since she moved in with the Stoakeses, since her mom was arrested, loosening a bit.

"But I don't *feel* normal. I live with people who call me their daughter and their sister and I don't even remember them," she said, almost with relief.

Naomi had so many feelings that she wouldn't dare share with anyone but her therapist or her journal. It was strange to finally say them aloud.

"Dawn tells me stories about myself . . . stuff I did when I was a baby, and it's like she's talking about someone else. I mean . . . I lived in another part of the country and lived a completely different life with Mom for almost fifteen years until the cops came. Until they brought me 'back home,'" she said, making air quotes. "I still feel like someone played a practical joke on me, dropped me off on some alien planet, and told me 'You thought you were human? No, stupid, you were really another intergalactic species this whole time!'"

Khalil looked at her with pursed lips, making her self-conscious.

Had she said too much? Maybe an emotional dumping on the first date wasn't the best idea.

"Well," he said. "I grew up with my mom and dad and I still feel like an alien around them sometimes. Like they don't know what I am or what the hell I'm talking about. I'll tell them about some cognitive theory I read about or how some doctors are using virtual reality for exposure therapy to help people with anxiety disorder, and my dad will just look at me and say, 'Boy, what are you saying? Speak English!'"

He laughed and Naomi joined him.

"So, *you* may not believe you're normal, but you're a lot more like the rest of us than you think," he said. "Just your background is a little different."

"A little?" she asked, incredulous.

"Well, *a lot* different but . . . it all evens out in the end. We're all different, right?"

Khalil reached across the table and placed a hand over hers and squeezed, catching her by surprise. But she didn't pull away. Instead, she squeezed his hand back.

17

KHALIL PULLED ONTO THE WINDING ROAD LEADING to the cabin just after eleven o'clock. All the lights inside the cabin were out. Only the porch light was on. As they drew closer, she could see Andre reclining in one of the Adirondack chairs. Bear was slumbering at his feet—from a distance resembling a misshapen orange fluffy rug—but the dog raised his head, alert, when Khalil's car approached.

"Good night," she whispered to Khalil after he parked. She opened the car door.

"I'll text you tomorrow. Maybe we can . . . uh . . . meet up again in a couple of days, if you want?" he asked hopefully.

She nodded. "I'd like that," she said, relieved that he wanted to see her again, that she hadn't ruined their date even though she'd told him so many intimate things. He still liked her.

She climbed out and closed the door behind her. As she turned away, Khalil rolled down the passenger side window. "Oh, and Naomi?"

She paused. "Yeah?"

"That smell in town," he said. "It isn't just in your head. You're not the only one who's smelled it."

She gaped. "Are you serious?"

"My nana says it all the time. She said she hates going near Sparksburg. She said it's given her bad vibes since she was a kid and the place stinks. 'Stinks to high heaven,' she says. But none of us can smell it. You're the first person who said they smelled it, too."

"I knew it!" It wasn't her imagination.

As Khalil drove away, Naomi climbed the wooden stairs to the porch and gave Andre a wave. "Hey."

"Hey," he replied with a yawn. "Had a good time?"

"Yeah." Bear walked toward her and licked her wrist. She scratched behind his ear.

"And that young man behaved himself?" Andre asked, narrowing his eyes.

"Yes, Khalil was a perfect gentleman." She gazed up at the cabin's darkened windows. "It looks like everyone else is asleep."

Andre glanced over his shoulder and nodded. "Mom went down early. Said she had a headache. Maya went to sleep not too long after. I made Blake turn off his video game and go to bed about a half hour ago. That kid would be up until dawn if he could, firing away at zombies."

"You didn't have to wait up for me," Naomi said.

Andre cocked an eyebrow. "Of course I did. Just wanted to make sure you came back safe and sound. Go ahead and get some sleep," he said. "We've got a busy day tomorrow. Hiking and whatnot. I'm going to head to bed soon myself."

"Okay, good night," she said.

"Hey, Cam?" Andre said as she stepped inside.

Naomi turned back toward him. "Yeah?"

Andre opened his mouth as if to say something, then abruptly closed it. He shook his head. "Good night, honey. Get a good rest."

She nodded. "I will."

18

NAOMI HADN'T MEANT TO LIE TO ANDRE. SHE'D HAD every intention of going to sleep after she'd brushed her teeth and put on her pajamas. But then, just when she was about to close her curtains and turn off her lamp, her eyes fell on her open satchel. She couldn't help opening it and taking out the book, especially after what Khalil had said about his great-grandmother and Sparksburg.

She said it's given her bad vibes since she was a kid and the place stinks. "Stinks to high heaven," she says.

Naomi wasn't the only one who could smell the stench, who got bad vibes here. Something was wrong with this town. She just couldn't figure out what it was. Maybe the answer was in its past. In Sparksburg's "dark history" as the title said.

She sank beneath her covers with the book and began reading.

First, she read the epigraph. It was a verse taken from a white poet who had grown up in a sundown town in the 1940s:

When the sun goes down in a sundown town
Be wise and beware.
When the sun goes down in a sundown town
Make sure you are scarce.

For when the sun goes down in a sundown town,
Only the foolhardy stay there.

Naomi got the same feeling now as when she read the blurb back at the bookstore, like a pile of bricks had been lowered onto her chest. She read page after page, chapter after chapter, learning more about the sundown town where she and the Stoakeses were now vacationing.

Naomi read about the upheaval during the Civil War and the immediate years after, and how the population of Sparksburg had been driven close to famine. Though most of the enslaved people in Sparksburg did leave with the Union Army, some stayed behind, and the formerly enslaved and their former slave owners had to navigate the new world in which they found themselves and try to rebuild.

The first signs of unrest started with a dispute between a formerly enslaved man named Jesse, who was working as a laborer for his former master, Henry Wainwright. When Jesse wasn't paid the wages he was promised, he refused to do any more work for Henry and sued him for back pay in the local court. His former master threatened that he would regret it. The day before Jesse was supposed to appear before the judge, he disappeared. His neighbors found his cabin empty, with a few embers still burning in his stove hearth. His one pair of shoes sat abandoned by the front door. Jesse was never seen again.

After that, more of the formerly enslaved who tried to assert their new rights as freed men and women began to disappear. Some left town on their own. Others would later be discovered drowned in a nearby creek or left in a hollow of the mountain to rot or be eaten by wild animals. In those cases, at least the families had a body to bury. But most weren't even granted that dignity and their loved ones were left to wonder what had happened to them.

That passage was particularly hard to read, and not just because of the brutality and bloodshed. Loved ones left to wonder about the missing. She couldn't help but think about Dawn and Andre. She wanted to stop reading, but plowed ahead.

When the Black community in Sparksburg tried to rally together to counter this terror, cabins were burned to the ground with families inside. The few remaining Black people who had stayed behind in Sparksburg soon left.

In the early 1900s, Black families started to slowly move into Sparksburg again. Maybe the memories of past terrors had been forgotten, or "time helped heal old wounds," as the saying goes. The Black population ballooned to nearly two hundred by 1910. But then World War I started and a few years later the Spanish flu hit, spreading through Sparksburg like a wildfire. Young men were drafted and never returned home. Families were mowed down like crops after the growing season by a disease that didn't discriminate between the young or old, rich or poor, or Black or white.

In his fiery sermons from the pulpit of the Pentecostal Church of Christ—the very same stone church the Stoakes had passed when they drove into downtown Sparksburg yesterday—Reverend and newly elected Mayor Charles Davis Meacham argued that the locals and the world were being punished for their heathen ways. God was smiting them for not protecting the customs of the past and respecting the purity of their town and "letting the Coloreds back in their borders with their heathen ways," he said. It would only be when they remembered the old ways and "got right with God" that the Spanish flu would disappear and the war would end.

Only then would Sparksburg become "great again," Reverend Meacham assured his congregants.

"Got right with God," Naomi murmured before flipping the page. "That's rich."

In 1921 Sparksburg legally became a sundown town, and the disappearances and murders resumed in Sparksburg with a new fervor. Those who defied the signs that were posted throughout town, saying non-white residents could no longer live within Sparksburg's borders, were punished brutally. Local law enforcement looked the other way when faced with the growing crime spree or sometimes joined in the violence.

All non-white citizens had to be outside the town limits by sunset. The iron bell in the town square would ring to notify anyone within listening distance that the perilous hour was near.

Now, at the mention of the bell, Naomi got a chill. She remembered how Blake had wanted to climb up the gazebo to touch it, to ring it himself.

Reverend Meacham would later die of a heart attack, though the rumor was that he'd been poisoned by his housekeeper, who sought revenge for a nephew who had disappeared.

Naomi could feel her eyelids getting heavier. She yawned and looked down at her cell to see it was a little after 2:00 a.m. Though she wanted to keep reading, her vision was starting to blur. Plus, she had to wake up in a few hours to head out with the Stoakeses to the hiking trail. She had to get some sleep.

Naomi sat the hardback on her small night table and walked to her sliding glass doors.

The moonlight was bright tonight. So bright that it was like having a spotlight in her bedroom. She began to close the curtains but stopped when she spotted a figure outside. Her heartbeat quickened when she saw who it was.

It was the girl. She was back and wearing the same flowing white nightgown, stained at the hem with crusted mud. She was standing several yards away from the cabin in her bare feet, just like the last time Naomi had seen her.

Naomi quickly slid open the door and stepped onto her balcony. "Hey," she called down to her. "Hey, do you live around here?"

The girl didn't answer her. She only continued to gaze up at Naomi silently, as if in a daze, letting her long hair float in the breeze.

"Is everything okay?" Naomi asked her. "My name is Naomi. Do you need help or someplace to stay?"

She didn't know how Andre and Dawn would feel about her offer but she knew the type of people they were. They wouldn't desert a teen girl in need, who was wandering through the forest at night by herself.

"I'll grab my robe. I can come downstairs and . . ."

Her voice trailed off when she saw it. The first spark on one side of the hem of the girl's nightgown. Then another. Then another. Like some unseen person was throwing lit matches at the cotton fabric. Within seconds, the entire hem was aflame.

"Oh my God!" Naomi shouted, lurching back from the balcony. "Oh my God!"

The flames began to grow and climb up the dress, fire latching on to the girl's legs. Then her arms. Then her hair. She lit up like a human candle, like she had been dropped into their firepit in the backyard. The fire and smoke billowed and waved. It was a riotous cacophony of color. Orange, blue, white, and black. Naomi could feel the searing heat from her balcony perch, like she was standing next to an open oven.

The girl in the nightgown didn't fight the blaze. She didn't whip her arms or flail or fall to the ground and roll in circles to put it out. She didn't run. She didn't cry or scream. Instead, she lurched toward the cabin almost drunkenly, even though she was on fire, even though her once beautiful skin was beginning to crack and char from the flames.

Naomi fled from the sight of the girl like she was chasing her, closing her eyes and scrambling blindly to her bed. She could smell the burning flesh. The singed hair. The smoke. Finally, she did hear a scream and realized it was coming from her own mouth. It was loud, shrill, and boundless, as if twenty voices were screaming all at once. Her bedroom door flew open.

"What happened? What's wrong?" Andre yelled.

Naomi opened her eyes to find Andre standing in the doorway in his boxer briefs, looking frantically around him. His body was tense and alert, like he was ready to charge into the room to rescue her or battle her attacker—whichever was required. Dawn was behind him with a silk robe dangling off one of her shoulders. She ran to Naomi's side and drew her close. Naomi couldn't help but tremble in her arms.

"The . . . the girl," Naomi stuttered, pointing at the open glass door with a shaky hand. "She's . . . she's on fire! She's on fire! We have to help her!"

"What?" Andre asked, his voice going up an octave. "What *girl*?" Andre pushed back the curtains. He stepped onto the balcony and leaned over the railing, peering into the night.

"Why is *everyone* shouting?" Maya asked, stumbling bleary-eyed into the room in a Hello Kitty nightshirt. Her eye mask was pushed to her forehead. "I'm trying to sleep."

"Is everything okay?" Blake asked worriedly, stepping from behind Maya. "I heard screaming."

"I don't see anything," Andre said, slowly shaking his head and turning back to them. "Nothing's out there."

"But she was there! She was *right there* and she was on fire! I saw her!"

"It was just a nightmare, honey," Dawn said, gently rubbing her cheek. "Sounds like it was a bad one."

"No! No!" Naomi pushed away from her. "It was the girl from yesterday. She was on fire!"

They were all staring at her now—Dawn and Andre in bafflement, Blake with unease, and Maya with unmasked loathing. Naomi ran to the balcony.

Andre was right; there was nothing out there. No girl. No fire. There were no signs that she had been there either; even the grass where she'd stood mere seconds ago was untouched. Naomi sniffed the air. The smell of smoke and burning flesh had disappeared. She only smelled the usual stink.

"B-b-but she was . . . she was there," Naomi said, turning to face them.

"Sure she was," Maya muttered. "This is stupid. I'm going back to bed. Come on, Blake. You should, too."

"But what about the girl?" he asked as Maya guided him by his shoulders.

"There was no girl. It was just Camryn being weird, per usual. She's addicted to drama. They call it 'main character syndrome,'" Maya said, shoving him down the hall toward their bedrooms.

"Main character what?" he asked, scrunching up his face.

"Forget it," Maya said.

Naomi heard their doors close a beat later.

"She was . . . she was out there. I—I swear," Naomi whispered, now confused herself. "I know how crazy it sounds but—"

"It doesn't sound crazy, sweetheart," Dawn insisted, rubbing Naomi's shoulders like she was cold and Dawn was trying to warm her. "Some dreams are incredibly vivid, and it sounds like you're having a recurring nightmare with this . . . this girl. It happens."

Naomi watched as Andre shut the glass door and the curtains. He gave the bedroom a quick scan. "Your light is on. Were you up reading again? Maybe you fell asleep mid-page and didn't even realize it."

Naomi's eyes were drawn to the night table where the book on Sparksburg sat on top of the haphazard pile of books assembled there. She had just finished the chapter about the murders and mysterious disappearances of the Black residents and had been reading about the cabins set ablaze before that. Could those images have been percolating around in her subconscious and she'd manifested this image of the burning girl? Had she been asleep the whole time like they said?

But then Naomi's gaze shifted to the closed curtains. "The sliding door was open," she argued. "If . . . if I was dreaming, then why was the door open? I wouldn't have fallen asleep with it open like that."

"Then that means you were sleepwalking," Andre said. "I had a friend who used to do it back at Columbia around exam time after we would pull all-night study sessions. People sleepwalk when they're sleep-deprived or under lots of . . . well, lots of stress. Come on, baby," he said to Dawn. "She seems better now. Let her get some rest."

Dawn seemed unsure whether she should stay longer.

"I'm okay," Naomi whispered. "Really."

Finally, Dawn let her go. Naomi fell back onto her bed and watched as they walked toward her door.

"Good night, honey," Dawn said, shrugging into her robe and tying the belt around her waist. "We'll be downstairs if you need us."

"She'll be fine," Andre said to Dawn, before turning to Naomi. "But it's important that you sleep, Cam."

Naomi nodded.

They shut the door and once again Naomi's eyes shifted to the closed curtains. She shuddered at the memory of the girl, of the twisting flames and billowing smoke, and the smell . . . that awful smell.

"It was just a dream," Naomi assured herself. She climbed beneath the covers and sank against her pillows. "I was sleepwalking."

She turned off her lamp, dropping the bedroom into darkness.

19

"JESUS! PICK UP THE PACE, CAMRYN," MAYA BARKED. "You're holding up the line, and I have to pee!"

Naomi blinked and glanced over her shoulder to find Maya glaring at her.

They were finishing up the last leg of Mary's Rock, a three-mile portion of the one-hundred-one-mile Shenandoah National Park section of the Appalachian Trail, but Naomi guessed she had stopped mid-hike to stare off into the distance at . . . *what* exactly? The scenery? She couldn't say. She gave herself a mental shake and nodded. "Yeah, uh, sorry. I was just . . . just . . ."

Maya flapped out her arms. "Just what?"

"Never mind." Naomi adjusted her backpack, faced the trail, and started walking again, even as Maya loudly groused behind her, swatting at the gnats and mosquitoes buzzing around her honey-scented braids.

Once again, Maya had worn something completely impractical: a one-shoulder tank top, jean shorts, and tennis shoes. The dirt, mud, and sweat from hiking painted her outfit with streaks and splatters of green and brown.

"Hey, Troy," Maya said to her boyfriend, who was on her cell screen. "Can I call you back later, babe? I'm being tortured at the moment and can't talk."

Serves you right for being such a bitch, Naomi thought as they trudged forward. *And I hope your bladder bursts.*

Naomi continued to walk, pushing aside a stray tree branch and making her way around an overgrown shrub so she wouldn't trip.

Focus, she told herself as they followed the rocky path downhill. *Put one foot in front of the other. You can do this.*

After dreaming about the burning girl and waking up the entire household with her screams, Naomi had managed to fall back to sleep—eventually. This time, there were no nightmares, but when she'd heard the persistent pulse of her alarm clock, she'd groaned. Morning had come way too soon. If it was up to her, she would have slept several more hours, but she didn't want to ruin the family vacation any more than she already had.

She'd tried to sleep as their SUV made its way along Skyline Drive, putting on her noise-cancellation headphones and using her hoodie as a makeshift pillow—only to get nudged awake by one of Blake's knobby elbows.

Now, no matter how hard she tried, her sleep-starved mind was still lost in a fog. While the Stoakeses had been captivated by the panoramic views of the Shenandoah Valley, taking selfies and videos of the undulating canopy of trees and misty clouds, Naomi had prayed she could finish the three-mile-long trek without stumbling over her own feet and twisting an ankle or accidentally walking off a cliff. So far, she hadn't, but the hike still wasn't over.

"We're almost there, y'all," Andre called back with a grin. He was at the head of the pack and waving them all forward. "I can see the visitors' center and parking lot from here."

"Thank God," Maya mumbled, wiping the sweat from her brow.

"You can always pee in the bushes if you're that desperate," Naomi said, earning another glower from Maya.

"I'd rather die," Maya said.

"We'll take a short break and use the bathrooms," Andre said, sounding more chipper than the Carolina chickadees overhead. "Then on to Rose River Falls! We'll eat and drink in the car on the way there."

A few minutes later, they crossed the parking lot and peeled off their backpacks, rotating their sore shoulders and tugging their now sticky T-shirts from their sweat-soaked bodies. Naomi grimaced as she pulled at her khaki shorts, which were chafing like crazy.

"Okay, everybody, let's meet at the car in fifteen minutes. Got it?" Andre said.

"Outta my way. Outta my way. Outta my way," Maya chanted before bolting past them all and beelining to the women's bathroom. She hurled her body against the steel door and ran inside. "Jesus Christ, it stinks in here!" Maya screeched seconds later. Naomi laughed.

"Are you as desperate as your sister to get in there?" Andre asked.

Naomi shook her head. "Nah, I'm good."

"Well, take Bear, will you? Your mom or I should be back in a sec."

Naomi nodded and took Bear's leash. She walked Bear through the grass and visitors' center lot, pouring him water from her bottle and letting him sniff along the curb and the side of the building. They made their way toward the series of bulletin boards along the entrance of the visitors' center where factoids about the Shenandoah National Park and flyers for local events were displayed.

Naomi spotted a familiar MISSING flyer taped to the board's glass case. It was the same flyer she had seen back in Sparksburg, the *same* one that Mayor Bartz had ripped down. She saw that the girl with dirty-blond hair blowing a sultry kiss to the camera was eighteen-year-old Amber Nash, and she hadn't been seen or heard from for more than a week.

Amber was last seen walking along Route 250, just outside of downtown Sparksburg on June 12, Naomi read. *She might have been hitchhiking. Before her disappearance, a man had been following her for weeks. She was last seen wearing a black halter top, denim skirt, and red sneakers. She has a heart tattoo on her right shoulder, the name "Jake" tattooed on her left hip, and a butterfly tattoo on her left thigh. If you've seen her, please call 555-237-2872 or the Sparksburg Sheriff's Office.*

Naomi didn't know why she did it, but she snapped a few pics of the flyer.

"Hey, what are you guys doing over here?" Dawn asked as she dropped to one knee and ruffled Bear's wrinkled face. "Catch any butterflies, buddy?" She looked up at Naomi. "Spot something interesting, Cam?"

"Huh?" Naomi asked, quickly tucking her phone into the pocket of her shorts. "What do you mean? Why did you say that?" For some reason, she felt guilty.

"Didn't you just take a picture of something?" Dawn asked, rising to her feet.

"Yeah, umm, just stuff about the park," Naomi said. "Like did you know black bears are the only bears in Shenandoah National Park? And . . . uh . . . uh, you can find at least one every square mile. Sucks that we didn't see any on our hike today, huh?"

Dawn looked confused, but nodded. "Yeah, I guess so." She took a step closer to Naomi. "Speaking of the hike, sweetheart . . . your dad and I could tell you were a little . . . distracted today. Did you ever get any sleep last night?"

"Kinda, but I'm fine," she lied.

"Well, if the nightmares come back, let Dad and me know."

"Don't worry. If they come back, you guys will definitely hear about it. Everyone will." Dawn only sighed at Naomi's joke.

"I'm serious, Cam. If you—"

"Hey, strangers!"

Naomi and Dawn turned to find their neighbors, Krissa and Cheryl Jamison, sauntering toward them arm in arm across the parking lot—one short and squat, the other tall and willowy. Their daughter, Elly, was once again clad in head-to-toe black, and trailed behind them.

"We thought it was you!" Cheryl cried cheerily. "I told Krissa, 'That looks like the Stoakeses over there!'" She looked down. "And who is this handsome fella?"

"This is Bear," Dawn said, smiling at their dog. "We just finished hiking Mary's Rock and were waiting for the rest of the family to freshen up before we drove to the next trail."

"Oh?" Cheryl said. "We were about to start Mary's Rock, then head to Stony Man after that."

Krissa shook her head. Her pixie cut swayed. "No, we're headed to Whiteoak Canyon Trail next, babe."

"Nooooo," Cheryl said, blue eyes wide. "I'm pretty sure we agreed on Stony Man, hon."

"No," Krissa argued, "we said we'd try Stony Man later this week, before we head back to Washington Sunday to beat the traffic."

"Well, anyway, we came over here to ask what you think about Sparksburg and Shenandoah so far?" Cheryl asked.

"Have you had a chance to go kayaking?"

"Not yet," Dawn said, "but we plan to go tubing next week."

"You should try the company we used! It was called Raft Adventures or Canoe Adventures." Cheryl snapped her fingers. "What was it called, Krissa?"

"No idea. I just know it cost us an arm and a leg," Krissa said with an eye roll. "The creek was nice but not *that* nice."

"Oh, come on!" Cheryl said, playfully slapping her arm. "We had a good time!"

Naomi listened to the women talk. What was it about old people? They found the most boring things interesting to go on and on about.

Naomi strolled toward Elly, who was leaning against the side of the visitors' center, chewing her nails, which were chipped and painted an iridescent green. The dark-haired girl lowered her hand from her mouth as Naomi approached.

"Hey," Elly said, looking up at her through her heavy bangs.

"Hey." Naomi leaned against the stone wall beside her.

"Are they still talking about the kayaks?" Elly asked.

"Seems like it."

"We were on the water for two hours, saw a deer poop in the water, and I got sunburn." Elly pointed to her pink forearms, where some of the skin was already starting to flake. "Trust me. I'd pass."

"Maybe hiking will be better for you guys," Naomi ventured. "We did it today and I didn't think it was that bad."

"Maybe. But honestly, I'm just ready to go home. My friends are vacationing in Paris and LA this summer, and I'm stuck here. This place blows, and it creeps me out."

Naomi did a double take. *"You too?"*

Elly nodded. "It's not so bad during the day, but at night . . ." Elly's voice trailed off. She started to chew her nails again.

"When it gets dark, I see things, you know. In the trees. Outside. There's some weird stalker who's been hanging around our cabin."

Naomi felt like her heart momentarily stopped. Her mouth went dry.

"I can see them outside my window sometimes," Elly went on.

"Is it a girl? A girl in a nightgown? Did you see her, too?" Naomi asked, now almost excited.

But Naomi's excitement quickly faded when Elly shook her head, looking confused.

"No, I don't think it's a girl. Definitely not a girl in a nightgown. The person was a lot bigger than any girl I've seen, but I can't make out who it is, even when I turn on the lights outside. It's some guy, I think." She glanced at Krissa and Cheryl. "I told my moms that a strange rando has been hanging around the cabin, but they said it's probably just a hunter cutting through the property. But why would he do it *every* night?"

Naomi shrugged. "I don't know."

"That day we first stopped at your cabin, I wanted to warn you about him . . . about the guy, but it was too . . . you know . . . bizarre to just bring up. I guess you haven't seen him though."

"No. No, I haven't," Naomi said.

"Camryn," Andre called. "We're headed to the next trail! You ready, kid?"

"Look, umm, that's my dad. I've gotta go. Hope your vacation sucks less before it's over."

"Yeah, me too, but I doubt it."

Naomi ran across the parking lot toward the car, giving Elly one last look. She climbed inside the SUV, and a minute later, they were heading toward Skyline Drive.

20

"YOU TWO HAVE BEEN HAVING THE SAME DREAM?" Khalil asked a couple of days later, glancing at Naomi as he drove. "You're seeing the same girl outside your windows at night?"

"No, I was the only one having nightmares about the girl. Our neighbor Elly said she's been seeing a guy at night near her cabin in real life." Naomi adjusted the visor to block out the sun's glare. "She doesn't know who it is though. She can't make out his face in the dark."

They were on their second date, and thankfully Dawn and Andre hadn't made her promise to check in with them this time. Khalil wouldn't tell her what they were doing or where they were headed. He'd only told her to "bring sunglasses and wear comfortable clothes and sturdy shoes."

Now that they were driving there, Naomi kept trying to trick him into revealing their destination, but Khalil remained tight-lipped. Instead, he distracted her by asking about all that had happened over the past few days: the nightmare that made her wake up everyone in their cabin, hiking in the Shenandoah Valley, and the story Elly had told her about the mysterious guy lurking around the Jamisons' cabin.

"That's weird as hell. She really has no idea who the stalker could be?" Khalil asked.

"It doesn't seem like it." Naomi shrugged. "It could be anybody."

"You know what she should do?" Khalil mused. "She should put her camera phone in her window at night and press record. Let that thing run all night. Maybe the camera can see more than she can, and she can show her moms the footage."

Naomi thought about it. "You know what? That's a good idea." She patted his shoulder. "I knew you were smart, Khalil."

"Yeah, I say it all the time, but nobody listens to me." He laughed.

"I'll tell her your camera phone idea when I see her Friday. The Jamisons invited us to come to their cabin for dinner. They're preparing a big meal before they drive back to DC on Sunday."

"Cool! Sounds like a plan. Let me know if she sees anything."

A few minutes later, Khalil pulled off the highway and followed a bumpy gravel road until they passed a large green sign on the shoulder that said MURRAY'S TREETOP ZIP-LINING.

"Zip-lining?" Naomi cried in surprise. "You're taking me zip-lining?"

He grinned, showing off the dimples she was growing to love. "Yeah! Have you ever been zip-lining before?"

"No, I haven't."

"Me neither. I'd thought it'd be fun though."

"Yeah, it's an awesome surprise but . . . what if I had a fear of heights?"

"Oh, damn." Khalil's grin faded. "I didn't think of that. *Do* you have a fear of heights?"

Naomi gave a nervous giggle. "I don't think so."

Unfortunately, she was wrong. Naomi realized that a half hour later, after the zip-line instructor checked the straps on her helmet and her harness, after she and Khalil made the thirty-foot climb with a mother and daughter duo to the first zip-lining platform.

When they reached the top, Naomi looked around at the awe-inspiring view of the Appalachian Mountains and the seemingly endless blue sky—and the football field of open terrain that lay between them and the next platform. Her vision started to go topsy-turvy like the platform was moving up and down, like she was walking through the fun house at the carnival her mom had taken her to when she was seven years old.

This was different from when she'd climbed up the mountain cliffs with the Stoakeses a couple of days ago. Then, Naomi hadn't been expected to hurl herself off the side of the summit. Now the idea of jumping off the platform and trusting a rope, harness, and steel clips to keep her safe made her heart race and her stomach queasy. She had to take several deep breaths to stay calm.

"You ready?" Khalil asked. He had no idea how panicked she was.

Naomi forced a smile. "Yep!"

Khalil and Naomi stood back as the mother and daughter went first. The mother leaped only after saying a quick prayer and making the sign of the cross. They could hear the woman's scream echo across the mountaintop as she flew to the next platform. Her daughter, a blond girl who had to be eleven or twelve, went next. She excitedly pumped her fists before leaping off the platform with a banshee cry when the instructor finished his countdown. Her pigtails flew behind her as she sailed across the field with arms outstretched like a superhero.

"All right, who's up next?" the instructor asked, gazing expectantly at Naomi and Khalil.

Their instructor resembled a fit Santa Claus with his white fluffy beard and muscles.

"Do you want to go first?" Khalil asked her. "Makes no difference to me."

She gazed at the field again. The world was starting to tilt and spin again. Naomi gripped the railing to steady herself. It felt like her feet were about to go flying from underneath her.

"Umm, I don't . . . I don't think I can do this," she whispered to Khalil.

"Huh? I didn't hear you. Did you say you're going first?" Khalil asked, leaning closer to her.

"I don't think I can do this. I thought I could, but I'm . . . I'm freaking out."

"Still deciding, folks?" the instructor asked.

"Uh, yeah," Khalil said to him, plastering on a fake smile. He turned to her and placed a hand on her shoulder, now looking concerned. "Do you wanna walk back down?"

She glanced at the rope ladder and winding staircase leading to the ground below and had to squeeze her eyes shut. "I don't think I can do that either."

"Whoa, you really are freaking out, huh?"

"I'm so sorry. I don't know what it is." She cringed. "I—I thought I could do it, but I can't. I just can't!"

"It's okay, Naomi. Just take deep breaths. Deep breaths."

"This is crazy! I mean, who does this? I'm not some adrenaline junkie. I don't wanna die in—"

She stopped short when she felt his lips against hers. It was a quick kiss, only a few seconds, but she blinked in shock.

"Did you just kiss me?" she breathed.

Khalil nodded. "You were spiraling. I thought you were going to have a panic attack. I read once in this psychology book that one way to stop a spiral is to refocus your attention, so I thought, 'Why not kiss her?' Did it work?"

Naomi thought for a moment. It *did* work. She was definitely less concerned about falling to her death. Khalil had *actually* kissed her. Her first real kiss.

Naomi's cheeks . . . her entire face was still flushed but now for a very different reason.

"Hate to break in on you lovebirds," the instructor said, "but one of you is going to have to go next. The ladies on the other side are waitin' on us."

"I'll go," Naomi said shakily. She wanted to do it before she lost her nerve. Plus, her neck and chest were starting to feel hot and getting hotter every second Khalil looked at her.

"Well, let's get at it! I'm gonna count down for you. And when I hit three, I want you to step off the platform, tuck your feet beneath you, and let gravity do the rest," the instructor said. He locked her harness onto the rope that would take her to the other side, then tugged at it to make sure it was secure. "One . . . two . . . three!"

He kissed me, Naomi thought again dreamily, right before she took the leap. *He really kissed me.*

She felt braver now. Naomi forced herself to keep her eyes open so she could see it all. The sky, trees, and mountains rushing past her at warp speed. The way the mountain dew on the leaves sparkled in the sunlight like jewels. She was moving so fast, it felt as if she was flying. That she was weightless.

She let out a delighted scream like the girl in pigtails. For a fleeting moment, she felt a bliss that she hadn't felt in quite a while.

When her feet landed on the next platform thirty seconds later, she was breathing hard and her heart was still beating rapidly in her chest. A man stepped forward—one of Murray's Treetop's employees, to unhook her from the harness. She saw the girl and her mother were already descending the ladder to the ground below.

She turned and watched as Khalil zip-lined toward her. His arms were spread wide. His long legs were tucked underneath him. His oversize T-shirt billowed around him like a cape. He looked like a superhero preparing to land.

When he did hit the platform, he was grinning just as much as Naomi was.

"Gotdamn!" he shouted as his harness was unhooked. "That was crazy! Wasn't that crazy? It felt so . . . so . . ." He struggled to find the right words.

"Free," she finished for him.

He nodded eagerly. "Yeah, exactly!"

Naomi had felt true freedom as she flew over the canopy, like she was no longer shackled by her past or present. She wasn't some kidnapping victim who was trying to connect with the family she didn't remember. She wasn't the girl who still yearned for her mom. She wasn't terrified of being recognized in public and worried her life would never be normal again.

"You did look happy. I was worried you'd be crying the whole way across, but you were fearless once you took the leap. It was cool to watch you glide."

"Yeah," she said, her grin slowly evaporating.

"What? What's wrong?"

"I just . . . . I just hate that it had to end, you know? I was floating up there like nothing mattered. It was . . . nice."

"Well, the date isn't over. Wanna go again?"

"Yes! Yes!" she said, practically racing him to the ladder. "Come on!"

21

AN HOUR AND A HALF LATER, NAOMI AND KHALIL strolled down the mud-crusted driveway back to his car. As he kicked at pebbles, she kept her gaze on the sunset. Today was amazing, from the zip-lining to the kiss. She remembered the fleeting sensation of his full lips against hers, of his mustache tickling her nose, and it made her giddy.

My first real kiss, she kept thinking over and over again.

"Sorry for scaring you at first," he said, shoving his hands into his jean pockets.

"It's fine. Every new thing is scary at first, but once I got over being nervous, I was glad I did it." She turned away from the sunset and gave him a side glance. "Thanks for . . . you know . . . helping me . . . with . . . with all that."

He slowed his steps as they neared his car. "You mean thanks for kissing you?"

She giggled and nodded, feeling her cheeks warm again. Thank God for her brown skin or her cheeks and neck would be so red right now.

"Yeah, I took a chance with that one. I was hoping you wouldn't slap the hell outta me." He leaned against the side of the car. "It gave me a good excuse to shoot my shot though, you know?"

"So you didn't do it to just keep me from freaking out up there? You wanted to kiss me?"

He laughed and nodded. "Well, yeah! I wanted to kiss you back on our first date but you said you were mostly home-schooled and didn't have a lot of friends. It sounded like you were pretty isolated, so I guess that meant you haven't done a lot of dating either. I thought you'd think I was moving too fast if I went in for a kiss at the mall."

He was right. She would've.

"So, I took a chance today." He pushed himself away from his car and drew closer.

She worked up the nerve to meet his gaze. At this angle, the sun gave his tight curls and long eyelashes brown and golden tips that were mesmerizing. His dark eyes were so warm and intense, her stomach flip-flopped.

"I'd like to kiss you again, Naomi, if that's okay with you."

She took a shuddering breath, hoping her racing heart wouldn't seize up.

"Sure," she whispered. "That would be . . . umm . . . nice."

He stepped forward, cupped her face, and lowered his head. She closed her eyes as their lips met and she swore she saw stars. She felt the butterflies in her stomach that she kept hearing about in films and books. Naomi swore they were trying to flutter their way out because their invisible wings were beating so fast.

When he pulled away a minute later, she smiled.

He trailed his thumb along her lower lip. "I should get you home. Your dad is probably on the front porch waiting for you again."

"Probably, but . . . one more kiss before we go?"

Khalil nodded before kissing her again, and this kiss really did take her breath away.

22

"CAM, CAN YOU GRAB THE BOTTLE OF WINE CHILLING in the fridge for me?" Dawn asked Friday night.

Naomi nodded. She spotted the bottle of sauvignon blanc and sat it on the granite island.

"Thanks, honey," Dawn said as she placed a napkin around the basket filled with freshly baked dinner rolls.

"Where'd you get the wine?" Naomi asked, bracing her elbows against the counter and examining the orange label. "Looks fancy."

"At Sunny Market. You know? That little grocery store in town. We went there yesterday to grab more supplies. The store owner, Nelson, recommended this vintage. I just hope the Jamisons like white wine."

"Not much of a choice if they don't," Andre said, strolling into the kitchen and kissing Dawn's cheek. He reached for a dinner roll but Dawn slapped his hand away. "We should get going if we're going to make it there by seven, baby."

"I know." Dawn tucked her hair behind her ears and smoothed out the wrinkles in her shirt.

Dawn and Andre had ditched their vacation gear for business casual clothes tonight. Dawn was even wearing a little makeup. "I'm ready if you guys are."

"Guys!" Andre shouted up the spiral staircase. "Let's go! We need to head to the Jamisons' *now*!"

Ten minutes later, they were all piled into the SUV with the exception of Maya.

"Where the hell is she?" Andre asked. "That child said she would be down five minutes ago."

"Getting ready is a big production for her." Dawn sighed. "If she manages to get her clothes on and her hair and makeup done in less than an hour, I consider it a victory."

"I could be playing *Zombie Reign* right now!" Blake flailed dramatically and let out a long, tortured groan.

Everyone else was annoyed with Maya, but for once Naomi didn't mind her older sister's diva antics. Instead, she was staring wistfully at the sky.

She was still thinking about Khalil and the many kisses they'd shared at the park. They'd even managed to sneak in a few more during the drive back to the cabin. Naomi had been floating on a cloud ever since. She'd lie in bed listening to the same love song playlist that played on the radio during their drive back, letting it run in a loop.

Kiss me, your lips taste of honey
Songbirds and bees start a-hummin'

It made her remember the way the dew drops twinkled off the leaves as she flew over the trees and the warmth of Khalil's full lips. "Why do you keep giggling?" Blake had asked her yesterday with a frown. "What's so funny?"

"Just grown-up stuff, Blake," she'd said with a wink before twirling away. "You wouldn't understand."

Khalil had invited her to come with him to a cookout one

of his uncles was throwing tomorrow. Naomi couldn't wait to see him again.

"There she is! Finally!" Andre cried, snapping Naomi out of her blissful daydream. She'd been fantasizing about her and Khalil lying on a blanket in the grass, kissing beneath the branches of a grand oak tree.

Maya was wearing a blue miniskirt, platform sandals, and matching off-the-shoulder top. She'd pulled her braids into a long *I Dream of Jeannie* ponytail that showed off the oversize gold hoops dangling from her earlobes.

It never failed. Maya insisted on dressing like she was going to an exclusive exotic cruise or a new nightclub. Naomi guessed Maya hadn't gotten the memo that they were only headed to a family dinner at their neighbors' cabin.

"I'm here!" Maya said, getting into the car. "Sorry I took longer than expected, but I couldn't decide on what top to wear. I settled on the one you bought me last summer, Mom. You like it?"

"Yes, it's very cute, Maya," Dawn said flatly. "But please be more thoughtful of your family and the people who invited us to dinner next time you're deciding on your wardrobe. It's rude to keep everyone waiting."

Maya's smile faded. "Sorry, Mom," she whispered.

THEY ARRIVED AT the Jamisons' five minutes later, just as clouds gathered overhead, darkening the sky. It had been easy to find their cabin once they got off the main road. The layout of the property was almost identical to the Stoakeses' vacation house, except the Jamisons' also had a small pond.

She noticed that all the windows were dark. It looked like no one was home.

"Honey," Andre began as he parked a few feet away from the cabin's stairs. He leaned toward the windshield and frowned. "Are you sure the dinner was scheduled for tonight?"

Dawn nodded. "Yes, she said Friday night, seven o'clock."

"Then why are all the lights out?"

"I have no idea. Cheryl said to come here tonight at seven." Dawn pulled out her phone and showed him the text.

Naomi eased forward in her seat to read the text, too.

We'd love to have you guys for dinner Friday. How does 7 PM sound?

Andre's frown deepened. "So did they forget about our dinner plans? Or maybe an emergency came up and they had to leave town early." Andre tapped his fingers on the steering wheel and took a deep breath before unbuckling his seat belt. "I'll try ringing the doorbell. Maybe they're just in another part of the house or in the backyard."

Naomi watched as Andre took the cabin stairs two at a time. He left his car door yawning open so the open-door alarm began to ring as they waited. A few fireflies floated by the driver's-side mirror.

Naomi gazed around at the empty yard and cabin. Under the shade of nearby trees, shadows stretched across the gravel driveway and the front porch, making objects that would seem sedate during the day, like the ceramic bullfrogs by the foot of the stairs and the wicker chair by the front door, look almost spectral and forbidding, like prop pieces in a haunted house.

A slow chill made its way up Naomi's spine. The hairs on her arms began to stand on end. She waited for someone else to speak. For Maya to make one of her snarky comments. For Dawn to start her usual "concerned parent" small talk and ask them how they were feeling and if they were enjoying their vacation so far, but no one said anything. She wondered if they felt the burgeoning disquiet, too, as if it had climbed into the driver's seat in Andre's stead.

Naomi remembered the chapters she'd read in her book about the families that had disappeared in Sparksburg more than a hundred years ago and how only traces of them had been left behind. Was that what it was like inside the Jamisons' cabin right now? Was the television still burning bright in Elly's bedroom or makeup and hair brushes still sitting next to one of the bathroom sinks where Cheryl or Krissa had gotten ready that morning? Had they disappeared, too?

Naomi suddenly wished Andre would run back to the SUV and drive far, far away from here.

But he didn't.

All that was in the past, like Khalil had said. Sparksburg wasn't like that anymore. So she bit down on her bottom lip as Andre pressed the glowing yellow doorbell. She clenched her hands in her lap as he waited for a beat before pressing the doorbell again. After about a minute or so, he turned to the car and shook his head. "No one's answering," he said.

"Are we going home now?" Blake asked, saying out loud what everyone else in the SUV was probably thinking.

The Jamisons obviously weren't there. There was no point in lingering.

Dawn smiled. "I guess so, buddy. Looks like we're eating leftovers tonight."

Naomi breathed a sigh of relief when Andre got into the car.

"I just hope everything is okay," Dawn said as they backed out of the driveway.

"I'm sure they're fine, honey," Andre said. "Plans change. That's all."

Naomi took one last look out the rear window and watched as the Jamisons' cabin grew smaller as they drove away.

23

"CAMRYN!" DAWN CALLED OUT THE NEXT DAY. "Khalil is here!"

"Coming!" Naomi called back, closing her novel just as the warriors began a battle to the death that would determine the fate of their two villages. She wanted to find out what happened next, but wanted to see Khalil more, so she raced down the hall to check her reflection in the bathroom mirror. Naomi shifted her headband and swept her long curls forward toward her face, then changed her mind and flung them over her shoulders before adjusting the spaghetti straps of her sundress.

Her hands shook with nervous energy. She took a deep breath to calm down and quickly dabbed her usual Vaseline concoction in her nose before meeting Khalil at the front door. He was talking to Dawn and Andre. Naomi had to restrain herself from leaping into his arms and planting kisses on his face. She'd been fantasizing about doing that for days.

"Hey," he said.

"Hey!" she gushed.

"Well, shoot, baby," Andre said, snapping his fingers and giving Dawn a sly smile. "Cam made it downstairs before we could break out the baby pictures."

"You wouldn't dare," Naomi grumbled. Andre chuckled.

"I know the perfect one. It's one of Camryn when she was

eight months old," Dawn said. "She'd grabbed the baby powder when I wasn't looking and blasted herself in the face. She looked like a demented pastry chef. It was so cute."

"I'd love to see that one," Khalil said.

"No!" Naomi ushered him outside before Andre and Dawn could embarrass her any more. Dawn and Andre laughed hard as Naomi and Khalid jogged down the cabin stairs.

"Have a great time at the barbecue, guys!" Dawn called after them.

"We will!" Naomi shouted back.

They'd certainly have a better time than the family had yesterday, eating leftover pizza after being stood up by the Jamisons for dinner.

Dawn had texted them during the drive back to the cabin. Cheryl texted an hour later apologizing profusely, admitting they'd completely forgotten about their dinner plans.

Here Naomi was thinking something nefarious had happened to the Jamisons, when the truth was Cheryl was just a scatterbrain.

"You know the drill. Home by eleven at the latest," Andre now said from the doorway. "Both hands on the wheel and eyes on the road with my little girl in the front seat. Okay, Khalil?"

"Got it, sir." He gave Andre a salute. Khalil raced around the car to open Naomi's door so she could climb inside. As soon as they were out of view of the cabin and hit the main road, Naomi leaned over and planted butterfly kisses on his cheek, neck, and ear. He burst into laughter.

"Hey! I'm drivin' here!" Khalil said, giving her a grin. "Are you trying to make me swerve off the road?"

"Of course not." She slid back into her seat. "I was just excited to see you again."

"Well, we can skip the cookout, pull over, and you can keep

showing me how excited you are if you'd like. I won't mind. Trust me."

Naomi's mouth fell open. Her cheeks flared with heat as she slapped his shoulder. "Khalil!"

"Okay, okay," he said, laughing again. "You know me. I had to shoot my shot." He pulled her close, kissing her quickly before returning his attention to the road. "Cookout it is."

Khalil's Uncle Otis was throwing the barbecue. He lived two towns over, even higher up in the mountains than the cabin where the Stoakeses and Naomi were staying. They drove for about thirty minutes along the mountainside, giving them breathtaking views of the steep valley below. Naomi noticed higher up in the mountains that the perfume in her nose wasn't necessary. The foul smell of Sparksburg was gone. They took a back road that led to a path dense with trees. Their heavy canopy blocked out most of the sunlight. She wondered if Khalil was going to have to turn on his headlights to see the rest of the way. It was like someone had carved out the path with bulldozers and excavators, but hadn't bothered to clean up the road when they were done, leaving behind six feet of exposed roots, rocks, leaves, and earth.

"Where are we going?" Naomi asked uneasily. "Your uncle seriously lives up *here*?"

"Yep! Don't worry," Khalil said. "We're almost there."

She heard the music first. The thumping beat of an old R&B tune that was so loud it made the windows rattle. Then it was like someone suddenly pulled back a heavy curtain, and she saw the sun and blue sky again. There was an open field littered with cars, mostly pickup trucks and SUVs. A crowd of what had to be at least fifty people was slowly walking uphill.

At the top of the hill was a gargantuan rambler decorated in all things red, white, and blue for the upcoming July Fourth celebration next week. There were balloons, streamers, American flags, and pinwheels.

"Wow," Naomi said, following the rest of the crowd, "there are a lot of people here, Khalil."

"I've got a big family." Khalil shrugged. "We come here every summer. Uncle Otis's annual cookout is like our family reunion."

"What's up, Big K!" someone called to him.

Khalil raised his arm and waved. "What's up, Dee!"

For once, Naomi wasn't focused on whether someone would recognize her. Instead, she was more worried about fitting in. She liked Khalil and wanted to be accepted by this sprawling network of aunts and uncles, cousins and grandparents.

"Don't worry," he said, seeing the bewildered look on her face. He gave her a quick kiss, then squeezed her hand. "They're chill people. And if *I* like you, they'll like you," he said, reading her mind.

She smiled.

They reached the house and rounded the corner to the backyard, where even more people were congregating around picnic tables and milling about the deck. At the grill stood a tall man with a backward-turned cap. A group of teenage boys were playing football on the other side of the field, shouting and laughing. Some people were doing a line dance, shuffling their feet and wiggling their hips to the music.

"Khalil!"

A girl her age raced across the yard, darting her way through the crowd. She was short and buxom and wore her hair parted into two afro puffs. Her low-riding jeans revealed a belly ring. When she drew near them, she leaped into Khalil's arms, catching him off guard. He shouted out in surprise. The girl wrapped her arms around his neck and squealed excitedly. A group of guys trailed behind her, forming a semicircle.

Naomi stared at the young woman, unnerved by the way she was clinging to Khalil. Who was she? Judging from her body language, Naomi supposed she was an ex-girlfriend.

Khalil disentangled himself and turned to Naomi. For the first time, the young woman noticed her standing there.

"Naomi, this is my cuz Alexis," he said, gesturing to the girl at his side. "Well, not my real cousin. I just call her that because our parents have been friends since before we were born. She lives around here."

"Hi," Alexis said, resting her hand on one hip and fluttering her fingers in greeting.

"And that's my real cousin Darius," he said, pointing to a guy in cornrows. "That's my cousin Hakeem, my cousin Chris, and that goofy ass over there is my little brother, Antonio," he said, jabbing his thumb toward a dark-skinned boy who looked to be thirteen or fourteen years old, with braces and short dreads with blond tips.

"No disrespect, Naomi, but you must be desperate if you came here with this dude," Antonio said, causing the cousins to hoot and cackle.

"Shut up," Khalil said, punching his brother in the shoulder. He grabbed Naomi's hand again. "Come on. Let's get away from these clowns." He steered her across the yard. "Let me introduce you to everybody."

She met his mom and dad. His mom was plump with a wide smile that seemed to take up the entire bottom half of her face. Naomi could see where Khalil got his dimples.

"Well, ain't she just the cutest little thing!" his mom drawled before enveloping Naomi in her thick arms that smelled like cocoa butter. "As pretty as can be, too!"

His dad was tall and lean, with chestnut colored skin. He looked like an older version of Khalil with his same long eyelashes and roman nose, except his dad had a bald head and not Khalil's afro curls and clean shape-up.

"We haven't scared you off yet, have we, Naomi?" he asked.

She shook her head bashfully. "Not yet . . . I mean no, sir."

"Just call me Mark."

He turned to an elderly woman sitting in a wheelchair beside him. "And this here is Nana, my grandmother and Khalil's great-grandmother."

Her hair was stark white and parted into two long braids that were pinned in a bun at her crown. She was wearing capris and a short-sleeved peasant blouse, revealing the liver spots and ropey veins on her frail arms and legs.

He placed a hand on her shoulder. "Nana, this is Khailil's friend Naomi."

So this was Nana, Naomi thought, gazing at the old woman with fascination. The one who avoided Sparksburg because she could smell the stench like Naomi could, who also said the town gave her bad vibes.

"Hello, ma'am," Naomi said, bending down slightly so that she was eye level with Nana. "It's a pleasure to meet you."

Should she ask her about Sparksburg? After living near the town for so long, did the old woman know more about Sparksburg than what Naomi had read in her book?

Nana squinted up at Naomi with eyes that were almost gray from cataracts. She raised her hand to her ear. "What you say?"

"She said hello, Nana!" Khalil's mother shouted into Nana's ear before giving Naomi a shrug. "She's a little hard of hearing."

"Oh," Naomi said. So much for asking his great-grandmother questions about Sparksburg.

Naomi met more of Khalil's relatives, including Uncle Otis, who was the guy in the backward baseball cap manning the grill. He assembled a plate for her, proudly pointing to the barbecue ribs.

"I let those bad boys marinate for three days. You'll wanna slap your mama with how good they are," he promised. "If you're brave enough, I've got some rabbit and venison, too. Hunted them myself right here in the valley."

"And he only hunts the best," Khalil's Aunt Loretta said, placing a hand on Uncle Otis's shoulder. "My man's one of the best trackers in the county!"

Naomi forced a polite smile. "I'll just take the ribs for now."

Though she honestly couldn't see herself requesting a sample of Bambi and Thumper when she got seconds.

Laden down with plates and drinks, Naomi and Khalil made their way across the yard to one of the picnic tables. As soon as they sat down, Khalil's cousins all piled around them.

"Hey!" Khalil yelled as his brother, Antonio, snagged one of Khalil's hot dogs, roughly bumping Naomi as he did.

Alexis sat on the other side of Khalil, practically plastered to his side. She held out a slice of watermelon. "They ran out ten minutes ago, but I grabbed you some before they did," Alexis said. "I know how much you like it."

"Thanks, Alexis!" Khalil took a bite before turning to Naomi. "Did you want some, too?"

"No, I'm good." Naomi tried not to look annoyed.

After that, she and Khalil barely said a word to one another. It was almost impossible to hear each other over all the shouting at the table.

"You should've seen me smoke all of them in a hundred-yard dash before you got here, K," his cousin Chris said.

He was light-skinned with freckles. His orangish-red hair was in cornrows.

"Man, stop lying," Darius said, sucking his teeth. He was much darker and wore braces. "You ain't smoke nobody. You cheated!"

"I did not!" Chris rose to his feet.

"Oh, here we go," Khalil said with a laugh, rolling his eyes.

"Yes, you did, bruh!" Darius shouted. "We said 'go' on the count of three. And you started on one."

"No, I didn't! Just admit y'all can't keep up with me, son." Chris popped the collar of his polo shirt, leading to a chorus of outrage.

As the two cousins continued to argue and the rest joined in, Naomi leaned toward Khalil's ear.

"I'm going to the bathroom, okay?" she said.

"Huh?" he shouted, leaning closer to her.

She cupped her hands around her mouth. "I said I'm going to the bathroom!"

He nodded and Naomi eased off the wooden bench and headed toward the house in search of a bathroom, and, more importantly, someplace that wasn't pulsing with so much noise and people.

Being around Khalil's boisterous family reminded her that she was a girl who'd grown up in mostly solitude and quiet. It was all getting to be a little too much. She needed to find a place where she could be alone just for a few minutes.

24

NAOMI EXCUSED HER WAY PAST UNCLE OTIS, WHO was flipping another batch of burgers on the grill, and Aunt Loretta, who was shimmying to music. She barely dodged getting sprayed with water guns by a bunch of five-year-olds before she slid open the screen door and stepped into a deserted kitchen.

She was relieved to find it empty. All she saw were piles upon piles of dirty dishes and half-filled Tupperware. No people. She took a deep, calming breath.

"Hey! Hey, chile!" At the sound of snapping, Naomi turned around. Khalil's nana sat in a wheelchair in the living room.

So much for finding a moment of quiet. "Yes, ma'am?" Naomi said, giving a tentative smile.

"Turn this up for me, will you?" she croaked, pointing at a dusty floor fan nearby. "It was too hot out there. Told one of the boys to bring me inside and it's just as steamy in here. I need some air."

"Umm, sure." Naomi walked into the living room and adjusted the knob on top of the fan to high. "Is there anything else I can get you?" Naomi asked.

The old woman frowned and narrowed her eyes up at Naomi. "You Khalil's girlfriend, ain't you?"

"Girlfriend?" Was that what his family was calling her? Her cheeks reddened. "Well, umm, I don't know if I'd say girlfriend. We've only been on a couple dates and—"

"I heard you live in those new cabins in town," Nana interrupted. "Is that true?"

Naomi nodded. "Yes, ma'am. We're . . . uh . . . we're vacationing there. Me and my . . . uh, my family."

Nana slowly shook her head. "Y'all shouldn't be there. None of y'all should be staying in that town. I told my grandson when they were building those cabins that it wasn't safe for folks like us."

Naomi's polite smile faded. "Why? Because it used to be a sundown town?"

The old woman leaned forward. She seemed to regard Naomi more keenly with eyes that probably were once brown, in her youth, but were now gray—almost milky white. "You know about that?"

"Yeah . . . I mean yes. There's a book about the town by Joshua Ellington."

"Who?" She went silent and paused to think for a bit. "Never heard of the Ellington family. Are they from 'round here?"

"No, Joshua Ellington is a historian from the University of Virginia, ma'am. I saw the statue of Reverend Charles Davis Meacham in the town square and . . . and the bell they used to ring when the sun went down," Naomi went on, growing more and more nervous under Nana's intense gaze. "I noticed Mayor Meacham on the cover of Ellington's book, so I bought it. You see, I'm . . . I'm a big reader. I love books . . . stories."

"So you know what they did to the Black folks? How they scared them out after the Civil War?" Nana asked.

Naomi nodded.

"Did you know they kept the children though? Killed their

mamas and daddies, but made the children into their own little slaves."

Naomi stilled. "No, I read that they all left Sparksburg and didn't come back until the early 1900s."

"Is that what you read? Humph." Nana grunted and pointed to a nearby leather recliner. "Have a seat, girl. I've got another story to tell you."

Naomi sat.

"My great-grandfather Bill was one of them," Nana began. "One of the children. He and his twin sister, Willamena. Their daddy was hung. They never found out what happened to their mama. Grandpa Bill went to work for Old Man Butler. Willa was sent to work for the McDougalls. But she wasn't good at housework. She was never the same after she saw what happened to her daddy. Willa stopped talking after he was strung up. Wouldn't utter a word anymore. Sometimes she would start hanging clothes on the line and forget what she was doin' midway and just wander off. She'd drop dishes she was washin' because of how distracted she got. It made her clumsy. Willa got punished by the McDougalls when she made a mistake. Got punished real bad."

Naomi cringed, imagining the poor young girl being forced into labor after her parents' murder and then having to suffer abuse at the hands of her "employers."

Glorified kidnappers, Naomi thought with disgust.

"They kept Grandpa Bill and his sister apart for nearin' five years. When he was old enough to leave . . . when the town *made* him leave, he went lookin' for her. They said she'd run away, but he knew it wasn't true. She would never leave without him. Without telling him where she was going." Nana sighed, making her nostrils flare. "She disappeared like her mama did."

Naomi felt a chill snake its way down her spine. She couldn't help but shiver.

"After a while, people forgot the past or tried to forget it. One by one, Black families moved back in town and tried to start fresh. Bought farms, built homes, and tried to make what they could from the land. But when Mayor Meacham took over Sparksburg back in the '20s like some king, instead of Black folks moving in, people started to leave again. They had to. Anybody who wasn't white . . . anybody who *they* felt wasn't fit to live in their town, had to be out of city limits by sunset. They had patrols to make sure. But some would ignore the rules. They'd stay an extra hour or two to finish field work or to finish a drink at some juke joint three towns over and have to cross through Sparksburg to get home—and they'd pay the price for it.

"My cousin Jimmy did it back in '57. He was seventeen years old. His friends dared him to sneak into Sparksburg one night. He made it back the first time. Had his chest all puffed out. Won three dollars that day. Then they dared him to do it again. Except this time he had to stay there until dawn. They waited for him at the border, laughin' and drinkin', watching for him to come smilin' and waving over the hill. But when the sun came up, Jimmy didn't come back. We never saw him again."

"I'm so sorry," Naomi whispered.

"He never should've gone there. He knew what could happen. But now people are floutin' the rules again. My grandson was working there after dark, building those cabins. Now your family is staying there. I don't like it. I don't like it at all. You don't set foot in Sparksburg after dark."

Naomi hesitated, wanting to take the old woman seriously, but if she did, that meant Naomi and her family were in danger. They'd have to leave town immediately. "I get what you're saying, ma'am. Really, I do. I was scared, too, when I read about what happened in Sparksburg decades ago. But we've been there for more than a week and nothing has happened to us. And your family stayed here," Naomi countered. "There must be something good about the area. It can't be that bad."

"We stayed for the dead, chile. First, hoped they'd come back home. Then when we figured out that wasn't gonna happen . . . that they were never coming home, we stayed to pay vigil for the ones we lost. So that the ghosts who can't leave, who are chained to the soil, won't get lonely here."

"Ghosts?" Naomi gaped. "You mean, like *real* ghosts?"

"Do you know any other kind?" Nana asked, tilting her head. "I can smell 'em, you know? Those spirits rotting like a body in the open while they wait for a proper burial. Waitin' to be sent home to glory by their loved ones. It's a god-awful stink."

Naomi raised her hand to her nose.

So, that's what she was smelling in town? The dead? She remembered the burning girl she'd seen outside her cabin window days ago. She hadn't seen her since then and had convinced herself that it had all been a dream, a nightmare brought on by the stress of missing her mom and her old life. It had been conjured by the gruesome stories about Sparksburg that she'd read for hours before falling asleep. But now Naomi was starting to doubt that.

Had the burning girl been a nightmare or was she one of the tragic ghosts Khalil's great-grandmother was talking about who haunted the town of Sparksburg?

"Nana, stop scaring the girl." Naomi startled at a deep baritone suddenly rumbling behind her.

She looked over her shoulder to find Khalil's dad sliding open the screen door and stepping into the kitchen. He was carrying an aluminum tray filled with spare rib remnants and barbecue sauce, probably in search of a refill to feed the growing crowd outside.

"I'm not trying to scare her, Mark. I'm trying to warn her. She and her family shouldn't be staying in that town. It's not safe! They could disappear like all the rest."

"All *what* rest? Most of that stuff happened over a hundred years ago, Nana. That girl who disappeared in Sparksburg two weeks ago ain't even Black. She's probably just a runaway."

The girl who disappeared two weeks ago? Was he talking about Amber Nash, the eighteen-year-old Naomi had seen in the MISSING flyers?

"People go missing all the time all over the country," Khalil's dad continued. "Sparksburg is no different."

"It *is* different," Nana said. "And y'all know it! That place is not good. History just keeps repeating itself there. You should be teaching the young ones like I taught you. It'll keep them safe!"

Khalil's dad shook his bald head in exasperation before turning his attention to Naomi. "Thank you for keeping Nana company, but I bet you're eager to get back outside with Khalil and the others," he said. "I'm sure he's missing you out there."

Naomi turned to Khalil's great-grandmother. "It was nice meeting you, ma'am."

Naomi began to stand but stopped short when Nana suddenly reached out and grabbed her arm. Her hands felt dry and calloused against her skin. Naomi gazed into her milky-white eyes and felt her stomach flip then flop.

"Tell your family to get out of there while they still can," she said in a hoarse whisper. "I'll pray for you."

Naomi nodded blankly, then pulled her arm away when Nana loosened her hold. Naomi walked out the house, closing the screen door behind her.

25

NAOMI STUMBLED INTO THE BACKYARD IN A DAZE, reeling from everything that Nana had told her about Sparksburg and hearing her dire warning echo inside her head.

Tell your family to get out of there while they still can.

Were they really in danger? Should she tell her parents? But even if she did tell them what Nana had said, they would never believe her. They'd excused everything else so far, from the smell in town to the mysterious girl she kept seeing near the cabin.

But I've got to at least try, she thought.

Naomi searched for Khalil so he could take her home. She found him where she'd left him sitting at the picnic table with his cousins and Alexis glued to his side.

"Hey!" Khalil shouted over the music. He strolled across the yard toward Naomi, tugged her toward him, and gave her a lip-smacking kiss. "You were gone for a while. Did you get lost on the way back from the bathroom?"

Naomi shook her head. "I'm actually not feeling well. It might be all the noise or maybe the heat. If it's okay, I'd like to go home now."

Khalil frowned. "But we just got here like an hour ago. You sure you don't wanna eat something? You barely touched your food. It might make you feel better."

"No. I'm not hungry."

"They're going to start the karaoke machine soon. You don't wanna miss my Uncle Ty singing his favorite nineties hits and doing his dance moves. It's pretty epic."

Watching Uncle Ty's dance moves was at the bottom of her list when her family could be in danger.

"I just want to go home, Khalil. Please. Can we go?"

She'd shouted the last part. He glanced around them and saw that some of his family was staring now. Were they making a scene?

His shoulders sank. Gradually, he nodded. "Okay, let me tell my fam we're leaving and then we can head out."

"It wasn't Otis's burgers, was it?" Khalil's dad asked. "I told him they were undercooked."

"No, I bet the poor thang was wilting in all this heat," his mom said with a concerned frown. She waddled toward Naomi, scanning her face. "You sure you just don't want an ice pack and sit for a while, honey?"

Naomi shook her head. "No, ma'am."

His mother hugged her and whispered in her ear, "Is it that time of the month? I'm sure we can dig up some Motrin for you if you need it."

"I think it'll be better if I just lie down and recover at home," Naomi said, happy to use menstrual cramps as an excuse.

They said their goodbye soon after.

FOR MOST OF the drive to her cabin, neither of them spoke. Naomi could feel the tension in the car, but Khalil kept his eyes focused on the road, leaning over to change a song on the radio every now and then while Naomi gazed out her window.

"What was that about?" he asked out of nowhere.

Naomi shifted in her seat to look at him. "What was *what* about?"

"You seemed like you were having fun, disappeared for twenty minutes to use the bathroom, came back, and said we had to leave. What was that about, Naomi? What happened?"

"I told you. I'm not feeling well."

"Yeah, well, I don't believe you. You're acting weird, not sick, and I wanna know why. Did I do something? *Say* something? Was someone at the cookout rude to you?" He eyed her from the driver's seat. "You can tell me, you know."

She exhaled, sinking back into her seat. "There was just . . . just a lot going on."

"Like what? Tell me."

"First off, you have a big family and it can be a little overwhelming, Khalil," she grumbled. "I felt out of place there. You spent the whole time hanging out and talking to your cousins anyway."

"*Huh?* No, I didn't. I kept trying to include you. You left the table. Besides, if you thought I was ignoring you, you could've just said something."

"You're right, I should've. But that wasn't the only issue. It wasn't the reason I wanted to leave."

"What else happened?"

Naomi gnawed her bottom lip. "Your great-grandmother. She said . . . she said my family shouldn't be staying at our cabin because it's too dangerous for Black people to stay in Sparksburg. She said the town is haunted by the ghosts of the people who were murdered there, Khalil, including some of your family."

"Naomi, Nana says weird shit like that all the time. She told me once that when she was little she saw a guy shrink and climb into a bottle when it was raining. Everybody else in our family knows to just ignore her. She's going senile."

"Well, if she's going senile, I must be going senile, too. Both of us smell the same stink coming from that town. And I've been . . . I've been seeing things, too. I'm starting to think that the girl I saw, who I've been seeing for more than a week, isn't some recurring nightmare. I really could be seeing her."

He turned away from the road to stare at her, wide-eyed. "You mean you think the burning girl is a ghost? You're serious? You really think you're seeing ghosts now?"

Naomi threw up her hands. "I don't know! I told you I know it sounds strange, but I—"

And that was when she saw her. The girl. She was standing in the middle of the road like she had been standing there the entire time. Or as if they had summoned her like a genie from a bottle.

The girl was wearing her cotton nightgown again. Now, in the afternoon sun, Naomi could not only see the tattered, mud-splattered lace along the hem, but also her features in more detail: her pert button nose, her parted pink lips, and her doe-like eyes glazed over them like she was lost in a dream. Naomi could even see the color of the ribbon in her hair was a sage green.

When Naomi realized that the girl wasn't going to move . . . that they were going to run straight into her, she screamed.

"Khalil, watch out!" she yelled, pointing in front of them.

He whipped the wheel to the right, slamming the brakes.

Naomi braced her hands against the dashboard and felt her seat belt tug roughly against her chest as the car began to spin. The tires squealed and Khalil shouted as he struggled to regain control of the car. The rocky face of the mountain, the pine trees, the hollow below, and the blue sky spun around her. Again and again. Mountain. Trees. Sky. Mountain. Trees. Sky. She was riding a carousel at rocket speed.

This is it, Naomi thought. They were going to die up here. She and Khalil would become some tragic, cautionary tale of two teenagers who plunged to their deaths on the mountainside. They would tell their story at school assemblies and driver's ed classes throughout Virginia as a warning to kids to "keep their hands on the wheel and both eyes on the road."

But then, miraculously, the spinning ended as the car came to a screeching stop. She opened her eyes.

"Shit!" Khalil said breathlessly. "Are you okay?"

Naomi let go of the dashboard. She nodded shakily. "Y-y-yeah. I'm—I'm okay."

"Did you see something in the road? A deer?" he said, looking around them.

She looked around as well, but the girl was gone. Once again, only Naomi had seen her.

"Y-y-yeah, a deer," she lied. "I guess—I guess it r-r-ran off."

She gazed in front of her to see where the car had stopped and her heart lurched in her chest again. They were only inches from the cliff's edge, a heartbeat away from nose-diving into the hollow below. She stared at the trees, shrubs, and rock. Among the green, gray, and shadows, she spotted a bright shock of blue and glinting metal.

Khalil took a deep breath. "Okay, I guess we're good now. Damn, that was scary. But we're okay. We're fine." He put the gearshift into reverse and began to slowly back away from the edge of the cliff.

"Wait!" she shouted, making him slam on his brakes again.

"What?" he asked. "What's wrong this time?"

"There's something down there."

"Huh?"

Naomi opened her door and gingerly stepped onto the gravel-and-pine-needle-strewn shoulder. She walked toward the edge, holding on to the hood as she leaned over and peered into the depths below.

There it was: the blue Naomi had spotted a minute ago. But now she could see the black of a rear bumper and the treads of a tire as well.

"There's a car down there, Khalil!" She pointed over the mountainside.

"There is?" He hopped out of the car, rushed around the rear, and met her on the other side. Khalil braced his hands on his knees, bent down, and squinted, following the path of her finger. "Yeah, I see it, too!"

Behind the leaves and twigs, she spotted more blue and more of the rear bumper. Naomi read the words *Capitol Hill Half Marathon* now splattered with mud, and her breath caught in her throat. Beside it were more bumper stickers.

She recognized that car: It was the Jamisons' SUV.

26

NAOMI RAISED THE ZIPPER OF HER HOODIE AS SHE sat in the back seat of the Stoakeses' SUV. It was approaching evening now, hours after the discovery of the Jamisons' car at the bottom of the ravine. She stared out the window at all the cop cars and police officers standing near the cliff's edge, watching the climbers in their harnesses who were examining the vehicle. Dawn and Andre stood a few feet away from the car, talking to one of the officers, who was nodding and scribbling in a notebook.

Khalil wasn't there; he'd driven home hours ago. He'd wanted to call the police himself, to tell them what they found, but Naomi had talked him out of it. She'd convinced him that it was better to tell Dawn and Andre first and let them handle it.

The truth was, Naomi was always tongue-tied when she spoke to police, probably because her limited experience with law enforcement had been far from good. They were the ones who made her watch helplessly from the back of a police cruiser as her mom was taken away in handcuffs.

What if they wanted to question her? Take her to some cinder-block room with no windows and record testimony of what she'd found? Could she go through that again?

Even now, watching the accident scene, Naomi's grip

tightened on the door's armrest. Her knees jittered with nervous energy. She silently told herself not to panic at the sight of the kaleidoscope of flashing lights and tan uniforms, but she couldn't slow down her racing heart. Not only was she worried about Elly and Elly's moms (How long had they been down there? Were they all dead or seriously injured?), but she was also having flashbacks to more than a year ago, to the last day she saw her mom.

A few minutes later, Andre and Dawn shook the officer's hand, waved goodbye, and walked toward the SUV.

"What did the cops say?" Naomi asked, easing forward as Andre and Dawn climbed into the front seat. "Why isn't an ambulance out there? Is Elly okay?"

She suspected she knew the answer to her question, but she wanted to hear them say it.

Dawn looked over her shoulder at her. "Elly wasn't in the car, honey. Cheryl and Krissa though . . ." She grimaced. "The cops said they died from their injuries or maybe on impact."

Naomi sat back. Her brows furrowed in confusion. "So, where's Elly? In her cabin?"

"The cops don't think so. They said some officers went to the Jamisons' cabin and no one was there. They're getting out a search team to look for her," Andre said as he began to back their SUV away from the police cruisers. "Maybe she was with her parents, survived the crash, and got out of the car, but got lost out there in the woods."

"But wouldn't she have found help by now?" Naomi asked.

This was mountain country, but they weren't completely isolated out here. Even Khalil's uncle only lived five or so miles away.

"Those cops have been here for the past three hours," Naomi

went on. "Elly should have heard the sirens and shouts by now. Seen their flashing lights."

"Not necessarily, Cam," Dawn said as Andre made a U-turn that put them back on the road. They were finally headed to their cabin. "Elly could be disoriented, suffering from a concussion or blood loss. Who knows, sweetheart. But don't worry, they'll find her."

"Yep! There's plenty of them out there looking for her now. I'm sure they will." Andre smiled at Naomi in the rearview mirror.

But Naomi wasn't as convinced. Was Andre putting on a brave front for her sake, or did he truly believe the police would find Elly?

"Elly told me she saw a guy hanging around their cabin after dark. Maybe he had something to do with this. He could've . . ."

Naomi's words trailed off when she saw something else in the rearview mirror that made her eyes widen and her pulse race again. She whipped around to look out the rear window.

This time when she saw the girl in the nightgown, she didn't yell out like she had with Khalil. She clamped her lips together to stifle the scream.

She could see the girl standing casually among the police officers, but they were all oblivious to her. They were walking around her, talking to each other and barking into walkie-talkies. Meanwhile, the girl stood near the cliff's edge, gazing at the hollow below, where the Jamisons' SUV was.

Oh, yeah, she's a ghost, Naomi thought. *Either that, or I'm going completely nuts.*

Naomi saw the ghost look up in their direction, staring as their car drove away.

Why was she standing there? Had she been standing in the middle of the road on purpose to get Khalil and Naomi to swerve and discover the SUV? Did she know what happened to Elly?

"What were you saying, honey?" Dawn asked. "What guy?"

Naomi faced Dawn again, now dazed. "Huh?"

"You were saying something about a guy around their cabin."

"Yeah. Yeah, she said he . . . he scared her," Naomi said, now scared herself.

"Are you okay?" Dawn eyed Naomi from the front seat. "You don't look good, Cam. Is all this too much for you? I know today was very traumatic."

Naomi shook her head. "No, I'm okay. Just . . . just a little tired."

"Well, we'll be at the cabin soon," Dawn said. "Don't worry. Then you can climb into bed and rest."

As they rounded the bend and the patrol cars and the girl disappeared, Naomi slumped back in her seat. She highly doubted she'd get any rest tonight.

27

Tuesday, July 2

Dear Mom,

Do you remember that time when we had the break-in at our trailer back in Mesa? We weren't home when it happened, but they had kicked in the door and stolen our TV and that little stereo you kept on your dresser. They dug through our drawers and left our underwear and clothes spilling out.

Remember how I couldn't sleep for weeks after? Even when I went to bed with my favorite stuffed animal, Mr. Blinker. I'd wake up in the middle of the night screaming because I thought I heard them kicking open the door again. I thought this time, they wouldn't just steal things. They were going to kill us. I didn't get a good night's sleep until we moved out that trailer two months later.

I'm having recurring nightmares again. This time, it's because of our vacation neighbors, the Jamisons.

Khalil and I found their SUV three days ago near the bottom of a hollow. They're dead, Mom! Cheryl and Krissa Jamison. Their daughter, Elly, has gone missing. It's so fucked up! The cops said their bodies were inside the SUV, but Elly wasn't there. She's missing. She's the second missing girl in

Sparksburg that I've heard about since we got here. Wondering what happened to her keeps me up at night.

I keep dreaming of her screaming for help in the dark. I can't see her, but I can hear her.

I've been thinking of these different scenarios of what could've happened. Elly told me she thought someone was stalking her and her family, the last time we spoke. That some guy was lurking outside her cabin window at night, watching her. What if he took her and killed her parents? Maybe caused the accident.

I know it sounds far-fetched. I tell myself that a story like that is just too crazy, but then I think about my own life. I think about the ghost I keep seeing. Nothing seems too far-fetched anymore, Mom. Why couldn't Elly have been kidnapped?

What if she's still alive out there and we just have to—

"Cam! Cam, breakfast is ready!" Dawn called up the stairs. "Are you finally coming down?"

Naomi stopped writing. "I'm coming!" she yelled, shoving her notebook into her satchel.

A minute later, Naomi strolled downstairs, surprised to find that only she was still in her pj's; everyone else was dressed in their summer gear already. Andre and Blake had finished their waffles and bacon and were rinsing off plates in the sink and loading the dishwasher. Dawn looked as if she was almost done with her breakfast, too. Maya nibbled at her waffles while taking selfies and smiling at her cell camera as she ate.

"Honey," Dawn said with a frown, "why aren't you dressed? We're leaving in like"—she glanced down at her smartwatch—"fifteen minutes."

Naomi shook her head in bewilderment. "Leaving to go where?"

"To the caverns," Andre said. "Remember? That's what's on the itinerary for today, kid."

Naomi stared at them, stupefied. She must have heard him wrong. "We're still going to tour the caverns today after what happened to the Jamisons?"

Everyone fell silent. Even Bear stopped panting.

"You guys are kidding, right?" Naomi asked. "Elly is still missing!"

Dawn and Andre exchanged a look across the kitchen island.

"We know that, honey," Dawn began. She sighed. "We just figured with all this crazy stuff happening right now that you kids might need a mental health break. To do something fun, you know? A little distraction. That's all."

"A distraction?" Naomi cried.

How could she possibly get distracted from something that was causing her night terrors?

"Oh, come on," Maya said. "We've been stuck in this cabin for the past two days, Camryn, watching the news about the search. We barely knew those people. Why should what happened to them stop our vacation plans?"

"You didn't even want to come on this vacation," Naomi argued, glaring at Maya. "You've been whining this whole time about being stuck in 'butthole Virginia.' And you barely knew the Jamisons because the only people you care about are yourself, your Insta followers, and your stupid boyfriend!"

"Hey, now," Andre said, holding up his hands, "that's enough. I understand you're upset, but that doesn't mean you can pick a fight with your sister."

"Doesn't anyone care that two women are dead?" Naomi shouted. "That their daughter is still missing? We should be out there looking for her, not spelunking through caves!"

She thought Dawn and Andre would at least understand.

They'd had to deal with a missing daughter for fifteen years, worrying if she was okay or if she was still alive. They should get how serious this was.

"Cam, we told you we reached out to Sheriff Turner and offered to help with the search, but she turned us down and for good reasons, sweetheart," Dawn explained. She gently rubbed Naomi's arm. "We're inexperienced searchers and we don't know the terrain out there. We could injure ourselves on that mountain, or maybe even trample over important evidence that could help them find Elly."

"It's better to leave something like this to the experts," Andre added. "Leave it to the Sheriff's Office and the state police."

"So that's it?" Naomi crossed her arms. "We just go about our lives like nothing ever happened?"

"What are you suggesting, honey?" Dawn asked. "Do you want us to end our vacation? You really want us to pack up and head home now? What about Khalil? You guys really seem to be hitting it off."

Naomi hesitated. She had considered telling Andre and Dawn that maybe it was time to leave after Nana told her the story about Sparksburg, about it being a haunted sundown town. But she didn't get the chance because finding the Jamisons' SUV had seemed more important. If she left now, she would have to say goodbye to Khalil and may never figure out what happened to Elly. She might never understand why the girl in the nightgown kept appearing.

But what if Nana was right? What if the disappearances were starting again in Sparksburg and their family was next, and they had the chance to escape the town but didn't?

"I don't know," Naomi said. "Maybe it'd be for the best."

"Aww, man!" Blake groaned. "I didn't even get to go tubing!"

Andre scratched his goatee thoughtfully. "Look, y'all, we

spent a lot of money on this cabin and paid for outdoor activities in advance, but we aren't going to force you kids to stay here if you don't want to. If you want to pack up our things and head back to Silver Spring today, we will. We'll just eat the cost."

"No, Dad! Please!" Blake begged. "I don't want to go yet."

"We're almost halfway through the trip," Maya said with a casual shrug, scrolling through her phone again. "We might as well stay."

Andre sighed. "Your brother and sister want to stay, Cam. I'm sorry, but you've been outvoted."

"Typical," Naomi said, annoyed that the fate of the entire family had come down to cave tours and tubing, that no one else seemed to understand how dire the situation was.

"Camryn!" Dawn called after her, but Naomi ignored her and stomped up to her room.

28

"CAMRYN," DAWN SAID TEN MINUTES LATER, GENTLY knocking on her door. "Cam, honey, can I come in?"

"Yes," Naomi murmured, raising her head from her pillow.

She couldn't help find Elly. Her family refused to leave Sparkburg. It was all so pointless.

"We're headed to the caverns, but I wanted to check on you first," Dawn said. She took a seat on the bed beside Naomi. "I know how upset you are."

"I'm not just 'upset,'" Naomi said, pushing herself up to her elbows. "I don't understand why you guys can't see what I see. Two girls have gone missing. Elly said a guy was hanging out by her cabin before it happened. It's obvious we shouldn't be here. This town is messed up! I can feel it. Can't you?"

Dawn shook her head. "No, honey. I don't. But I understand how something like what happened to the Jamisons could make you feel that way."

"It's not just me. Even Khalil's great-grandmother said it. Sparksburg has been like this for centuries. She warned me and I . . ."

I keep seeing that girl. I think she may be trying to warn me, too. Naomi wanted to tell Dawn, but she knew what Dawn's reaction would be. Concern. Unease. But she wouldn't believe her.

"And what, honey?" Dawn asked.

"And I . . . I read about it. About Sparksburg." She picked up her book from her night table and handed it to Dawn. "It was a sundown town. This is hostile territory. They don't want us here!"

Dawn read the title and the blurb on the back. She handed the book back to Naomi. "You're right. That is some really messed-up stuff. But, Cam, honey, you *live* in a sundown town, too."

"What?"

"Yeah, Silver Spring. It started as a sundown town. The landowners who developed it in the early 1900s said it was whites only," Dawn explained. "It was even written in the land deeds to keep anyone else from selling to buyers who weren't white. It didn't change until almost the 1970s. Now there are all types of people from all races and nationalities who live there. So, you see," she said with a smile, "this kind of 'dark history' is hiding *every*where, but we can't let it rule our lives. We can't let it dictate our present either, or you could miss out on some really amazing places and people. Are you sure you don't want to come with us?"

Naomi slowly nodded. "I'm sure."

"Okay, well, we should be back from the caverns by four o'clock at the latest. We'll check in with you throughout the day, okay?" She gave Naomi a quick peck on the cheek. "Try to chill out. Watch some TV. Eat some junk food, but not too much. Maybe give Khalil a call." She paused. "You know, I really like Khalil. It's nice to see you two together . . . to see you going out and doing things. Exploring. I know the life you lived before with . . . with her . . ." Dawn winced when she said the word *her*. "I know that it was very . . . well . . . isolated. The homeschooling. The constant moving. The lack of friends. But you're finally blossoming, Cam." She walked toward the bedroom door. "So please, don't obsess about the search and what happened to the Jamisons. It's very sad. I know, sweetheart. No, we didn't know them well, but Cheryl and Krissa seemed like really nice people, and I hate the idea of poor Elly out there wandering around in the woods alone. You may think your dad and I don't understand, but we do. I know what it's like waiting around to hear news about someone. It's agonizing to feel . . . well, powerless."

Naomi looked at her lap, loath to witness the decades-old pain flicker in Dawn's eyes.

"But I can say from experience that you've gotta accept that some things are out of your control," Dawn went on. "You have to continue to live your life as best you can. Okay?"

Naomi nodded grudgingly.

A minute later, she heard the SUV engine rev as the Stoakeses drove away. By then her stomach was growling. She went back downstairs and made herself breakfast: a bowl of cereal and a cup of orange juice. She parked herself on the sofa next to Bear, who was sleeping contentedly. She turned on the flat-screen in the great room and flipped channels until she landed on a teen comedy—one of her all-time faves. She watched the movie and then another, but couldn't fully lose herself in the films.

Even though Dawn had told her not to, Naomi kept thinking about Elly. She remembered how Elly had nervously confessed about the guy she saw out her window every night.

Elly had tried to talk to her moms, too, and tell them something was wrong, but they hadn't listened. Just like Dawn and Andre weren't listening to Naomi now. Parents—adults—thought they knew everything, but sometimes they had blind spots. Blind spots they weren't willing to admit to because that would mean they'd made a mistake, that they were wrong.

And the ghost had led her to the Jamisons' SUV. Why would it have done that if it wasn't trying to help her save Elly?

She grabbed her phone and flipped through her photo library before landing on the picture of the MISSING flyer for Amber Nash.

Amber was last seen walking along Route 250, just outside of downtown Sparksburg on June 12, the flyer said. *She might have been hitchhiking. Before her disappearance, a man had been following her for weeks.*

Amber had also disappeared near a roadway and just like Elly, she was being stalked before she disappeared. There had to be some connection between the disappearances of the two young women.

Naomi paused for only a few seconds before dialing the number on the flyer. She listened as the phone rang once . . . twice . . . before someone on the other end picked up.

"Hello?" a male voice answered.

"Umm, hi . . . my name is . . . my name is . . . umm, Kelsey . . . Kelsey Donovan."

She didn't want to give her real name. What if it got back to Andre and Dawn?

"Yeah?" the voice asked, sounding suspicious. "Can I help you?"

"Actually, I'm hoping we can help each other. You're looking for Amber Nash. Well, I'm—I'm looking for someone who disappeared in Sparksburg, too."

29

You did WHAT?

NAOMI SANK EVEN LOWER BENEATH HER SHEETS and grimaced when she read the text from Khalil. Within seconds, her phone started to buzz. Reluctantly, she pressed the green button and his face appeared on the screen.

"Are you serious?" Khalil shouted. "Tell me the text you sent me was a joke, Naomi. Why would you call some guy, asking him about a missing girl? Why would you give him a fake name?"

She raised her finger to her lips. "Shush! They'll hear you." She turned down the volume slightly on her phone.

It was late. The Stoakeses had arrived home hours ago and were exhausted from their tour of the caverns. They ate an early dinner before heading to their rooms to veg out and rest, but Maya or Blake might still be awake and overhear.

Khalil sucked his teeth. She could see that he was also in bed. Her eyes widened in surprise when she realized he was shirtless. Pillows and a slumbering orange tabby were in the background. For a few seconds, Naomi couldn't remember what their conversation was about. All she saw was glossy dark skin and muscular arms, pecs, and abs. So this was what was hiding under all those oversize T-shirts?

"Naomi. Naomi! Did you hear what I said?"

She blinked and raised her hand to her mouth. Was she salivating? "No, what?"

"I said I don't get it." Khalil lowered his voice. "I know you're worried about your neighbor being missing and all, but—"

"I did it because I think the two disappearances are related, Khalil. The circumstances, I mean. What was happening to Elly and what was happening to this missing girl when they disappeared is too similar. I think it might be the same guy."

"So tell the cops that!" he argued, leaning in closer to the screen. "Tell them about Elly's stalker. Let *them* make the connection."

"But what if they're like Andre and Dawn? What if they think I'm just flipping out, grasping at straws, and don't believe me?"

"So the only other option was to give this dude a fake name and tell him you're a true crime podcaster? How the heck did you even come up with that anyway?"

"I don't know," she said, flopping back against her headboard. "The guy . . . his name is Tate Carroll. He was friends with Amber, the other missing girl. He was the last person who saw her before she disappeared. I had to come up with something to keep him from hanging up. He got excited when I told him I had a podcast, that I wanted to do an interview with him for the story I was working on. I need more information from him before I can even think about going to the Sheriff's Office with my idea about the stalker."

"Information like what?"

"For starters, he said some guy had been following Amber

around for weeks. Could it have been the same guy Elly saw around the cabin? Does he have any idea who that guy was? What he looked like? If I shared that with the police, it could make my story more credible. Maybe if they find the guy, they could find out what happened to Amber. It could help them find Elly."

"Well, I hope he gave you the answers you needed, because this is wild, Naomi. You're lucky he didn't figure out you weren't who you said you were."

"Tate *will* give me answers," she began tentatively. "He hasn't done it yet. I'm gonna need your help for that."

Khalil squinted on-screen. "What do you mean?"

She hesitated. If Khalil had freaked out before, he definitely would after she told him this part. Best to just say it.

"Umm, I'm supposed to meet him in person tomorrow to interview him and I need you to take me there," she blurted out in one breath.

"*What?* No! Hell no!"

"It's the only way, Khalil. Please! I don't have a car. I can't ask Dawn or Andre to take me, and I can't do this by myself."

He closed his eyes. "This is crazy. You know this is crazy, right?"

"Please," she begged. "I can't just sit in this town going about my vacation like nothing happened. Maybe we could help save Elly. I keep thinking about her alone out there. If I'm stuck here in Sparksburg, I have to at least try."

She watched as he opened his eyes. "I still think this is crazy, Naomi, but yeah. Okay, I'll do it."

"You will?" she squeaked.

He nodded. "Who knows what trouble you'll get into if I don't go there with you."

30

WHEN THEY PULLED INTO THE PARKING LOT OF THE Starlight Diner, nine miles outside Sparksburg, Naomi flipped down the sun visor mirror and stared at her reflection. She adjusted her glasses. She had decided not to wear her contacts and had pulled her hair back into a tight bun. At the right angle, she thought she looked almost identical to Dawn. "How do I look?"

Khalil turned off the engine. "You look fine," he mumbled.

He'd tried more than once during the drive there to talk her out of meeting Tate, but Naomi had refused. She wanted to find out more about Amber, about the man Amber believed was stalking her before she disappeared. Naomi was convinced this was her only hope if they were going to help find Elly.

"Just fine?" Naomi asked, flipping up the mirror. "I wanted to look like a podcaster."

Khalil narrowed his eyes. "What exactly does a podcaster look like?"

Naomi thought for a minute, then shrugged. "I don't know. *More mature?* I wanted to look like I was in my twenties."

"Well, I hate to break it to you, but you look like a sixteen-year-old wearing glasses and her hair pulled back. I don't think you're foolin' anybody that you're in your twenties."

Her shoulders sank. "Either way, I'm going inside," Naomi said, deciding to just take the plunge before she lost her nerve. "I should be back in an hour, maybe less. Okay?"

He nodded from his perch in the driver's seat. "I'll wait for you out here."

She started to climb out of the car but paused when Khalil called out, "Hey, Naomi?"

"Yeah?" she asked.

"If this Tate guy seems sketchy . . . if shit gets weird or goes left in there, don't stay. Just leave or . . . or text me. I'll come in there."

She smirked. "You gonna rescue me?"

"I'm serious. This isn't a joke! If you get scared in there, let me know."

Naomi cupped his face, and gave him a kiss. "I will."

A minute later, Naomi stepped through the door of the crowded diner. The smell of coffee, hamburgers, and the faint hint of industrial cleaner wafted toward her. She gazed around her, on the lookout for Tate Carroll. He had told her that he'd be wearing a black baseball cap. She had told him she would be wearing a blue headband.

"Can I help you?" the hostess asked. The hostess's gray hair was pulled back into a scrunchie. A notepad was in the front pocket of her apron. A name tag that said MAVIS was pinned to her chest.

"Is it just you in your party or are you waiting for someone else, hon?" she asked, reaching for a stack of laminated menus.

"Actually, my guest is already waiting for me," Naomi said, noticing a guy in a tattered baseball cap sitting alone at one of the booths, staring out the window. He was nursing a beer. "Back there." She pointed across the diner.

"Well, go right ahead," the hostess said. "I'll bring ya a cup of water."

As Naomi walked across the diner, she got a better look at Tate. He had to be in his early twenties but his expression seemed world-weary, like he had seen a lot, like he was much older. He was wiry-thin with about a dozen piercings in his ears, septum, and bottom lip. He also sported a lot of tattoos. She couldn't see them all but they spanned from his wrists to the edges of his short sleeves. She could see even more peeking out the V-neck of his black T-shirt. When Naomi approached the booth, Tate turned to her warily.

"Hi," Naomi said with a wave and her best imitation of a confident smile, "I'm Kelsey from *Hot Case Files* podcast. We . . . uh . . . we spoke on the phone yesterday."

"*You're* Kelsey?" Tate asked, sounding incredulous. He lowered his beer bottle and looked her up and down. "I thought you'd be older."

"Most people do, but I'm still in college," Naomi lied, adjusting her glasses and sliding into the booth. She tried not to cringe when she felt something sticky underneath her thigh as she sat down.

"You don't say," Tate muttered as the hostess sat a menu and a perspiring glass of ice water in front of Naomi.

Naomi whispered her thanks.

"Your waitress will be with y'all soon," the hostess drawled before walking away.

Tate snorted. "Don't count on it. The waitstaff in this joint moves slower than my grandma on gummies. It took me about twenty minutes just to get a Bud Light."

"It's fine," Naomi said. "I'm not really hungry anyway."

"You know," he began, watching her as she opened her

satchel and took out her notebook and pen, "I looked up your podcast online, but I couldn't find it. Not one single link." He tilted his head. "But you've gotta be for real, because I feel like I've seen you somewhere before."

Naomi's smile tightened.

Damn, she thought. The last thing she needed was for him to recognize her, to remember her real name.

She cleared her throat. "You've probably seen me in our social media ads. We're gearing up our promotional campaign, but we're not launched on all platforms yet. We just posted the first couple of episodes but we're planning to expand and share more episodes soon. Speaking of," she said, changing the subject and setting her phone in the center of the table, "I'm ready to start the interview if you are."

He slumped back in the booth and stared at her for an unnervingly long time before finally throwing up his hands in surrender. "Shit. I'm here. Might as well." He gestured to her phone. "Go ahead."

She pressed the record button on her cell app and glanced down at her notepad, where she had her list of prepared questions. Naomi had sat through enough in-depth interviews as a former missing girl to know how these things went, though she was usually the person being interviewed, not the other way around. The reporters always came with recorders and notepads filled with questions or sent questions in advance. They sometimes came with a photographer or cameraman. They smiled a lot and nodded encouragingly as you talked. It was their job to make you feel relaxed, like you were just gabbing with a friend—not a journalist. Now she would have to do the same with Tate, disarm him so she could get the answers she needed.

"Thank you so much for agreeing to speak with me today. Like I said over the phone," she began, "I'm researching the recent disappearances of two young women in Sparksburg, Virginia. Police believe Elly Jamison went missing four days ago, after she and her parents were in a car crash."

"Yeah," he said, "I saw it on the news."

"Can you tell me more about Amber's disappearance? About her? You said in your flyer that she disappeared on June twelfth."

"Yeah, thereabouts," he said, taking a drink.

"How do you know Amber?"

Talking about his friendship with Amber would calm him, like talking about fond memories of her mom always did during interviews. It would warm him up for the more direct questions.

"We were both foster kids. Ended up at the same foster home back when she was eleven and I was fourteen," he said, scratching the hairs of his five-o'clock shadow. "It could get pretty rough in there sometimes with the other kids, so it helped to have someone watchin' your back. I watched Amber's. She was different then. Cute but real quiet. Kinda shy. An easy target. She got tougher over time, but back then, she needed me."

"Was she your girlfriend?" Naomi asked, scribbling notes as he spoke.

"She was in the beginning, but then we figured out we've got the same shitty taste in men," he said with a wink.

"Oh," Naomi said with a nod. "And you guys stayed in touch as you got older?"

"After we aged out, we tried to hold down jobs but it's hard when you don't have a car or a place to stay. You practically need a job to *get* a job. So we lived on the streets together. We found ways to make it work. To survive."

Naomi stopped taking notes. She looked up at him. "What does that mean?"

"Well, we had to eat, didn't we? So we did things that weren't . . . well, always legit. I won't go into detail. I don't need the cops on my ass any more than they already are. And the way Amber looked, she could always get guys who wanted to spend money on her . . . to pay her for her time and her . . . let's just say, her company."

Naomi could feel her cheeks going pink, but she forced her expression to stay neutral. She was mature. Sophisticated. She could do this.

"That's how we ended up out here," Tate continued. "Amber had a guy who reached out to her online back in May. He said she could stay with him for a few days. They could party. She asked me to come with her just in case the guy turned out to be a psycho. He would never send her pictures of himself or give his real name, which wasn't too off base with the guys she hooked up with. Most of the time, she wouldn't find out what they really looked like until she met them in person. This guy sent her a hundred bucks and said she'd get twenty times that if she came out here to spend the weekend with him while his wife was out of town. It was too good to turn down. I'm glad I came with her though, because when we got here, he ghosted her. We thought he stood her up at the bus station but turns out he saw us, but we didn't see him. He saw she wasn't alone and was PO'd. He just left. He didn't want me here. We came all this way, and he wouldn't even pay for her ticket back home.

"He told her to leave but she stayed in town just to piss him off. We camped out in the woods. We decided to make a vacation of it," Tate said with a snicker. "He must have seen us around because that's when he started harassing her . . . harassing us. A truck would drive by our campsite in the middle of the night, shoot its high beams at our tent or start beeping its horn, scaring the shit out of us, then he'd just drive off. And he kept sending her these texts, you know? He'd tell her he'd have her arrested if she didn't leave town and the county. He said if he saw her around Sparkburg again, he'd throw her ass out of town himself. I told her we should just leave. Between his bullshit and other things . . ." Tate slowly shook his head. "I was over it. I was ready to go home. But Amber can get so damn stubborn. She wanted to stay."

"What do you mean other things?"

He grew quiet and seemed to consider whether he should say what he was about to say next.

"Look," Tate began, leaning forward, "Amber and I are used to bunking down in some strange places. We've slept on park benches. Under overpasses. We even stayed in this abandoned house once or twice. But camping in those woods in Sparksburg was . . . different. The vibe was just off, you know what I mean? It didn't feel good to be out there." He stared out the window, then down at his beer bottle. "That guy was messing with our heads and I guess it worked, because at night . . . at night, I always felt like we were being watched. Like someone else was there. Like the woods were haunted." His brown eyes darted up from the bottle to look at her. "It sounds crazy, doesn't it?"

"No, it doesn't," she said, validating him and once again her own suspicions about Sparksburg.

"Well, anyway," he said, nervously licking his lips and staring out the window again, "after Amber disappeared, I told the cops about him. How'd he been stalking her for weeks, but I couldn't say for sure who he was, so they wouldn't listen. They just wrote her off as some junkie prostitute who skipped town, but Amber wouldn't have left without telling me. That's not like her."

"So, you think he's the reason she disappeared? You think he kidnapped her?"

"I'll be honest. I hope that's the worst thing he's done to her. I hope she's still alive."

Naomi went cold for a couple of seconds.

"Uh, do you know anything else about him?" Naomi asked. "Where he lives?"

"I don't know where he lives. We never made it to his house. And I told you, he never gave her a pic of himself. He was just a blank avatar, but he told her to call him Bobby." Tate took another sip of beer. "I remember that truck though that kept coming to our campsite. It was black. Big. I haven't seen it since she disappeared, but I still get this bad feeling like he's still around sometimes, like his truck could pop up outta nowhere," he said, scanning the parking lot.

Naomi stopped writing. "Did you say it was a black truck?"

Tate lowered his bottle back to the table and nodded. "Yep."

A black pickup truck.

A black pickup truck had tried to drive Andre off the road when they first arrived in Sparksburg less than two weeks ago.

"Thanks for agreeing to talk to me," Naomi said, reaching for her phone and ending the recording. She started to put away her things. "This information is really helpful."

"At least you're willing to listen. Doesn't seem like anyone else is."

"What are you planning to do now? Are you staying in town?"

"Until what money I have left runs out. If I leave, they forget about her. But if I stay on their asses, keep making a stink, maybe somebody will finally do something. Maybe your podcast will help too, and bring more attention to her disappearance."

Naomi slid out of the booth, feeling guilty about pretending she was a podcaster. She considered telling him the truth but reminded herself that she was going to use this information to help find Amber and Elly, if she could. She hadn't wasted Tate's time.

"You know the messed-up part? Amber always wanted to be famous," he said, making Naomi pause. "She talked about it for years. She wanted to be in the movies or a model. She was even happy to end up on TMZ. Now she's on missing flyers. You'll be talking about her on a podcast." He exhaled loudly. "She might get that fifteen minutes of fame she wanted, but not the way she thought. I guess that kind of fame isn't what it's cracked up to be, huh?"

"It never is," Naomi said morosely, relieved that he hadn't put together this whole time he'd been talking to the famous missing girl Naomi Ward / Camryn Stoakes. "Thanks again for doing the interview. If you think of anything else, please don't hesitate to reach out."

He nodded, then returned to drinking his beer and gazing out the window as she left the diner.

While walking to Khalil's car, she saw a dusty pickup truck pull into the parking lot.

Naomi's palms began to sweat.

Not only had a black pickup truck tried to drive Andre off the road when they first arrived in Sparksburg, a black pickup truck had almost hit Blake, too, and the driver was Travis Meacham.

Were Travis and this mysterious "Bobby" one and the same?

31

"COME ON, Y'ALL!" ANDRE CALLED OVER HIS SHOULDER. "Pick up the pace. We need to move it along if we want to find a good spot to set up our seats."

"We're trying, Dad!" Maya grumbled as she juggled a tote bag, her foldable tailgate chair, and a battery-operated fan. "It's not like we haven't seen fireworks before," she mumbled under her breath.

Today, the Stoakeses and Noami had made the pilgrimage—with more than half the town it seemed—to the Sparksburg Fairgrounds to watch the July Fourth fireworks. They'd had to leave Bear back at the cabin since the dog wasn't a fan of fireworks or loud noises.

Naomi looked around her at all the people streaming toward the outdoor stage covered with American flags and *This land is your land . . . This land is my land* and *Honor our founding fathers* banners. Cutout silver stars were attached to the black backdrop. In front of the backdrop was a papier-mâché reproduction of Mount Rushmore about the height of a grown man, and in front of mini Mount Rushmore were ten chairs where people were sitting or standing while talking to one another. Naomi spotted Mayor Bartz among them. Center stage, she saw a miked podium.

The whole setup looked cheesy compared to other July Fourth celebrations she'd attended, including the one last year with the Stoakeses in DC, but the crowd seemed genuinely excited to be here. They'd come in their red, white, and blue garb. One man had painted his face in patriotic colors like he was cheering on his favorite sports team.

Naomi wished she could say she was just as excited, too, but she wasn't. She was focused on something else.

She glanced down at her phone, annoyed to find there were no new messages or calls.

She'd called the Sheriff's Office hours after her interview with Tate Carroll, wanting to tell them her hunch about Travis Meacham and his possible connection to Elly's and Amber's disappearances. No one had answered, so she'd left a voicemail. Even though today was a holiday, Naomi had called again this morning only to get the Sheriff's Office's scratchy automated message again. She'd left another voicemail and had been checking her phone religiously to see if someone had listened, heard the urgency, and decided to call her back.

"He's probably busy with his family, honey," Dawn said beside her. "I bet they're celebrating July Fourth, too."

"Huh?" Naomi asked with a wrinkled brow. She looked up from her phone to find Dawn giving her a knowing smile. "What are you talking about?"

"Khalil. You're looking to see if he texted you back, right?" Dawn placed a warm hand on Naomi's shoulder. "He's probably celebrating with his family now, Cam. That's what I mean. But I'm sure he will get back to you by tonight or tomorrow morning. No worries."

Actually, Khalil was two counties over, spending July Fourth with friends from school. He'd invited Naomi to come along but she said her family had plans today. She knew he was calling her later tonight. That wasn't the issue, but she couldn't tell Dawn that.

"You're right," Naomi said, dropping her phone back into her satchel. "He'll call me later."

"This spot looks good," Andre suddenly announced.

They were about ten yards away from the bandstand where a six-piece brass band made up of high schoolers was currently setting up their instruments. The Stoakeses weren't near the stage—those spots had been taken by folks who'd come much earlier—but they were close enough to see the show.

As soon as Andre set down the cooler, Blake flipped open the lid and got one of the ice cream sandwiches they'd brought with them. His eyes practically gleamed as he peeled off the wrapper.

"Not too much sugar, buddy," Dawn warned. "You can have one and one only. We don't want you up all night on a glucose high."

"But it's July Fourth . . . Independence Day," Blake whined. "It's a special occasion, Mom!"

Andre chuckled. "He has a point."

"Fine," Dawn said, setting her foldout chair on the grass, "but save the second bar for *after* the fireworks. Okay?"

AFTER THE SUN had set, the lights over the stage were turned on and the official ceremony began. An older woman with curly white hair and wearing a visor walked up to the podium. She adjusted the mic, causing ear-piercing feedback.

"Hello out there!" she said with an exaggerated wave. "I want to thank all of you for coming out here for Sparksburg's fifty-third Annual Independence Day Fireworks Celebration.

How about we give a round of applause to America!"

Most clapped politely. Naomi heard a few whistles and chants of "USA! USA! USA!" She resisted the urge to roll her eyes.

"I'm Maggie Dunn, the chairwoman of the Independence Day Celebration Committee. An event like this is a big undertaking and couldn't be possible without the hard work of so many people. I can't name them all, but many of them are sitting here onstage. Please give them a round of applause as well," she said, gesturing to the row of people beside her. "Stand up, folks! Take your bow!"

The audience clapped again. Some onstage seemed to rise from their seats reluctantly but most, who were older ladies like Chairwoman Dunn, basked in all the praise.

"To kick off our celebration," the chairwoman continued after they'd sat back down and the applause ended, "we'd like Mayor Robert Bartz to come up here and say a few words. Mayor Bartz?"

The mayor shot to his feet and strode to the podium. He sported the same Ken-doll haircut as the last time Naomi had seen him, but he'd swapped out the red polo shirt for a blue one and khaki pants for khaki shorts. He shook the chairwoman's hand and kissed her cheek before stepping behind the podium and adjusting the mic for his height as she sat down in one of the empty chairs.

"Hey there, folks!" He held his hand over his eyes and peered into the crowd. "I know many of you know me well, but I spot a few new faces out there, which makes me happy. Very happy, indeed. I know some of you newcomers are just vacationing in our fair hamlet this summer, but I hope you come back to Sparksburg next summer and the summer after that and the summer after that. Maybe someday you'll even consider moving up here with your families or retiring here to breathe in that mountain air. We could use fresh blood in this town!" he said with a grin.

Naomi swallowed.

"Sparksburg was founded more than three hundred years ago by German immigrants, including my ancestors—the Bartzes, searching for a place they hoped was better than the old country. They were looking for opportunities . . . for freedom, and they found it here on this patch of land in Virginia," he said, pointing down at the stage. "This town embodies American, Christian values that so many have forgotten. We know our neighbors, but are welcoming to outsiders. We believe in hard work and just reward. We pray over meals and aren't ashamed to say, 'Merry Christmas'! Not any of that 'Happy Holidays' nonsense."

Someone behind them let out another whistle and this time Naomi did roll her eyes.

"We are proud of who we are. We are proud of our country. We are proud of our forefathers," he said, pointing to the papier-mâché Mount Rushmore and the banners behind it. "We don't tear down statues around here. We lay wreaths on them every year because we thank those brave soldiers and American heroes for the sacrifices they made and the battles they fought to make this country what it is today."

Naomi glanced at Andre and Dawn to see how they were responding to Mayor Bartz's speech. She was relieved to see they, too, were getting uncomfortable.

"Tonight," Mayor Bartz said, "we commemorate those battles with fireworks, harking back to the cannon explosions those great men and women witnessed firsthand. Men like Francis Scott Key, who was inspired to write the poem the 'Defense of Fort McHenry,' which became our 'Star-Spangled Banner.'"

Naomi sighed. That year in American history class she'd read about how Key believed Black people were so inferior they couldn't be incorporated into American society and would be better off shipped back to Africa. Of course Bartz would reference a racist like Francis Scott Key in a deluded speech like this.

"I want you to think of those men and women tonight," Mayor Bartz said. "Honor their memories even as you admire all those sparkling lights in the night sky. Thank you, and God bless America."

As he walked away from the podium, the crowd broke into uproarious applause. A few even rose to their feet to give him a standing ovation, though the Stoakeses all remained seated. The band began to play "The Stars and Stripes Forever," and the first firework shot into the sky.

As the crowd stood shoulder to shoulder and gazed at the colorful light display, *oohing* and *aahing*, Naomi felt a buzz on her hip. She pulled out her cell phone and saw that Tate was calling, not the Sheriff's Office. Had he remembered something about the last day he saw Amber or some other important detail about the mysterious Bobby after their interview?

Naomi stuck a finger in her ear, and answered. "Hey, Tate. What's up?"

"Cam, why are you on your phone?" Andre asked when he turned away from the fireworks and found her hunched over trying to listen. "Tell Khalil or whoever it is to just call you back."

Naomi wouldn't point out that Maya had been surreptitiously texting her boyfriend, Troy, the whole evening, while she was only taking one phone call. She strained to hear Tate on the other end of the line. "Tate?" she repeated.

She thought she heard scratching sounds just before the phone line went dead.

Naomi stared at her phone, confused, wondering if Tate had accidentally butt-dialed her.

"Are you done now?" Andre asked, eyes wide. "Would you like to return to the festivities with the rest of us, child of mine?"

She nodded and Andre threw an arm around her shoulder, pulling her in close as the fireworks boomed overhead.

32

"YOU HAVE REACHED THE SPARKSBURG SHERIFF'S Office," an automated voice answered. "If this is an emergency, please dial 911. If you are trying to reach the—"

"Arrrgh!" Naomi yelled, hanging up and slamming her phone down on her night table.

This was the seventh call she'd made to the Sheriff's Office over the past two days, and still no one had called her back. Didn't they understand how important this was?

Maybe Tate was right. Maybe the cops really didn't care about what had happened to Amber, and now Naomi would never be able to help find her or Elly.

Naomi flopped back on her bed, closed her eyes, and let out a low, tortured groan.

"Camryn?" Dawn asked before opening the door.

"Yes," Naomi answered.

"I'm headed downtown for a couple hours to go antique shopping," Dawn said, making Naomi's eyes flutter open. "I noticed a few little shops while I was there and thought I'd check them out. I just wanted to tell you if you wondered where I'd gotten off to. Dad and Blake are watching some action movie downstairs and Maya is out back shooting a video for—"

"Can I come with?" Naomi asked, springing up.

Dawn adjusted her hobo bag on her shoulder and stared at

Naomi in surprise. "You want to come with me? To go *antique shopping*?" she asked.

"Yeah," Naomi said. "I'm crazy about antiques."

The truth was she'd rather stab herself in the eye than go antique shopping, but Naomi thought she might stand a better chance of someone listening to her at the Sheriff's Office if she went there in person. She could always sneak off to town hall while Dawn was engrossed in her knickknacks and candlesticks.

"You know," Dawn said, thinking aloud, "a girls' day shopping for antiques might be fun." She nodded. "Okay, why not? Let's go."

They arrived downtown twenty minutes later. For about an hour, Naomi trailed behind Dawn from shop to shop, nodding with approval or shaking her head whenever Dawn showed her some find she was excited about.

"Hey, I saw something at the last shop we went to that I might wanna buy," Naomi said out of nowhere as Dawn examined a vintage mantel clock.

"Oh?" Dawn set the clock on the shelf between a vase and a rusted wind chime. "Well, we can go back there if you want. I'll just—"

"No, you can't! I think it might be the perfect gift for your birthday. I don't want to ruin the surprise. I'll pop in and pop out. It shouldn't take more than fifteen minutes."

"All right," Dawn said, looking skeptical. "I guess I'll wait here for you, then. Do you need my credit card?"

"No, it's a gift. Besides, the cash I have should be enough." Naomi backed toward the shop door.

"What cash? You haven't gotten your allowance yet this week."

"I still have some left from last week. I'll be back in fifteen minutes. I promise!"

NAOMI MADE SURE to keep her pace casual as she went past the shop window, but switched to a run and then a sprint when she neared town hall, where all of Sparksburg's government offices were located, including the Sheriff's Office.

She tugged open one of the double doors and walked inside. It was easy to find the Sheriff's Office. Not only did a dust-covered felt board near the entrance list the room numbers for all the offices in the building in plastic letters, but an officer in uniform also came strolling out a door toward the end of the corridor. He was sucking his fingers like he'd just finished eating something either very sweet or slathered in sauce. He was gazing down at his cell. The name tag on his chest said B. PACKARD.

Naomi hesitated, unsure if she should just walk up to him.

The last time she'd had any interaction with cops, they had put her sobbing mom in handcuffs before carting her off to jail. They'd dumped Naomi in the back of a police cruiser, refusing to answer any of her questions. Without explanation, they'd taken her away from everything and everyone she'd known.

I have to try, she reminded herself.

"Umm, excuse me," she said, making him look up from his phone. "My name is Naomi Ward and I've left like six messages with you guys. I've been trying to reach someone at the Sheriff's Office to talk about the search for Elly Jamison. Her parents were killed in the car crash on the edge of town."

He took the thumb out of his mouth and hooked it in his belt loop. "Yeah, I know who she is. We all do. We have a tip hotline the public can call for that. You should probably give that a try. It takes a while to sift through all of the tips but we'll reach out if it's viable."

"But why do I have to call a hotline if you guys are right here? Can't I talk to someone at the Sheriff's Office?"

He eyed her. "What did you say your name was?"

"Naomi." She cleared her throat. "Naomi Ward."

"I take it you're not from around here."

She shook her head. "No, I'm vacationing here with my parents. We're from Maryland. Silver Spring."

He smirked and nodded. "Like I thought. Well, Naomi, back in Maryland you might have big police forces who can listen to every single person who comes in off the street. You may want to talk to a police officer right away, but we can't do that in Sparksburg. Each officer is doing the job of five men. So, like I said, I suggest you call our tip line. All right?"

"If I waited for someone from the tip line to call me back, Elly could be dead by then!" she argued. "Elly was being stalked by a guy before she disappeared, before her mothers were killed. I think it's the same guy who was stalking Amber Nash when she disappeared, too. He could've kidnapped them both!"

"That's quite a theory," she heard someone say behind her.

Naomi turned to find the sheriff striding through the front doors. The older woman removed her cap, tucked it under her arm, and cocked a dark eyebrow. "A very elaborate theory, too, young lady. Based on what information?"

"Elly told me before she disappeared that some guy was hanging around their cabin at night, staring through the windows, and I talked to Tate Carroll. He's a friend of Amber's. He said something similar happened to her. That she was being stalked by a guy."

"Ah, Tate Carroll," Sheriff Turner said with a chuckle. "He's quite the character. We arrested him and his friend Amber three weeks ago for trespassing and possession of an illegal substance. They were released on bond. Did he tell you that?"

Naomi shook her head, though she didn't know how Tate's arrest was relevant to what she was saying.

"Didn't think so," Sheriff Turner said as she looked at the other officer. "I'll take this one, Sergeant Packard. You can go ahead."

The officer nodded before glancing once more at Naomi, then heading through the double doors.

Sheriff Turner inclined her head toward the end of the hallway. "Young lady, you can follow me. I'd like to hear more."

33

NAOMI LOWERED HERSELF INTO ONE OF THE CHAIRS facing Sheriff Turner's grand oak desk. She looked down at her phone and saw that nine minutes had already passed from the time she'd left the antique store. Dawn would be expecting her back soon—or Dawn would start going through shops, searching for her. Naomi hoped she could get this done quickly.

Saying what I have to say shouldn't take that long.

"I've met you before, haven't I?" Sheriff Turner asked, squinting at her as she opened a desk drawer and pulled out a yellow steno pad. The sheriff nodded, answering her own question. "Yeah, your parents are Dawn and Andre Stoakes. They were the ones who spotted the Jamisons' car in that ravine."

"Uh, yeah. I mean, yes, that's . . . that's them."

"Want something to drink?" Sheriff Turner asked. "I've got a few bottled waters in my fridge."

"No, thank you," Naomi said. She took slow, deep breaths.

Sitting in the office now surrounded by Fraternal Order of Police plaques and hearing the low murmur of the dispatcher calling out codes over the radio on the other side of the room was starting to bring back bad memories. Her eyes drifted to the line of pictures behind the sheriff's desk, finding those less overwhelming. A few were of Sheriff Turner posing in her uniform with other officers, but she saw one pic of her in a flowery dress with her hair down. The sheriff appeared much younger in the photo. She was posing with a smiling redhead in a wedding gown holding a bouquet of baby's breath and pink roses. Naomi leaned in closer to look at it.

"We were cuties back then, weren't we?" Sheriff Turner asked with a self-deprecating laugh while gesturing to the picture. "That's me and my little sister, Jodie, the day she got married. She and Liam were so happy that day. It feels like a hundred years ago."

Naomi thought for a bit. "Liam. You mean the guy at Sunny Market? She's married to him?"

Sheriff Turner's grin evaporated. She went somber and nodded. "They were. But Jodie died four years ago. She was coming home late one night from a friend's house and got hit by a drunk driver. She died later at the hospital from her injuries. A guy from DC on a hunting trip. She used to work at Sunny Market with Nelson and her husband, Liam." The sheriff sat down at her desk and gazed at the photo of her and her sister. "We all took her death pretty hard. I don't think we'll ever be the same now that she's gone, but it's like that when you've lost someone you love."

"I know," Naomi said softly.

Her mom hadn't died, but some days . . . *some* days, it felt like she'd died, especially when Naomi knew it would be years before she could see her again.

"Well, enough about that." Sheriff Turner set the picture in its original spot on the console behind her. "You're not here to listen to me take a sad trip down memory lane. You're here to tell me more about this theory you have that Elly Jamison and Amber Nash were supposedly stalked by the same man. Though, frankly, I'm confused because I don't remember your parents ever mentioning anything about a stalker when we questioned them."

"They wouldn't have because they didn't know about it. Elly told me—not them. She told her moms, too. She said a guy would come out of the woods at night and lurk around their cabin. She said it creeped her out. Her moms just dismissed it as some random hunter. And Tate Carroll said that Amber was being stalked, too, by a guy before she disappeared. This guy named Bobby had been texting her and would terrorize her and Tate at night at their campsite with his black pickup truck."

Sheriff Turner leaned back in her chair. "Honestly, I'd take whatever Tate Carroll said with a grain of salt. The kid is trouble. He has a rap sheet as long as my arm. And though he posted those missing flyers of Amber, there is no reason for us to believe she's actually missing. Those two had a big argument before she left town," she said.

"I didn't know that."

Sheriff Turner grunted. "Seems like good ol' Tate left out a few important details. Amber probably got mad and ditched him. Plus, she was facing a marijuana charge. I'm not shocked she skipped town."

"But what about the guy who was stalking her? *Stalking Elly?* Isn't it worth following up about? This Bobby guy and his pickup truck?"

"What is there to 'follow up'? There are millions of Bobbys in the world and thousands of people in Virginia alone who own black pickup trucks."

The sheriff was right, but Naomi could recall one person in particular in Sparksburg who owned a black truck that had raised her suspicions.

"I think . . . I think Travis Meacham did it," Naomi whispered. "He took Elly and maybe caused her moms to go over that cliff."

"*Travis Meacham?* Those are some pretty serious allegations."

Sheriff Turner narrowed her eyes. "Why do you think he did it?"

"His truck fits the description," Naomi explained. "And he has a lot more than speeding tickets." She held up her phone, showing a screenshot of Travis's criminal charge history in West Virginia that she'd found online that morning. "Nine years ago, he was charged with second-degree assault and harassment."

"That's still not kidnapping, Naomi."

"And there's just a . . . a feeling I have about him."

She remembered Travis Meacham's cold stare. The way he'd spit tobacco on the ground only about a foot away from her and Blake, and how he'd railed about newcomers to Sparksburg.

You people come here and think you own the goddamn place!

Plus, he had the evil Mayor Charles Davis Meacham's blood coursing through his veins. She could easily believe that someone like Travis would be capable of kidnapping teenage girls who he felt didn't belong in Sparksburg.

"Young lady, I can't bring in someone for questioning, let alone arrest them because of decade-old charges and a 'feeling.' Look," Sheriff Turner said, sitting up in her chair, "I'm only telling you this because from what I understand someone at the county's medical examiner's office already leaked this to the press, but we ordered a postmortem toxicology test on the bodies of Cheryl and Krissa Jamison, just to understand why they may have gone off the road. They both had high levels of sedatives and painkillers in their system. That would definitely impact their driving and could explain the accident."

Sedatives and painkillers? But Elly's moms had seemed like such responsible people. Why would they drive around like that?

"Now, we still haven't accounted for Elly, and I understand you're worried about your friend. We're doing everything we can to find her, but do me a favor and leave the detective work to the people who were trained to do this. Okay?"

Naomi grimaced.

"Okay?" the sheriff repeated.

Naomi forced herself to nod. "Okay," she said, though she might as well be crossing her fingers behind her back because she wasn't going to listen to Sheriff Turner. She was already planning her next steps. She wouldn't give up on trying to find out what had happened to Elly and Amber. Not yet anyway.

"HEY!" NAOMI SHOUTED to Dawn, skidding to a stop near the antique shop's door only four minutes late.

Dawn had stepped out of the shop with the mantel clock she'd been eyeing earlier clutched in her arms and a canvas bag filled with other antique finds dangling at her side.

"Let me take that for you," Naomi said, lifting the heavy clock out of Dawn's hands.

"Thanks, sweetheart, but where's your bag? You decided not to buy anything?"

Naomi wrinkled her nose. "It wasn't as cool as I thought it was when I got a chance to see it the second time around."

The lies were rolling off her tongue so easily now. She didn't like how good she was getting at this.

"Why are you sweating? And why is your face so red?" Dawn asked. "Did you run here?"

"Yeah, I didn't want to be late. I know how anxious you get when . . . well . . . when you can't find me. I didn't want to put you through that again."

Dawn gazed at her silently for a few seconds before suddenly wrapping an arm around her and kissing her on her cheek. "That was very thoughtful of you, Cam." She squeezed her shoulder. "Come on, let's head to the cabin."

34

"HEY!" KHALIL SAID, STANDING IN THEIR CABIN'S doorway the next day.

Naomi leaped into his arms and squeezed him tight.

"Nuh-uh, I better see some sunlight between you two," Andre joked.

Naomi released Khalil and stepped back.

She was just so happy to see him in person again, it was hard to hide it. It felt like forever since they'd been together, but it had only been a few days.

Was this what it was like to fall hard for someone?

"What plans do you guys have on deck today?" Andre asked.

When Khalil reached for Naomi's hand, she went gooey all over again. "It's your last week in Sparksburg, so I thought we might keep it chill and have a picnic. We can figure out the rest from there. Sound good to you?"

"Sounds perfect," Naomi said, resisting the urge to kiss him since Andre was watching them like a hawk.

And she already had in mind what they could do after that. She'd just have to convince Khalil or, worst-case scenario, trick him into taking her there—but she hoped it wouldn't come to that.

"Well, have a good time, y'all," Andre said. "See you later this evening, Cam."

When they got to the hilltop where they were to have their picnic, Naomi gasped as soon as she stepped out of the car. Maybe the views had been just as arresting when she'd climbed to the summit of Mary's Rock with the Stoakeses a week ago, but she'd been too exhausted to appreciate it. She certainly was taking it all in now though. The treetops looked like an undulating cloud of green below them. The blue sky and the even taller mountain peaks in the far-off distance looked almost surreal in their perfection.

"Whoa," she said in awe. "It's so pretty up here." She leaned back her head and closed her eyes, feeling the sun and breeze on her face.

"I know, right?" Khalil popped open the trunk and took out a picnic basket, an old quilted blanket, and a Bluetooth speaker. "My parents used to drag us up here when I was younger. It's an important spot for my fam. My dad said his great-great-grandfather used to hold sermons on this hilltop for the Black people in town before they got their own church built. I think Dad proposed to Mom up here, too."

"Really?"

"Yeah." He handed her the blanket. "Can you spread this out for me? You choose the spot."

Naomi took the blanket and looked around her. Now that she knew how much history and significance this hilltop held for Khalil's family, she wasn't sure where they should sit. It felt like all of it was sacred ground. What if that spot five feet in front of her was where Khalil's great-great-great-granddaddy used to quote the Bible and preach to his flock? What if she laid the blanket twenty feet to her left and that was where Khalil's dad had dropped on bended knee and proposed? Finally, she chose a spot near a large oak tree for shade and spread out the blanket there.

They unloaded the picnic basket that Khalil's mom had helped him pack. It was filled with thick deli sandwiches, fresh fruit, chips, and chocolate chip cookies.

"Mom made the cookies yesterday," he said, taking a bite. "They're better than anything you'll get off a store shelf."

They ate while hip-hop and R&B music played on the speaker. Naomi liked it up here. The atmosphere felt lighter and less humid than it did back in Sparksburg, though they were probably at the same elevation. The air was less oppressive; you could *breathe* here. She bet if she didn't have her usual vaseline and perfume combo in her nose, she'd find that it smelled better, too.

Maybe it was the ghosts in town that made it feel so heavy. Like a curse hung over the land.

When they were done eating, she absently pulled at tufts of grass while he lay on his back, staring up at the puffy clouds overhead.

"I'm going to miss views like this when we go home," she said, resting her chin on her knees. She watched as a butterfly flitted its way to a nearby stalk covered with vibrant colored lilies.

Khalil gazed up at her. "So you're just gonna miss the views?"

She shrugged. "Well, you know how I feel about Sparksburg, especially after what happened to Elly and her parents. I haven't exactly vibed with that place."

He cocked an eyebrow. "I wasn't talking about Sparksburg, Naomi. I meant are you gonna miss me?"

"Of course I'm going to miss you. You've been the best part of this whole vacation."

"Well, if that's the case, I was thinking . . ." Khalil slowly sat up.

"Thinking about what?"

"Marymount is only like a thirty-minute drive from Silver Spring. We could still see each other on the weekends. There's no reason to end this just because your stay in Sparkburg with your family is over."

"You really want to keep hanging out with me?"

He laughed. "Hell yeah! Why wouldn't I?"

She remembered how Alexis had looked adoringly at him, how'd she'd practically been glued to his side almost the entire cookout a week ago. Khalil was a cute guy and smart. Naomi was sure there would be plenty of girls on Marymount's campus who would adore him as well. Did he really want to be stuck with a high school girl he'd only known for three weeks?

"Yeah, but . . . I thought you might want to . . . to explore your freshman year. You know, meet people."

"Why explore when I've already found what I'm looking for?"

Khalil went to the orange lilies, picked one, and held it out to her. He dropped to his knees and leaned in close.

"I want us to be together, Naomi. I want you to be my girl."

Her chest tightened. She could barely breathe as he tucked the lily behind her left ear.

"Okay," she whispered just as he leaned in and kissed her. Once. Twice. He nibbled her ear and her neck before returning to her mouth.

All of Khalil's past kisses had been quick pecks or puckers with a sweep of the tongue that lingered on the lips as sweet as honey. But there was more power and passion this time, catching her off guard. He eased her onto the scratchy wool blanket and reclined next to her. She felt a mix of excitement and panic when they stopped kissing long enough for him to open one button at her collar, then another.

You're his girl now, she told herself as she closed her eyes. *It's okay. Relax.*

She'd seen it done on TV plenty of times. Read about it in books. She'd even seen it in person after walking in on Maya and her boyfriend Troy's make-out session months ago where they were practically gnawing each other's faces off.

But now she was the one kissing so hard that she could barely breathe. Her heart was pounding so fast she could hear the blood thrumming in her ears, and her body temperature was skyrocketing. Khalil's hand snaked its way to her bra cup. Alarm bells went off in her head even as goosebumps of anticipation puckered on her skin. When she felt a strap being tugged off her shoulder, panic won out and her eyes snapped open. She shoved him away and sat up.

"What?" he asked, showing his hands as she quickly closed her shirt. "What's wrong?"

"Can we slow down?"

He began to ease back from her. "I'm sorry. I thought you liked it. I wasn't trying to have sex. Not out here, Naomi. I wouldn't do that. But we can stop if you don't want to—"

"I don't want to stop. I did like it. Just not all at once. Okay? Can we . . . we ease into it?"

He nodded. "Of course."

She kissed him again. This time when he kissed her back, it was much more gentle, more tentative. This time, when her heart started racing, it wasn't out of fear but expectation as she eased him back to the blanket and the kiss deepened.

35

AFTER THEY'D PACKED THE CAR AND CLIMBED INTO the front seat, Khalil and Naomi exchanged a knowing look that made her giggle. She flushed at the memory of the thrills and sensations she'd been feeling for the past hour.

"Don't look at me like that," she said, slapping his arm, making him laugh, too.

It was official. She had a boyfriend. One whose hand she constantly wanted to hold, who she couldn't wait to kiss again.

"So where should we go next?" he asked.

Naomi's smile faded, his question knocking her off the cloud of bliss she'd been floating on.

She remembered the other place she'd planned to go today. The truth was that she'd looked up Travis Meacham's address online yesterday—as soon as she and Dawn got back from downtown Sparksburg. She wasn't too shocked to discover he lived less than three miles away from where the Jamisons had vacationed.

She knew if she told Khalil she wanted to do surveillance at Meacham's property, he'd instantly say no. She was even second-guessing now whether it was a good idea to go there, but she was sure there was a connection between Elly and Amber—and that the connection was Travis Meacham. She just had to prove it to Sheriff Turner.

"I'll give you the address," she began, "but . . . but the rest has to be a surprise."

"A surprise? Is this payback for zip-lining?" Khalil asked. "You aren't making me drive to some weird place, are you?"

"Maybe. Maybe not," she said in a singsong voice, hoping he wouldn't be too angry once he found out the truth.

"It's like that, huh?" He laughed. "Fine, then. Give me the addy."

IT DIDN'T TAKE them long to arrive at Meacham's property. For about a quarter of a mile, they drove along an old wooden post-and-rail fence covered with lichen and bleached by the sun. The fence was broken in some sections and overgrown with shrubs, weeds, and vines that looked like they could have inhabited an ancient, enchanted forest in one of Naomi's fantasy novels. Like they could come to life and reach out to grab a passerby at any moment.

Khalil slowly braked and wrinkled his brow when they reached the end of the fence and saw a rusted NO TRESPASSING sign nailed to a post near a long dirt road. They could barely see through all the trees and dense foliage, but she guessed Meacham's home was nestled somewhere in there at the end of the road.

"Naomi, what is this?" Khalil asked, turning down the volume on the radio and facing her. "Why did you want to come here?"

She took a deep breath. "It's the home of the guy I think may have kidnapped Elly."

Khalil didn't say anything at first. *"What?"* he finally uttered.

"It's the home of the guy that—"

"Yeah," he interrupted, "I heard you the first time. I wasn't asking you to repeat it. I'm just trying to figure out why we're here."

"I told you. Because he might have Elly. She might be in there."

Khalil put the car in park and shook his head in exasperation. "Naomi, even if you're right, which I don't see how, what are we supposed to do if she is there? Run in and *save her*?"

"No," she said, though honestly, she hadn't thought that far. "If we see signs that she's there or that he's keeping another girl there, we can tell the police. They can do it themselves."

"You know this isn't like Silver Spring, right? The folks up here are built different. They shoot at you just for walking on their property without permission and this dude clearly," he said, pointing at the NO TRESPASSING sign, "doesn't want any surprise company. I'm supposed to start my freshman year at Marymount in the fall. I'm only eighteen. I don't wanna die!"

"We're not going to die," she snapped. "Stop overreacting! I'm just going to look around. You can stay in the car if you want and wait for me. He won't even know we're here."

Khalil leaned forward, bracing his hands on the steering wheel. "First you pretend to be a podcaster so you could interview some dude about a girl on a flyer. Now you're snooping around a stranger's house in the middle of nowhere because you're somehow sure he kidnapped your neighbor. Do you realize how crazy all this sounds?" He shook his head. "You know doing this stuff isn't going to change anything, right?"

"What are you talking about? Change what?"

"You were a missing girl. *They're* missing girls. But saving them isn't going to change what happened to you, Naomi. It's not gonna rewrite anything."

She flinched as if he'd hit her.

"This . . . this has n-n-nothing to d-do with what happened

to me," she said. "You don't know what you're talking about!"

"I do. And I worry if you keep doing this stuff, you're gonna get hurt. It's getting obsessive. You've gotta stop."

Naomi felt her anger flare up like an oven burner. "You're not my dad, Khalil, and even though you want to be a therapist, you aren't one yet. I don't need or want a lecture from you." She threw open her car door.

"Naomi! Naomi!" he shouted after her, but she ignored him.

She wasn't doing this out of some misguided effort to change her past. She was doing this because she knew this was the right thing to do. Because the ghost of the girl had led her to the Jamisons' car and had entrusted Naomi to figure out where Elly was and who was behind this.

And I will, Naomi assured herself. She climbed over one of the broken fence rails and made her way through the shrubs and weeds, taking a less conspicuous path to Meacham's home than the main road.

36

FOR SEVERAL MINUTES, NAOMI WALKED CROUCHED low so that she couldn't be seen. She sneezed, sending gnats and pollen flying in all directions. She wished she'd taken an antihistamine and maybe brought some bug spray with her. Mosquitoes were buzzing around her bare arms and legs, practically eating her alive. She waved them away absently. As she brushed past a few leaves, she prayed to God that she wasn't wading through poison ivy, too.

Finally, through the tree branches, Naomi could see Meacham's truck. It was parked at the bottom of a hill in front of a rundown double-wide with a sheet-metal roof. Beside the truck was the skeleton of an old tractor on cinder blocks. She saw a white cat missing its left ear sunning itself on the front porch next to a broken lawn chair and an abandoned cooler. The trailer had a few windows but almost all the curtains were drawn. Only one was slightly parted.

Naomi drew even closer, then abruptly stopped. The cat wasn't Meacham's only pet. She could hear a dog barking inside the trailer. The canine was probably like Bear would be in this situation, trying to warn his owner that he could hear and smell an invader nearby.

Should she turn back?

Naomi gazed desperately over her shoulder. She couldn't see Khalil's car anymore at this distance, but she assumed he was still there, that he hadn't left her. She waffled for a minute or two, trying to decide whether to turn back or not. But she had come this far.

Better to just keep going, she thought.

After walking a few more yards, she wasn't hidden in the trees anymore, but out in the open, feeling the hot sun on her face and shoulders. The cat raised its head to stare at her. The dog's muffled barks became louder, more hoarse and insistent. She could hear a man's voice yelling at the dog to be quiet.

She knew she only had minutes, maybe less to look through the window before she had to run back into the trees.

Naomi quick-tiptoed across the yard, focusing on the window where the curtains were parted about two inches. The window was toward the farthest end of the double-wide, near a hibachi grill perched atop a card table. She stood on the balls of her feet and peeked inside.

She saw a German shepherd barking at the door, leaping on his hind legs and throwing himself against it in a desperate effort to get outside. At the far end of the trailer was an eat-in kitchenette. On the counter was a pile of dirty dishes. Closer to her was the living room. Naomi saw a battered tweed sofa where a dog bed with exposed cotton stuffing sat on one of the cushions. Beside the sofa was a small flat-screen TV where a baseball game was blasting at full volume. Facing the TV was Travis Meacham in a leather recliner, nursing a beer.

He seemed to be alone in the trailer. There were no signs of Elly or Amber.

"Henry, stop all that damn barkin', boy!" Travis shouted. "What the hell has gotten into you?"

Naomi leaned in closer. Was there a bedroom behind the door by the kitchenette? Could the girls be in there?

She lurched back in alarm when the dog raced across the living room and ran to the window. He barked and snarled, sending lines of drool and spit flying and splattering the glass.

Travis whipped his head to glower at the dog. "Henry!" he yelled just as his eyes locked with Naomi's.

She froze. Her breath caught in her throat.

"What the hell?" Travis rose to his feet.

Naomi stumbled backward, knocking over the grill and card table. She almost tripped over her own feet, but managed to stay upright. She turned and ran.

"Goddamn it, I saw ya!" Travis shouted seconds later, after throwing open the trailer's door. The dog's barks were even louder now. "What the hell were you doin' out here?"

Naomi didn't stop to answer him. She kept running, leaping over shrubs and darting through trees. She raced at breakneck speed back up the hill. Her side started to ache as she ran. Her throat began to burn from breathing so hard. Vines and branches whipped against her bare legs, leaving scrapes and cuts.

In less than a minute, she could see the road again and then the post with the NO TRESPASSING sign. Khalil was sitting on the hood of his car, casually scanning through his phone. When she came bursting out of the tree line, he hopped to his feet and stared at her, aghast.

"What's wrong? What happened?" he asked as she raced to the passenger side.

"Stop! Stop, damn it!" Travis boomed over all the barks and yips.

"Get in the car!" Naomi yelled. "Drive! Just go!"

But they were too late. The dog came charging at them,

barely being held back by his leash as Travis came running in his T-shirt, boxers, and bare feet.

Khalil jumped on the hood of his car to keep from being bitten. He pulled Naomi on top of the hood with him.

The hot metal burned her knees and shins, which were already covered with cuts and mosquito bites, but that pain was nothing compared to the prospect of getting mauled by Travis's dog.

"Oh no you don't!" Travis yelled. His wrinkled, gaunt face went crimson with rage. "You both get your asses down here!"

"He didn't do anything," Naomi shouted, her voice shaking with terror. "Let him go! It was me! It was just me! He didn't even want to come here."

Khalil wrapped his arms around her protectively. "Leave her alone!"

"Don't kill us!" Naomi pleaded, now teary eyed.

"Kill you?" Travis burst into laughter before roughly yanking the dog back again. His wiry, hairy arms strained with the effort. "Heel, Henry! Heel, damn it!"

The dog finally stopped barking but gave a low, menacing growl instead.

"I'm not gonna kill you, kid," Travis said with a yellow-toothed grin, "but I *am* callin' the police."

37

NAOMI LEANED AGAINST THE HOOD OF KHALIL'S car, stretching her legs, trying to keep the hot metal from burning the back of her thighs. She felt a bead of sweat roll its way down the side of her face and her neck. She tried to wipe the sweat away before remembering she couldn't—her hands were cuffed behind her.

Khalil was in handcuffs, too, but he wasn't fidgeting. He was a statue and just as stony-faced. He'd only said a few words since the two Sparksburg cops had arrived: his name, date of birth, "Yes, sir," and "No, sir."

Naomi had recognized one of the two officers the moment he got out of his cruiser. It was Sergeant Packard, the same cop she met yesterday at the Sheriff's Office. He was being just as much of an asshole today. He'd shouted at her and Khalil to get off the roof of the car, threatening that he would drag them down himself. He'd put them in handcuffs while he and the other cop questioned Travis about what happened, unwilling to listen to Naomi's explanation.

Were they really going to arrest them? What were Andre and Dawn going to say? This was worse than stealing money out of a wallet and trying to catch a train at Union Station in DC. Once they bailed her out of jail, would they ground her for life? Or send her off to some boarding school so they wouldn't have to deal with her drama anymore?

And what was going to happen to Khalil? How would his parents react to the news?

She glanced at Khalil now, trying to make eye contact. Was he as scared as she was?

When he wouldn't look at her, she leaned toward him.

"Khalil," she whispered.

He didn't respond.

She slid a little closer to him. "Khalil, I'm sorry."

"Stop talking," he snapped.

"Please don't be mad at me. I just wanted to say I'm sorry."

"I heard you. Stop talking," he whispered back.

"Look, I know it's all my fault."

"Yes, it is your fault, but right now, I'm more worried about getting shot by some racist redneck cop in the middle of Virginia, Naomi. I just wanna keep my mouth shut and make it home, though I'll probably lose my college scholarship because now I'll have a criminal record. This is fucked up what you've dragged me into."

Her lower lip began to tremble. She blinked back tears. "I didn't mean to drag you into it."

"Yes, you did. You told me to drive you here. You made me wait for you."

"You didn't have to wait for—"

"Yeah, right," he said, speaking over her. "Like you really thought I would leave you in the middle of—"

"Hey, shut up over there!" Sergeant Packard yelled, making them quiet instantly. He strode toward them, narrowing his blue eyes. "And stay two feet apart, like I told you!"

Naomi shifted to her left, away from Khalil. She swallowed, feeling her throat grow dry as a tear fell.

A minute later, she heard a siren blare. Naomi watched as another police cruiser stopped near Meacham's fence.

"Why the hell are these kids in handcuffs?" Sheriff Turner asked, stepping out of the police car.

Naomi sighed, now relieved. Their nightmare wasn't totally over, but at least she knew they stood a better chance of not going to jail with the sheriff here. The woman had been sympathetic to her so far.

Sheriff Turner looked at both officers expectantly. "Well, go on! Why are they in handcuffs?"

"For . . . uh . . . breaking and entering," Sergeant Packard said.

Naomi noticed that some of his bravado from earlier had disappeared. He seemed a lot more sheepish in front of his boss.

"Wait. These kids broke into your trailer, Travis?" the sheriff asked.

"No, but that girl over there ignored the sign telling her to stay the hell off my property." He pointed a gnarled finger at Naomi. "She hopped the fence and was looking through my window. Scared me and Henry half to death."

"Did she, now?" Sheriff Turner crossed her arms and faced Naomi. "Young lady, I thought we talked about this."

Naomi lowered her eyes.

"Take off the handcuffs," Sheriff Turner ordered.

Sergeant Packard said, "But they broke the law, Sheriff!"

"No, they didn't. There was no breaking and entering. She hopped a fence, and the young man didn't do a damn thing, according to Travis. Am I correct, Travis?"

The scraggly old man gave a grudging shrug. "I ain't see it, if he did."

"We'll just go with no. He didn't do anything. And the most you could get her on was unlawful entry on private property, and it's not worth the time or the paperwork," Sheriff Turner said. "I'm sure this whole episode scared the hell out of these kids. She won't do it again. Let 'em go with a warning and call it a day, officers."

Sergeant Packard's face flushed. He pursed his lips, forming a thin white line. He looked like his head was about to explode, but he kept quiet and removed the key chain from his belt.

"Turn around," he barked.

"What's your name?" Sheriff Turner asked Khalil as Packard uncuffed him.

"Khalil Crowley, ma'am," Khalil said, his voice a little shaky.

"And how old are you, Khalil? Eighteen? Nineteen?"

"I'm eighteen, ma'am," he said, rubbing his wrists as he turned around.

Sheriff Turner nodded. "Well, then I don't have to release you to your parents. You can go. This one over here, though." She looked pointedly at Naomi. "We're going to have a talk with your mom and dad."

Khalil looked eager to flee. He didn't even give Naomi a second glance as she said goodbye to him. She watched helplessly as he jumped in his car and pulled off.

"Sorry about all this, Travis," Sheriff Turner called out.

Meacham grunted in reply before yanking his German shepherd to his side. He headed back to his trailer.

"You come with me, young lady," she said to Naomi. "I'm taking you to the Sheriff's Office. You look like you can use some water and some AC. Your parents can pick you up from there."

Naomi nodded and reluctantly followed Sheriff Turner to her cruiser.

LESS THAN HOUR later, Naomi sat in one of the chairs outside of Sheriff Turner's Office, leaning toward the door. Dawn and Andre were in there with the sheriff. Naomi was trying her best to eavesdrop.

Dawn and Andre had arrived twenty minutes prior. When they walked into the lobby and saw Naomi standing next to Sheriff Turner, they had the same looks on their faces they had that day back at Union Station. They looked hurt. Disappointed. Sad. Sheriff Turner took them into her office, asked Naomi to wait outside, and shut the door behind them. She had been waiting for them ever since.

Suddenly, the door swung open and Naomi snapped back into her seat. She stared at the wall in front of her, pretending like she hadn't been trying to eavesdrop seconds ago. She watched as Andre and Dawn stepped out of the office first.

"Thank you, Sheriff Turner," Andre said as she stepped into the hall. He shook her hand. "Thank you for being so understanding and patient."

"Yes, thank you so much," Dawn said, shaking the sheriff's hand, too.

"No problem, folks. I hope your daughter's truly learned her lesson this time." She then turned to Naomi. Her pale, round face was grim. "I don't wanna see you here again, young lady. Do you understand?"

"Yes, Sheriff," Naomi whispered.

"Come on," Andre said. "Let's head back to the cabin."

Naomi slowly stood. She'd been terrified before of spending

a day in a jail cell. Now she was just as worried about what Andre and Dawn's punishment for her would be.

As she followed them on shaky legs down the corridor and into the lobby, she passed Sergeant Packard. He narrowed his icy blue eyes at her and shook his head. If it was up to him, she and Khalil would be getting fingerprinted by now.

She and the Stoakeses stepped out the double doors into the humid July sun. Naomi wanted them to say something. Anything. Tell her how disappointed they were. Berate her for embarrassing them. Instead, they wordlessly walked down the block to their waiting SUV. She brought up the rear. The silence and calm were starting to unnerve her. The knots in her stomach tightened painfully. She was starting to feel sick.

After they climbed inside the car and pulled onto Main Street, Naomi continued to wait for the lecture she knew would come.

"I never thought I'd ever be picking up one of my daughters from a police station," Andre finally said minutes later. "Now I've done it twice. The first time wasn't your fault, Cam. But this time definitely is."

Even though she'd been anticipating it, Naomi still winced at the emotional gut punch.

"And it's not just the fact that you could've been arrested. Do you realize what could have happened to you out there?" he asked. "Cam, you guys could have seriously been hurt. Killed! Those two cops who showed up before Sheriff Turner did could've shot you."

"I'm sorry," she said. She'd repeated those words so many times today, but each time they lost power and meaning. "I just wanted to find Elly. That's why I was there."

"You thought you could find Elly by stalking a complete

stranger?" Dawn asked, speaking for the first time.

"No, that's not . . . that's not what I meant. That's not what I was doing."

"I thought we were making some progress, Cam. We thought we could trust you! And you do this?" Dawn sucked her teeth. "Just so you know, you're grounded. Maybe until the end of the vacation. Maybe after. Your dad and I haven't decided yet, but we'll let you know when we do."

Naomi sank lower in her seat and stared out the window. Why bother to keep defending herself? Part of her knew that Andre and Dawn wouldn't listen anyway. Her plan to help find and rescue Elly and Amber had seemed solid, but it obviously didn't to anyone else. It was one of many ways Naomi felt misunderstood. By Sheriff Turner. By Dawn and Andre. Now even by Khalil, who she'd thought she connected with. No one understood her, and she was starting to suspect it would always be that way.

38

THUNDER BOOMED. NAOMI SLOWLY OPENED HER eyes to find drool pooling on the page that she'd been reading. She'd literally fallen asleep with her head in a book after being stuck in her room all day with nothing else to do now that she was grounded and couldn't leave the cabin.

She closed the novel, yawned, and pushed herself up to her elbows. She turned slightly to find rain pounding the sliding glass doors. Beyond that was the pitch-black sky. She sat up and reached for her cell, scratching at the mosquito bites on her knee and calf.

Khalil still had not texted her back despite the dozen or so messages she had sent him over the past two days. Had his parents found out what had happened and grounded him, too, or was he just refusing to ever speak to her again?

She couldn't blame him for freezing her out. He hadn't wanted to go to Meacham's house. He'd tried to warn her about searching the property. She knew the long list of awful scenarios that could've happened that day but luckily hadn't. And he'd been right. She put his scholarship and future in jeopardy because of her bad choices. She managed to gain and lose a boyfriend in one day.

Naomi sat her cell back on her night table and flinched at the lightning making its way across the sky, momentarily illuminating the trees and grass. An earsplitting boom soon followed and the rain seemed to come even faster.

God, how she hated thunderstorms, especially ferocious ones like this.

She marched to the sliding glass door to close the curtain but paused when she saw who was standing beneath her window.

The girl was waiting for her. She stood in the rain but an invisible bubble seemed to surround her, for not a single drop of water touched her body or hair. She stared up at Naomi with those haunting, dark eyes.

Naomi unlocked the door and opened it.

"I tried!" she shouted over the sound of echoing thunder. She thought she also heard the sound of a tolling bell, like the ones in church steeples, but she couldn't be sure.

Naomi blinked through the rain spraying her face.

"I tried, okay? But Elly wasn't there. Amber wasn't either. I could've gotten arrested. My boyfriend isn't even talking to me anymore because of what I made him do."

The girl didn't say a word, didn't move. She only gazed at Naomi.

"What do you want from me? I'm only sixteen. I don't have a friggin' car and now I'm grounded. Just leave me alone. Go haunt someone else!"

Lightning flashed again. Naomi jumped as the lights in her bedroom flickered. The sky shifted from black to slate gray, revealing the angry clouds overhead. The field went bright again and this time the girl wasn't out there alone. She was surrounded by more than fifty people.

Naomi saw a woman wearing her hair in a bun and a dark skirt made wide with petticoats. She saw a teenage boy with a pompadour wearing a T-shirt and jeans rolled up at the cuffs, and beside him was a man with a thick beard wearing denim overalls and a faded dress shirt rolled up at the sleeves. She saw a little girl in ankle boots and an apron, clutching a rag doll against her chest. Their gaunt brown faces were turned up to her. Their dark eyes were all locked on Naomi like she was a beacon that had guided them there.

"You're trying to scare me but it isn't going to work!" She backed away from her balcony, realizing who they all were. "Just . . . just leave me alone."

They were the tragic souls of Sparksburg that Khalil's great-grandmother had talked about, that she'd read had disappeared from their families in the middle of the night. These were the people. The ones who had been terrorized and murdered, who were locked to the land and could not leave.

The sound of the tolling bell grew louder and louder. Naomi clasped her hands over her ears to shut out the sound. She swore she could feel the bell's vibrations through the cabin walls. She could feel the banging and clanging in her teeth and her skull. She cringed at the pain.

"I can't do anything!" she screamed over the noise. Tears flooded her eyes. "I can't change anything! Pick someone else. Pick someone else!"

"Camryn?"

Naomi whipped around to find Blake standing in her doorway in his Spider-Man pj's.

"I was playing my video games and heard you shouting. Are you okay?"

The ringing had stopped. All she could hear now was far-off thunder.

"I'm . . . I'm fine, Blake." She faced him, sniffing and blinking tears away.

Blake gazed at her uneasily. "Who were you talking to?" He stepped into her room, staring out the window. He stepped closer. "Is someone out there?"

Could he see the ghosts, too, or was she still the only one who could? She *had* told them to haunt someone else. Would they latch on to Blake instead?

Naomi shook her head. She wouldn't drag her little brother into this.

"No one," she said firmly, shutting the balcony door and making him wince. She closed the curtains. "I wasn't talking to anyone, Blake. Go back to your video games."

"But—"

"*Go*, Blake!"

He lingered a little longer but nodded and left. When she heard his bedroom door close, she peeked between the curtains, relieved to see that all the ghosts were gone.

But will they return?

39

NAOMI SETTLED INTO ONE OF THE KITCHEN CHAIRS and plopped her bowl of cereal in front of her. She adjusted the straps of her bikini top beneath her T-shirt, then ate a few spoonfuls. Blake pantomimed eating his pancakes, staring at her like she could sprout a second head at any moment.

He'd been looking at her like that since he'd caught her yelling at the ghosts outside her window a couple of nights ago.

Now she met his stare, raising her brows in challenge. "My face can't be that interesting, Blake. Look somewhere else, okay?" she said, making his eyes dart back to his pancakes. He kept his head down as he finally took a bite.

"All right. Let's finish up, guys," Andre said, clapping his hands. He strode into the kitchen. "I want to get going soon."

Today, they were tubing on the Shenandoah River, taking another stab at this whole family-vacation thing. Though Naomi was relieved to finally get out of the cabin, she was depressed.

It was more than a week since Elly went missing and Naomi noticed how she was appearing less and less on the local news, getting pushed aside for other stories like a house fire, the devastating hurricane that hit South Carolina, and the latest presidential poll. Someone leaked the news that her moms had been under the influence of sleeping pills and painkillers when the car accident happened. It was like everyone was blaming Elly's disappearance on bad parenting. And Naomi hadn't heard back from Khalil, despite all of her calls and texts. She was starting to feel like a stalker. Maybe it was time to give it up, to just leave him alone and accept their relationship was over.

I couldn't even keep a boyfriend a full day, she thought miserably.

"Your cereal is getting soggy, Cam," Dawn said, gesturing to her bowl. "Not much of an appetite today?"

Naomi swirled her spoon, watching as the rainbow-colored marshmallows turned the milk from white to gray. "Not really."

"Well, try to eat something. You don't want to be in that hot sun on an empty stomach. Maybe grab a banana and granola bar and eat it in the car," Dawn suggested.

Naomi nodded before dumping her cereal into the kitchen sink.

THEY ARRIVED AT the waterfront twenty-five minutes later and walked toward a small boathouse filled with canoes, kayaks, inner tubes, and paddles. A woman in a fisherman's hat, wearing a T-shirt with *Great Water Adventures* plastered on the front in fading letters, explained that they'd be taking a 1.3-mile circular course for tubing on one of the more tranquil stretches along the Shenandoah River.

When they got to the rocky riverfront, all wearing life vests and dragging their inner tubes behind them, Naomi gazed at the water. It seemed to stretch past the horizon with the sun reflecting off the rippling waves. She took a picture with her cell and pushed her inner tube into the river before climbing inside and joining the Stoakeses and the rest of their group as the current ushered them downstream.

They floated for a quarter of a mile before hitting small

rapids. Five minutes later, they reached another placid stretch. Naomi pulled out her phone again.

She snapped a photo of Maya taking pucker-lipped selfies. Maya stopped mid-photo to scream when Blake floated by and splashed her with water. Maya kicked water back at him and they began a splash fight that had them both breaking down into squeals and laughter. Several feet away, Naomi saw Andre reach out his hand to Dawn. They linked fingers and he slowly drew her toward him. Dawn smiled and leaned her head toward his. Naomi snapped another photo just as they shared a tender kiss.

She felt removed from both scenes, not only by distance but by connection. She felt like she wasn't there, like she was in some dark movie theater watching a loving family on-screen. It was yet another reminder that the Stoakeses had so much history together, a tapestry of moments she'd never witnessed and memories she could not share.

After about an hour, they reached the end of the course. Frankly, too soon for Naomi's liking. She and Blake were the stragglers. Dawn, Andre, and Maya were already carrying their inner tubes up the grassy hill. The other families were assembling them in piles along the shoreline where workers for Great Water Adventures were dragging them to another boathouse.

When she neared the shore, Naomi was surprised to see Mayor Bartz. He was helping a tawny-haired boy out of the water. The mayor must have been with another group or taken another course.

This was the first time Naomi hadn't seen him in a polo shirt or khakis. Instead, he was wearing only black swim shorts, and no shirt to cover his pale chest and hairy potbelly.

Beside him stood a pretty blond woman in what looked like a designer pink bikini—one that you could probably only buy at a high-end department store—and beside her was a seven- or eight-year-old girl in a baby-blue one-piece who was darker haired like Mayor Bartz, but had the woman's facial features.

"You had fun, buddy?" the mayor asked the boy just as Naomi and Blake reached the shore. One of the workers leaned down and offered Blake his hand to pull him up.

Naomi watched as the boy grinned and nodded in reply to the mayor's question. He was shivering as he took off his life jacket. The boy then turned to the blond-haired woman. "Mommy, I'm cold," he said through chattering teeth.

"I know, honey," the woman said. "We all are." She looked up at the mayor. "Bobby, can you take care of the tubes while I head to the car with the kids and grab some towels?"

Naomi did a double take.

Bobby? His name was Bobby?

Of course, she thought. *Robert Bartz. First name Robert—or Bobby, for short.*

However, Mayor Bartz couldn't possibly be the same mysterious Bobby that Tate had told her about. The one who had invited Amber to "party" at his secluded home in Sparksburg, all expenses paid, while his wife was away. The one who had harassed and tried to intimidate them into leaving the town. But then Naomi remembered how the mayor had angrily ripped down Amber's MISSING flyer, balled it up, and tucked it into his pocket. She still didn't know why he'd done that.

Maybe because he didn't want her to be found.

"Camryn, are you getting out?" Blake asked.

She turned away from the mayor and his family to find Blake already standing on the shore. He was unbuckling his life vest beside a crew member who was offering his hand to her. The crew member was waiting for her to climb out of the river.

"Oh. Umm, yeah," she said, holding out her hand. "Yeah, thanks."

40

"WHY ARE YOU WALKING SO FAST?" BLAKE ASKED, scrambling to keep up with Naomi.

Blake didn't know it, but they were trailing after the mayor, who was heading toward the parking lot while loudly talking on his cell.

She and Blake had already dropped off their inner tubes, and the entire time Naomi had stayed at a safe distance so the mayor wouldn't know she was following him, but she didn't want to lose sight of him either.

"We need to get back to the car, don't we?" Naomi asked. "Mom and Dad are probably waiting for us."

When they neared the lot, Naomi could see the Stoakeses standing near the SUV two rows down, toweling off and putting on clothes over their bathing suits. Andre looked up and waved at them.

"Cam! Blake! Over here," he said.

She shoved Blake in that direction. "Go ahead. I'll be there in a sec," she said.

Blake asked, "You aren't coming?"

"Yeah, I just have to talk to someone first," she said, still watching the mayor from the corner of her eye. "Tell Mom and Dad I'll be there in a couple minutes. Okay?"

She didn't wait for Blake's response before racing across the lot. She wanted to catch Mayor Bartz before he reached his family. What she had to say to him, she wanted to do without an audience.

"Mayor Bartz," she called out just before she pressed the record button on her cell. "Mayor Bartz?"

"Hey, Ted, let me call you back. Right . . . Right. Will do . . . Talk to you soon," the mayor said, lowering the phone from his ear. He gave her a perfect politician smile: all bleached teeth and surface-level friendliness. "Yes, how may I help you, little lady?"

Naomi blinked. She opened her mouth and closed it, struggling to find the right words as the gravity of what she was about to say . . . of what she wanted to ask suddenly set in.

She could be standing in front of Amber's kidnapper. He may have taken Elly, too. But the spirits of Sparksburg had been stalking her, downright imploring her to do this. This might be her only chance to find the two girls and bring a criminal to justice.

She forced herself to speak. To say something. *Anything.*

"Where were . . . where were you on June twelfth, Mayor Bartz?" she asked.

He laughed and squinted at her. "Excuse me?"

"The day that Amber Nash went missing. Where were you? Can you account for your whereabouts the day she disappeared?"

His smile faded. "I'm afraid I have no idea what you're talking about."

"No, I think you do, *Bobby,*" Naomi went on, gaining more confidence. "That's what you told Amber to call you, isn't it?"

Naomi saw something flicker in his blue eyes at that question. She wasn't sure if it was anger or irritation but it quickly disappeared as he shook his head.

"Again, I have no idea what you're talking about. I'm afraid you've mistaken me for someone else," he said, turning away from her.

"I don't think so," Naomi insisted, following him. "You invited her down here to Sparksburg. You said you'd give her money . . . two thousand dollars if she stayed with you for the weekend, but then you ghosted her because she brought a friend along."

At that, he stopped walking. She saw the muscles in his bare back go rigid. He took a deep breath and started walking again.

"When they wouldn't leave the valley and camped out in the woods, you harassed them," she said, running after him. "You called and texted her and showed up in the middle of the night in a black pickup truck to scare them off. Her friend remembers the truck. He knows it was you!"

The mayor whipped around and she knew for sure this time there was pure hatred in his eyes. His face and neck were beet red. His lips were pinched. He jabbed his finger at her as he marched toward her.

"Now look here, you little bi . . ." Mayor Bartz began through clenched teeth, then caught himself.

People were staring at them now, including his wife in the designer bathing suit. She looked at the mayor and Naomi curiously.

Mayor Bartz lowered his finger. He regained his calm. "I don't know who Amber Nash is, nor do I own a black pickup truck. I've never heard of her friend Tate either."

"I didn't tell you his name," Naomi said. She watched as the mayor's eyes narrowed into slits.

"Little lady, I am an upstanding citizen and the mayor of this fair town, and I'm going to politely ask you to stop following me, or I will contact security at this site. Maybe even the police. Do you understand?"

She didn't budge. She didn't answer him either. He turned around again and walked toward the blonde, who whispered something into his ear. He quickly shook his head, wrapped an arm around her tan shoulder, and steered her toward their vehicle, where the boy and girl stood waiting.

It wasn't a black pickup truck. It was a midnight-blue pickup truck with tinted windows—a truck that could easily appear black in the dark to two frightened campers.

She pressed the button on her screen to end her recording. It was only then that she finally turned and walked away.

41

"CAMRYN, GET DOWN HERE, PLEASE!"

Naomi had just finished eating breakfast and was brushing her teeth when she heard Dawn's call. She was still wiping minty toothpaste from her mouth with the back of her hand less than a minute later when she saw the cabin's front door was sitting open. As she drew closer, she could see a Sparksburg police cruiser parked in their driveway. Naomi stepped onto the porch and found Sheriff Turner there, talking to Dawn and Andre. When they saw her, they stopped talking.

So the sheriff must have gotten her message about Mayor Bartz.

Naomi had called the sheriff yesterday and gotten her voicemail. She'd left a message, telling her she'd been wrong about Travis Meacham, that the mayor was a much better suspect in Amber's disappearance and maybe Elly's as well. She'd even given the reasons the mayor was the likely culprit and said she could give Sheriff Turner the recording proving as much.

"Camryn," Dawn began, "Sheriff Turner told us you did something yesterday that was . . . that was . . ." She closed her eyes and grimaced. "Frankly, I'm just at a loss, honey. I don't even know how to say this."

"Well, I'll say it," Andre said. "Our kid harassed the town mayor and accused him of kidnapping."

"I didn't accuse him of anything. At least, not to his face. I just asked him where he was when Amber Nash went missing and proved that he knew her," Naomi said, crossing her arms. "He lied and said he didn't know her at all. Mr. God and Country . . . Mr. Upstanding Citizen tried to hire a teen sex worker and now wants to cover it up. That's probably why he kidnapped her in the first place, so that no one would know he—"

"Camryn, do you hear yourself?" Dawn groaned. "You can't just say things like that!"

"*Why not?* It's the truth!"

"Young lady, let me stop you there," Sheriff Turner said, stepping forward. "It is *not* the truth. It is a false allegation against Mayor Bartz that could destroy his reputation. He called me too, and told me what happened. He was very upset."

"Of course, he's upset because he's being called out! He knows what he did. He's trying to hide what he did. He used his real nickname Bobby for his screen name when he contacted Amber."

Sheriff Turner sighed deeply. "Bobby is a common nickname. One of our officers . . . Sergeant Packard's nickname is Bobby. You think I should bring him in for questioning, too?"

"But the mayor knew Tate Carroll's name without me even saying it! You don't think that's a weird coincidence?"

"Camryn, I came here strictly as a courtesy to your parents," Sheriff Turner said, not answering her question. "The last time we spoke at my office, they explained to me . . . well, your whole situation. Your background. I understand that you were kidnapped yourself when you were a baby and all the trauma you went through. That you're *still* going through."

Naomi froze.

Was that why they were in Sheriff Turner's office with the

door closed for twenty minutes? They'd been discussing her, sharing the tragic tale of baby Camryn, who was taken away from her family at a grocery store by a mean, crazy lady and now she was a fucked-up teenager, barely passing her classes and always getting into trouble, becoming a growing burden on her parents.

Naomi glared at Dawn and Andre, feeling betrayed.

"I even understand that you're doing all this with the best of intentions," the sheriff continued. "You have my sympathy, which is why I've tried my best to be patient with all these antics, but my patience is wearing thin. You are not a detective. You aren't a police officer. If you were, you'd understand the concepts of probable cause and search warrants, of which you've had neither. But that didn't stop you from going onto Travis Meacham's property and scaring the hell out of him and his dog. It didn't stop you from following Mayor Bartz around, asking him out-of-line questions in front of his wife and children. This is your *last* warning," she said, holding up a finger at her. "One more strike . . . your *third* strike, and you're out. If I find out you've done anything like this again . . . if you decide to reinsert yourself into this investigation of Elly Jamison's disappearance, I will have no choice but to arrest you and charge you accordingly."

"But if you would just listen to the recording," Naomi urged.

"Camryn," Dawn pleaded, "you're not listening. Didn't you hear what she just said?"

"Yes, I am listening! No one's listening to *me*! If you'd just hear the recording, Sheriff Turner, you'd—"

"Camryn!" Andre barked. Naomi fell silent. He'd never used that tone with her before. "Go upstairs. *Now!*"

Naomi bit down hard on her bottom lip, feeling hot tears pool in her eyes. She turned and angrily walked back inside.

"She might not hear you, Sheriff, but we hear you loud and clear," she heard Andre say. "We can assure you this will not happen again."

"I hope so. I truly hope so, Mr. Stoakes," Sheriff Turner said just before Naomi slammed her bedroom door.

42

TWO HOURS LATER, THERE WAS A LOUD KNOCK AT Naomi's door.

"Family meeting downstairs in five minutes," Andre said. She listened to his heavy footfalls as he walked back down the stairs.

She raised her head from her tearstained pillow, sniffed, and wiped her face. She'd been crying out of frustration since Sheriff Turner had left their cabin. She suspected she had finally run out of tears.

It was pretty obvious to Naomi that this family meeting was going to be about her. About how she had disappointed Andre and Dawn yet again. About how they couldn't let her out of their sight for one minute without her doing something crazy or destructive.

But Naomi wouldn't apologize for what she'd done. Mayor Bartz had known Amber Nash and probably knew something about what had happened to her. He should be called out publicly.

Five minutes later, Naomi walked down the stairs to find Blake and Maya already sitting on the sofa. Blake looked worried. Bear rested his head in Blake's lap and Blake was rubbing his ear. Maya, as usual, seemed annoyed. Dawn was pacing in front of the fireplace. She seemed wired with nervous energy, cracking her knuckles and gnawing her bottom lip. Andre stood stoically with his hands linked in front of him, like a pallbearer at a funeral. When Naomi walked into the great room, they all turned to look at her.

"Good, you're here," Andre said as she took a seat on the farthest end of the sectional. "The family meeting can start."

"Are we still going hiking today, Dad?" Blake asked.

"Afraid not, buddy. It's almost noon. Too late for a hike." He glanced at Dawn, who gave a barely discernible nod. "Besides your mom and I talked about it and we decided that we're actually going to end our vacation a little early. We're going to keep it pretty chill today. No activities. We want everyone to start packing up your things so we can head out bright and early tomorrow morning. If the traffic isn't bad, we should get home well before noon."

"Wait, *what*?" Maya asked, uncrossing her legs. "We only have a couple of days left, and we took a vote, Dad. Majority won. We voted to stay until the last day."

"Plans have changed, sweetheart," Dawn said softly.

"Why?" Maya cried, before jabbing her thumb at Naomi. "Because the drama princess did something batshit crazy again, so we all get punished?"

"Maya," Andre began in a warning voice.

"No, Dad! We came here *for her*, and now we're leaving here *because of her*. Why does she get to dictate everything in this family? You have three kids, not one! And she doesn't even consider us her family. She's said it herself in that stupid diary that she scribbles in all the time."

Naomi stared at Maya. She started to tremble. "You read . . . you read my journal?" she choked.

"Yeah, I read it," Maya spat, raising her chin, "and I'm glad I did because unlike Mom and Dad, I know what a fake bitch you are!"

"Now that's enough!" Andre shouted. "Apologize to your sister, Maya. Do it now!"

"Oh, I forgot. Once again, I'm wrong and she's right! Huh? 'Apologize, Maya,'" she said in a high-pitched, simpering voice. "'You need to be more patient with your sister. She's been through so much.' Yeah, the same sister who doesn't even go by the name you gave her. She still calls herself Naomi. She talks shit about us in imaginary letters she writes to the psycho who kidnapped her. She tells her she still loves her, you know? That she's her 'ride or die.'" Maya snorted and Naomi's vision tinged red. "It's just pathetic and delusional, and I'm tired of it. I'm tired of her!"

Naomi didn't know what came over her. Maybe it was the discovery that Maya had been secretly reading and laughing at her all this time as she riffled through the pages where Naomi shared her inner thoughts, where she'd bared so much of her soul. Or maybe it was because Maya had ridiculed her one too many times, and had now turned her venom on Naomi's mom by calling her a "psycho," but Naomi shot up from the sofa, raced toward Maya, and shoved her with all her might. The shove knocked Maya off the sofa and flat on her butt. She cried out.

"Camryn, what the— Have you lost your damn mind?" Andre yelled. He wrapped his arms around her just as Maya leaped to her feet and lunged for Naomi.

Dawn got between the two, holding Maya back, while Blake scrambled off the sofa, seeking cover behind the kitchen island.

Bear jumped off the sofa and began to bark and pace, agitated by the frenzy.

"Girls, stop!" Dawn ordered. "Stop it right now!"

"She started it!" Maya yelled. "She attacked me. She's crazy, Mom! Just like that psycho who raised her."

"Don't you ever . . . *ever* call her psycho! Don't you ever talk about my mother like that again!" Naomi sobbed with tears streaming down her face.

"She's not your mother!" Maya shouted, still lunging over Dawn's shoulder. "She never was, but maybe you should have stayed with her. We all would've been better off. We should have just left you there!"

Naomi ceased kicking and squirming in Andre's arms. Her heavy breathing slowed.

"Maybe you guys should have," she said just as Andre loosened his hold around her. She eased out of his arms and fled upstairs to her room.

43

"CAM? *CAM?*" DAWN CALLED THROUGH THE DOOR AS she knocked. "Camryn, open up! We need to talk *now*," she said, knocking again, but Naomi didn't answer her.

"Camryn Destiny Stoakes, if you don't open up this door right now, I swear to God that I will—"

Naomi angrily stomped to her door, unlocked it, and swung it open. She returned to her bed and went back to ripping out page after page of her journal and tearing them to shreds.

Dawn stared down at the sea of ripped paper, looking horrified. "What are you doing?"

She was destroying it. All of it. She'd never felt so violated. Her words felt tainted now that Maya had seen them and talked about them openly. Naomi hated her journal as much as she hated Maya, as much as she hated being stuck here with people who, as Maya had rightfully pointed out, were much better off without her.

Same here, Naomi thought as she ripped out another page. *The feeling's mutual.*

Her mom might have been the one in prison but it felt like Naomi was also serving a sentence. At least her mom was given the terms of her imprisonment. Meanwhile, Naomi wasn't sure if her punishment would ever end.

"Camryn, stop!" Dawn shouted, moving toward her. "I said stop!" She snatched the journal out of Naomi's hands.

Dawn tossed the journal onto the bed and closed her eyes. She took a deep breath before opening her eyes again.

"Honey, your dad and I are trying our best to be understanding . . . to support you, but I can't support this behavior. You almost got in a knockout, drag-out fight with your sister. You accused *the mayor* of kidnapping and murder. You trespassed onto a stranger's property. You're lucky you haven't been arrested! And the sleepwalking hasn't stopped. Blake told us that he saw you at your window again yelling at someone who wasn't there a few nights ago."

"Wow." Naomi gave a hollow laugh. "So, everyone's a narc around here."

"It's not funny."

"I didn't say it was," Naomi replied tightly, kicking at the piles of paper shreds.

"Blake was worried about you, and frankly, so are we." Dawn took another deep breath. "Your dad and I think . . . We think all the stress is piling up and you may be having some sort of psychological break, honey. That's why we're ending the vacation early. We've already consulted with your therapist. We made an appointment for you to have another assessment and she can determine—"

"You guys think I'm going crazy?" Naomi asked, staring up at her in alarm. "You seriously think I'm crazy?"

"Honey, you've been through *a lot,* to put it mildly." Dawn's measured tone was starting to annoy her. It seemed more patronizing than calming. "You've tried your best to handle it. We can tell. But it's getting out of hand. We want to help you."

Naomi slowly shook her head and started laughing again.

Maybe she *was* going crazy. It certainly seemed like it.

"Cam, we don't know what else to do!" Dawn threw out her hands in surrender. "We just want you to be happy, but we're—"

"If you really wanted me to be happy," Naomi began, "you wouldn't have sent my mom to jail and cheered when she got her sentence. You would've let me stay with her, because that's where I was happy. That's where I belong . . . where I *always* belonged. Not here!"

Dawn flinched as if Naomi had struck her.

Naomi had seen hurt in Dawn's dark eyes before but never like this. It was so raw and vast that she had to look away.

"I'm sorry," Naomi whispered, not because she'd told her the truth, but for the way she'd said it. Naomi hadn't intended to sound so cruel, especially to Dawn. She didn't deserve that.

But Dawn didn't respond to her apology. She simply turned and walked out of Naomi's bedroom, quietly closing the door behind her.

For the rest of the day, no one else came knocking at Naomi's door, not even to ask her if she was coming down for lunch or dinner. In some ways, Naomi was relieved they hadn't.

She called Khalil one more time to say goodbye, to tell him that it was their last day in Sparksburg, but he didn't answer. After that, she spent the evening packing up her things. Naomi loaded her suitcase with her clothes and all her books, with the exception of *A Dark History of a Sundown Town.* She chucked that one into the trash along with her tattered journal and all its ripped pages.

She paused when she found in her night table drawer the orange lily—or Turk's-cap lily as she'd discovered through an online search—that Khalil had given her on their date. Even though Khalil obviously wanted nothing to do with her, she couldn't find it in her heart to throw it away. She put it in her satchel's front pocket instead.

With all her thoughts and regrets clamoring in her head, it

took her a long time to fall asleep. Mercifully, after midnight, she dozed off, only to be awakened almost two hours later by a series of dings from her phone. Someone was texting her.

Khalil? Had he read her text and was ready to forgive her, after all?

She reached blindly for her phone in the dark and looked at the glowing screen. She instantly sat up when she saw the message was from Tate.

Amber escaped. She got out, he wrote.

Under the text was an image of Amber Nash turning slightly away from the camera but even Naomi could see the tears in her eyes and the bruises and scratches on her cheeks. She looked like she'd been through hell.

Are you taking her to the hospital? Naomi quickly typed back. **How did she get out?**

She saw three blinking dots.

No hospital. We're headed out of town, he typed. **We have to leave or Bobby might track her down again. He'll kill her.**

No, Naomi thought. If they fled, police would never find out what happened and Elly was still missing.

You have to tell the police what he did! You can't let Bobby get away with this.

She stared at the screen, waiting for the three blinking dots again, but they didn't appear. Was Tate ignoring her? Had he turned off his phone?

No, we don't trust the police. They're only going to arrest us, Tate texted.

She wanted to convince him that wasn't true, but she remembered her last conversation with Sheriff Turner.

If Amber doesn't go to the police, do you think she'll talk to me? Naomi wrote. **I can record the conversation. She can tell**

me what happened. Then she can leave. I'll give the recording to the sheriff. It's our only chance to save Elly. PLEASE???

A full minute went by before Tate texted her back.

Amber said OK. She'll tell you what happened and where Elly is but it has to be tonight and JUST YOU, he wrote. **Either you do the interview tonite or NEVER.**

Naomi considered his ultimatum. Should she go? But how would she get there with no car? And what if she got lost wandering around in the woods in the dark?

There were about a thousand reasons for her not to do this, including the knot of anxiety and fear forming in the pit of her stomach. But this might be her last chance to prove to Dawn and Andre . . . to Sheriff Turner . . . to *everyone* that she wasn't lying or crazy.

Saving them isn't going to change what happened to you, Naomi, Khalil had warned her. *It's not gonna rewrite anything.*

But she wasn't trying to change the past. She was trying to clean up the mess she'd made in the present with the Stoakeses. With Sheriff Turner. She hadn't meant to cause hurt or chaos, but to find two missing girls. She wasn't losing her mind or imagining ghosts. She could see what they couldn't. This was her chance to show them the truth. Recording Amber and showing it to all of them would vindicate her.

Tell me where you want to meet, she typed.

44

NAOMI LOOPED THE BEDSHEET AROUND THE railing, pulled it with all her might to test the strength of the knot, and tossed her makeshift rope over the side. Though she had tied her sheet, a blanket, and even one of her hoodies together, the makeshift rope still hovered several feet above the ground. She hoped she wouldn't twist her ankle or even break a leg when she landed.

She sniffed the air and grimaced. The Sparksburg stench was strong tonight. Even the concoction in her nose didn't stand a chance against it. She shrugged. She would just have to brave the smell. She'd have to round up as much courage for what she was about to do next.

Behind her, she heard the squeak of a floorboard, making her practically jump out of her skin. She looked over her shoulder at her door, expecting Andre or Dawn to step through at any moment and ask her what the hell she was doing. But nothing happened. Her door stayed closed and the cabin went quiet again.

Naomi shut the balcony door, climbed over the side, and balanced on the edge of the railing. She felt the wind against her back and legs. Much like when she'd gone zip-lining with Khalil, she knew she couldn't hesitate. She just had to jump. She looped the rope around her left hand, closed her eyes, swung herself forward, and jumped.

She careened toward the side of the cabin. Naomi grunted as she thumped hard against the wooden beams. The impact left her a little dazed, but she hadn't broken her neck—she was still in one piece.

Unfortunately, she could hear Bear barking inside the house now. It wouldn't be long before either Dawn, Andre, or both would wake up and see what all his barking was about. She shimmied her way down the rope, praying the entire time that it would hold.

When she let go, she landed on her back, knocking the air out of her. But it took only a few seconds for her to regain her breath. Naomi grabbed her satchel and stood, wiping dirt from her knees. She turned on her cell light, raised it, then stopped. She saw a figure in front of her. The girl in the nightgown stood almost five feet away.

Naomi felt her blood drain from her head and limbs, only to pool at her feet.

The girl looked even more real at this distance. Like she was a living, breathing being.

"I'm . . . I'm doing what you . . . what you asked me to do," she whispered to her. "I'm going to find out what happened to Elly."

The girl didn't respond, even as Naomi gave her a wide berth as she made her way through the field to the forest. When she reached the trees, Naomi was hit by a wall of sound. Whirring cicadas. Chirping crickets. A hooting owl. Twigs snapping under the weight of creatures making their way through the foliage. It stopped her in her tracks.

Once again, she felt like she had stepped into one of her

fantasy novels, like she was beginning a journey but she had no idea what was waiting for her in the dark. This wasn't a book; this was real life.

Naomi took one last longing look over her shoulder at the cabin. All the lights were out, including in her own bedroom. Her makeshift rope still hung from her deck. She could still hear Bear barking. She wondered if he was trying to alert Dawn and Andre she was gone. Or maybe he was begging her to come back.

"I've gotta do this," she said, before finally stepping into the darkness.

NAOMI HAD BEEN walking for almost twenty minutes when she heard the boom. Her stomach sank.

"Shit," she said as she looked up and saw the first bolt of lightning illuminating the tree limbs overhead. She felt the first few raindrops pelt her face. She wished she'd taken her hoodie with her; instead, it was dangling off her balcony.

For most of the walk, she'd been using her map app and cell light to guide her way. More than once, she'd cowered or flinched at passing shadows or a phantom sound. She yelled out or trembled when she felt something rub against her arm or over her foot. Now she had to contend with thunder, lightning, and rain, too. Naomi started to shiver again.

She knew instinctively that there weren't just furry creatures she should be concerned about out here. Tate had been right—this forest had a bad vibe. Out here, her childhood fears were taking on new forms and ferocity. Lightning *was* the stalking creature that could very well kill her. The unseen eyes she'd vaguely felt following her in town were closer in the woods. Close enough to touch. For the umpteenth time, Naomi considered turning around and heading back to the cabin, but how would she get inside? She couldn't very well climb up the rope to her balcony. Dawn and Andre would realize she'd snuck out, be even more pissed, and worse—she'd have nothing to show for it.

Better to ask for forgiveness than for permission, Naomi thought, *especially if you're doing it for a good reason.*

Naomi took a deep breath, counted down from ten, and forced herself to keep going.

She just had to make it to the main road, near the exit that led to the Stoakeses' cabin. That was where she'd agreed to meet Tate and Amber. She glanced down at her phone. She had less than a quarter of a mile to go. She was almost there.

Naomi walked a little farther but stopped and screamed. The girl was standing in front of her, even closer this time. Her mouth was open, like she was trying to speak.

"What?" Naomi squeaked. "What's wrong?" She looked down at her cell screen. "Am I going in the wrong direction?"

But no sound came out. The girl began to fade, going from opaque to translucent as a mist. Gradually, she disappeared.

Naomi kept walking, feeling her tennis shoes sink into the mud as the rain came down faster and faster. Her shivering was starting to get worse. Finally, she spotted blacktop through the trees. Relieved, she sped toward the steep hill that would take her to the roadway and began to climb, slipping slightly on wet leaves and pine needles. When she stepped onto the asphalt, the girl appeared again only inches away, making Naomi lurch back. Her arms windmilled wildly as she almost fell down the hill.

"Jesus!" Naomi shouted, clutching her chest where her heart was racing. "Stop . . . doing . . . that!" She took a gulping breath and glared at her. "*What?* What do you want? I'm doing what you asked! I'm going to find Elly. I'm trying to save her!" Naomi yelled.

The girl began to shake her head slowly just as a car turned on its headlights. It had been sitting almost fifteen feet away, hidden in the trees on the opposite side of the road.

Naomi squinted through the downpour, her eyes struggling to adjust to the sudden brightness. She started walking toward the lights.

"Tate?" she shouted. "Tate, is that you? Is Amber with you?"

Someone walked into the light.

She couldn't see the person's face. They were still just a dark figure set against the glaring headlights, but the build wasn't right. Naomi remembered Tate being slender, almost wiry when she'd met him at the diner. This person walking toward her was tall and broad shouldered. Almost stocky.

She took one step back, then another. *Where's Tate?* Who was this person?

"Just get in the truck," an unfamiliar voice said. "Don't make this harder on yourself."

Naomi's heart kicked into overdrive, blood whistling in her ears.

She wasn't here to meet Tate and Amber. Someone had managed to get Tate's phone and trick her into coming here. This was a trap.

Naomi bolted back to the hill and into the woods.

45

SHE COULD HEAR THE MAN'S THUNDERING FOOTsteps. She tried to run faster, but her shoes couldn't gain traction and she slid on her butt. She jumped up and blindly tore through the trees again, all while trying to dial 911.

But Naomi couldn't run for her life through the forest and rain *and* dial at the same time. Not while branches snapped and leaves rustled behind her. When she heard him curse and growl like some wild animal, her only thought was *Run! Keep running, for God's sake, and don't stop until you see another car or the cabin!*

Finally, her wet fingers managed to dial the last number she'd called. Naomi raised the phone to her ear and listened to it ring over and over again before the line picked up.

"Hey! It's Khalil. Leave a message."

"Damn it, pick up, Khalil! I know you're still mad at me but I'm in trouble!" she shouted after she heard the beep. She took a quick glance over her shoulder. She couldn't see the guy running after her anymore, but she knew he was out there. "He's chasing me! I need help! I'm—"

She stopped when she heard the sound of an approaching car. Naomi looked up and spotted headlights through the trees. She caught a glimpse of rotating red and blue lights.

Police lights, she thought. Naomi rushed toward them.

"Stop!" she yelled, running into the roadway and waving down the cop car. "Stop! Please!"

The cruiser skidded on the wet pavement, stopping only a few feet in front of her. Naomi leaped to the driver's side and saw the sheriff at the steering wheel.

"Sheriff Turner! Sheriff Turner, you have to help me!" she said, pounding on the glass.

Sheriff Turner lowered her window. "Young lady, what the hell are you doing out here? It's three o'clock in the damn morning and it's raining cats and dogs!"

"Someone was . . . a guy was chasing me! I was—"

"*What?* Just get in! I'm taking you back to your cabin."

Naomi ran around the hood. She opened the passenger door and hopped inside. When Naomi landed in the leather seat, her shoulders sank with relief.

"Why were you in the middle of the road?" the sheriff asked as she began to drive again. "You could've gotten hit by a car!"

"A . . . a g-g-guy was chasing me." Naomi pointed over her shoulder to the rear window with a trembling hand. The air-conditioning was on and she was starting to shiver again. Her teeth were chattering. "H-h-he's . . . he's back there! In the woods. He was parked in the trees not too far from the exit leading to our cabin. On the opposite side. I tried t-t-to . . . to call the police." She held up her phone and realized she hadn't hung up. She pressed end call. "But I couldn't dial it. I was too flustered. Too scared."

"Well, lucky you ran into me. Huh?" Sheriff Turner said, leaning down to press a button on the dashboard. The air coming out of the vents abruptly switched from cold to hot. "Let's see if we can warm you up."

"Th-thank you," Naomi whispered as her shivering gradually subsided.

"But why were you out there to begin with?" Sheriff Turner asked. "Were you running away from home again?"

"No, I got a text message from Tate." Naomi grimaced. "At least, I thought it was Tate. He said he had Amber with him. He even sent me a picture." She pulled up the image from her old texts and held it up for the sheriff to see. "That guy has her. He's keeping her prisoner. He might have Elly, too. We have to find him, Sheriff Turner!"

"Did you see who he was?" the sheriff asked. "The guy who was chasing you, I mean. Could you ID him? Did you get a picture of him, too?"

Naomi shook her head. "No. No, I didn't. I couldn't see him. It was too dark."

The sheriff pursed her lips and sighed. "We talked about this, young lady. I told you about getting involved in this investigation. It was too risky."

"I know. I know, but I . . ."

Naomi's words faded when she realized they had already passed the exit leading to her cabin.

"You've been warned so many times," the sheriff went on. "Given so many chances." She turned to face Naomi as she slammed on the brakes. Naomi jerked forward, the seat belt tightening painfully against her chest. "But like I said before. Three strikes, you're out, kid."

The passenger door whipped open. Naomi turned to find the man from earlier, reaching for her. This time she did see his face and she instantly recognized who he was.

She tried to scream, to kick and punch him away, but her voice was smothered by the cloth he slapped over her mouth and nose.

“This is the last one, Liam! I mean it!” Sheriff Turner yelled over the thunder. “I’m tired of cleaning up your messes. If you do this again, you’re on your own!”

“Yeah, yeah, yeah! I heard ya,” he said. “Don’t worry. I’ve got it this time.”

Naomi inhaled a clawing sweetness that almost made her stomach turn.

“Too bad you couldn’t mind your own damn business, kid,” Sheriff Turner muttered.

Within seconds, Naomi felt her limbs grow heavy. Her phone fell from her hands to the cruiser’s floor. Her head thumped forward on the dashboard as her body went limp.

46

"KHALIL, WAKE UP, BOY!" HIS DAD POUNDED ON HIS bedroom door. "It's almost noon. You gonna sleep the day away?"

Khalil slowly opened his eyes to sunlight piercing the blinds and playing on the ceiling of the guest bedroom in Grandma Regina's house where he'd slept every summer since he was three years old. Tigger, Nana's geriatric orange tabby, was slumbering on the pillow, using the crown of Khalil's head as a cushion. The tabby's tail was draped over his forehead and a paw was covering his mouth. Khalil moved the cat off him, causing Tigger to mewl with displeasure.

"Whatever." Khalil yawned. "You're gonna smother me in my sleep one day if you keep doing that. Then who's going to sleep with you all night, huh?" He scratched the cat's ear. "Huh?"

Khalil's past offenses now forgotten, the tabby purred contentedly and showed him his belly for a rub.

Khalil's phone buzzed. He reached down to the scuffed hardwood floor where it was charging, and wiped the sleep from his eyes. The screen glowed to life. He'd gotten a text message from his cousin Darius, asking him if he wanted to meet up later that day to play basketball. Below Darius's text was another notification. It was from Naomi. She'd called him at 3:27 a.m. She'd also left a voicemail.

Khalil rolled his eyes and grumbled.

He clicked on the voicemail and saw that the message was almost five minutes long. What could Naomi possibly be talking about for five solid minutes?

Probably just her rambling again.

Another long drawn-out apology and convoluted explanation of why she'd done what she did.

Naomi had sent Khalil so many text messages and voicemails in the past few days that he'd lost count. Though he'd deleted most of them, he had to admit that each one was chipping away at his anger and his resolve to ignore her. Yes, she'd almost gotten them mauled by a dog and arrested or even shot despite his warning her that going to that hillbilly's trailer was the worst possible idea. Sure, he could have lost his scholarship to Marymount and been grounded until he could legally drink. But he knew Naomi had only meant well with her harebrained plan—and despite everything, he still liked her.

He liked her laugh and the way she tucked her curls behind her ears when she got nervous. He liked how inquisitive she was. He even liked her bravery, though it got her into trouble. Talking to her was so easy.

He hadn't vibed with a girl that much in a while, which made the way things went down between them even more frustrating.

His finger hovered over the trash icon, but he hit the speaker icon instead.

"Simp," he muttered, before raising his phone to his ear.

Khalil listened to the full message. He blinked when it ended, wondering if he'd heard what he thought he heard. He listened again.

Naomi was screaming for help. She said someone was chasing her. He then heard Sheriff Turner's voice. The two were talking about the traumatic events of the night before the message abruptly ended, mid-conversation.

Khalil got tangled in his sheets as he tried to get out of bed. He dialed Naomi and listened as the phone rang.

"Hey! You know who this is and you know what to say," Naomi's voice answered. "If you don't, you've probably called the wrong number. If you haven't, then leave a message."

Khalil hung up and dialed her number again and again.

"Why aren't you answering?" he whispered before throwing down his phone in frustration. He swiftly put on a pair of jeans and a T-shirt and found his car keys.

KHALIL MADE THE drive to Naomi's house in less than thirty minutes—record time. He squinted at the multicolored rope he thought he saw hanging off the second-floor balcony. Two cop cars were parked in the Stoakeses' driveway.

"Naomi, what did you do?" he whispered as he parked behind the cruisers. "What the hell did you get yourself into?"

As soon as he stepped out of his car, Naomi's mom came racing out of the cabin toward him. Naomi's dad trailed behind her.

"Khalil!" she shouted. "We've been trying to figure out how to reach you. Have you . . . have you spoken to Camryn?" she asked. Her eyes were puffy from crying. "We were supposed to leave Sparksburg today, but we woke up and saw that she was gone! Just . . . just *gone*! I knew she was upset, but I didn't think she would . . . that she would . . ." Her voice drifted off.

"We were hoping she might be with you," her dad said.

Naomi's father was usually clean shaven but Khalil noticed today's whiskers were still on his cheeks. He was also wearing the T-shirt and pajama pants he'd likely slept in last night, despite it being almost noon.

Khalil slowly shook his head. "No. Sorry, Mr. Stoakes. She's not with me."

"Have you heard from her?" her dad persisted. "Did she text you? Tell you where she might have gone?"

Khalil opened his mouth to answer, but he stopped when he saw Sheriff Turner stroll down the cabin's porch stairs. She eyed him with interest.

"Hey, you're Camryn's friend, aren't you?" She nodded, answering her own question. "Yeah, you're the fella that was with her at Meacham's property. The one I sent off with a warning. What's your name again, son?"

He cleared his throat. "Uh, Khalil. Khalil Crowley."

"We were asking him if he spoke to Camryn . . . if he knew where she'd disappeared to," Naomi's dad explained. "But he said he doesn't know."

The sheriff inclined her head. "Is that true?"

Khalil paused, now confused.

Why was Sheriff Turner acting as if she had no idea what had happened to Naomi? He'd heard her on the voicemail. Naomi had used her name several times. She'd seen Naomi last night after she'd run away. Naomi had told her about the guy who was chasing her, but obviously she hadn't shared any of this with Naomi's mom and dad.

Something wasn't right about this. Not right at all.

Sheriff Turner raised her brows. "Cat got your tongue, kid?"

"Uh, no . . . I mean yes," he said, swallowing. "Yes, that's true. I haven't spoken to her. I don't know where she is."

The sheriff pushed up the bill of her cap. Khalil could see her green eyes now. They were focused on his face like she was searching for something.

He felt like he and the sheriff were playing a game of high-stakes poker. Though he was scared, something told him to keep his face neutral, to not look panicked.

"So why'd you come here?" Sheriff Turner asked. "If you haven't spoken to her, how'd you know she ran away?"

"I didn't," he improvised. "She texted me yesterday that her family was leaving Sparksburg, so I came to say goodbye."

"Humph," Sheriff Turner said before facing Naomi's parents. "Well, we're going to put out an Amber Alert. Hopefully, we'll get some bites from that."

"Just an Amber Alert?" Naomi's dad asked. "Why isn't your office and State Police out searching for her?"

"We are, Mr. Stoakes. My men know to keep an eye out for a girl fitting Camryn's description. We'll have patrols around town looking for her. But I'll be honest, thanks to the downpour last night and this morning, there isn't much of a trail out there in those woods."

Mr. Stoakes grimaced.

"Oh God," Mrs. Stoakes groaned, bringing a hand to her mouth.

"Wait, now. You didn't let me finish. On the bright side, you mentioned that your daughter ran away once before but called you to come home by the end of the day. Camryn might very well do that again. You said you had a big fight yesterday, right? She could just be blowing off some steam. I'd at least give it twenty-four hours before you get too alarmed."

Naomi's mom's face crumpled.

"Sheriff Turner, how can we *not* be alarmed? Our baby is out there," she said, gesturing to the trees in the distance, "somewhere, and we don't know if she's okay! We don't know if she made it to the main road and climbed into some stranger's car. She could be miles away by now or . . . or . . ."

Her voice faded again as she closed her eyes. She fell into her husband's arms and cried.

"God, I can't believe we're going through this again, Dre!" she sobbed. "I don't know if I can survive it this time."

"No, we will survive this because we have to." He rubbed her back. "We have two other children counting on us, and Cam *will* come home."

Khalil saw something flicker in the sheriff's eyes as she watched Naomi's parents console each other. Guilt or maybe regret. But she immediately wiped it away.

"Please let me know if you hear anything from her or if anything comes to mind that will help us in our search," she said. "I gave you my card. My cell number is on the back. You can call me anytime. I'll keep you updated on anything we find out on our end."

"Thank you, Sheriff," Naomi's father whispered.

Sheriff Turner faced Khalil again. "And you'll let me know if you hear anything as well?"

Khalil nodded. "Yes, Sheriff."

She gave him a stiff nod before heading toward one of the cruisers. A minute later, she and one of the deputies drove away, leaving Khalil alone with Naomi's family.

Mrs. Stoakes's tears finally subsided and she eased away from her husband. "I'm okay now," she whispered.

"No, you aren't," Mr. Stoakes said, still rubbing her back.

"Well, as okay as I can be, Dre," she said with a sigh.

"Uh, Mr. and Mrs. Stoakes," Khalil said, clearing his throat again, "I . . . I lied to you earlier."

They both stilled.

Her dad cocked an eyebrow and took a step toward him. "You lied about what?"

"I did hear from Naomi . . . I mean Camryn," he said. "I lied about that. She called me late last night while I was asleep. She left a message."

"What?" her father shouted.

"Khalil, why would you lie about something like that?" her mother cried. "You know we're looking for Camryn! Did she tell you where she is? Is she okay? Is she—"

"I don't know where she is, Mrs. Stoakes, and I only lied about hearing from her because Sheriff Turner was lying, too," Khalil insisted.

Mr. and Mrs. Stoakes went silent, now looking even more alarmed.

"Did we hear you right?" Mr. Stoakes asked. "Did you say the sheriff lied to us?"

"Yes, sir. I wanted to tell you guys the truth, but I didn't want to say it in front of the sheriff, because I know for a fact she saw Camryn last night. She spoke to her. Camryn came to her for help and she's pretending like she didn't for some reason."

And he suspected the reason was that Sheriff Turner knew where Naomi was but she was hiding it.

Naomi's mom slowly shook her head as if in a daze. "Khalil, we don't understand what you're saying. How do you know for sure the sheriff spoke to Camryn? How could you even know that unless you were there?"

"Because I *heard* her," he said, pulling his cell from his back pocket. "Please, just . . . just listen. She's in the voice message. Camryn is, too."

They leaned down as Khalil played the voicemail, listening to what could be the last time they would ever hear their daughter's voice.

47

NAOMI DREAMED. SHE DREAMED THAT SHE WAS back on the Shenandoah River, floating in an inner tube. She could see the cloudless sky above her and the water—the sunlight sparkling off the rippling waves and the little bubbles created by the fish and fauna swimming underneath the surface. She could feel the warmth of the sun on her face and the river against her legs and her hands as she dragged them in the water.

Dawn, Andre, Maya, and Blake were even farther away than they had been that day. She could barely make out their features. She watched as Maya snapped selfies, then got in a splash fight with Blake. It left them both squealing and laughing. Her view then switched to Dawn and Andre as they shared another tender kiss.

Then she heard it. The sound of the tolling bell. She turned her head in the direction of the sound and noticed that Dawn, Andre, Maya, and Blake did the same. The ringing seemed to be getting closer and louder, like an approaching storm. Naomi clapped her hands over her ears and sank lower in her inner tube.

It began to rock and sway. The water around her suddenly became more turbulent as Naomi was tugged into the rapids.

The rocking made it hard to hold on to the handles of her inner tube. She dipped and rose, twisted and turned, like she was riding a bucking bronco. She closed her eyes and sputtered as water slapped her face and went up her nose.

A huge wave came barreling toward her and tipped her over. She tried to float on her back, remembering she was wearing a life vest, but too late Naomi saw the vest was gone. Panicked, she struggled to right herself in the inner tube, but it was ripped away. She flailed and kicked. She called out for Dawn to help her. For Andre. She even called out for her mom, all the while feeling water flood her throat and then her lungs as she sank under the surface.

Naomi lurched awake in the dark, coughing and gasping for air. Liquid exploded out of her chest. It wasn't river water but vomit.

"Oh, look, she's up," a girl's voice said flatly.

Naomi emptied her stomach until all she had left was bile and spit. After she finished retching, she slowly climbed to her knees. She tried to stand, but her legs were wobbly underneath her. She fell back to the packed-dirt floor, landing in something wet. It made her cringe.

"It's the knockout drug he uses," the voice explained. It sounded like it was coming from the other side of whatever room or space this was. "That's why you're puking. I didn't know it was possible to puke that much." She snorted.

Naomi squinted, willing her eyes to adjust to the darkness. She thought she vaguely saw a figure several feet in front of her but she couldn't be sure.

Where was she? How did she get here?

The memory of what had happened to her all came flooding back. Being chased through the woods by Liam, Sheriff Turner's brother-in-law. Being relieved when she ran into Sheriff Turner, only for the sheriff to return Naomi to Liam's clutches. He'd used the knockout drug in the cruiser. Naomi had no memory of what had happened to her after that.

How much time had passed? Had he done anything to her while she was unconscious?

Naomi touched her face. She ran her hand over her chest and legs. Her satchel was gone but she was still wearing all her clothes, though they were damp from the storm. Nothing felt sore or bruised. She was just lethargic and disoriented. She felt so weak, and being stuck in this pitch-black wasn't helping.

Why hadn't Liam killed her? Why was he keeping her here? Did he plan to torture her? Had he tortured the others?

"Are . . . are you Amber?" she asked the voice in the dark. "Amber Nash?"

The room went quiet again. After a few seconds, she heard what sounded like clinking metal and footsteps, drawing closer. "How do you know my name?"

"I've been looking for you," she said, relieved to have finally found her. "I've been looking for you and my neighbor Elly. My name is Naomi. I mean Camryn. I go by both. You were kidnapped weeks before my neighbor. Back in early June. Elly was being stalked before she went missing. Tate said you were being stalked, too. He put up flyers around town for you."

"Tate was looking for me?" Amber sounded shocked, even touched. "We argued. He said he didn't care about me, that he didn't care what I did. I thought he hated me."

"No, he doesn't hate you. He's still looking for you! He's really worried about you, Amber. He tried to tell the cops that something was wrong, but they didn't listen."

Now Naomi understood Sheriff Turner probably knew all

along where Amber was and had been trying to throw Tate and later Naomi off the trail.

"But Liam, the guy who kidnapped you, must have gotten Tate's phone because he texted me from that number," Naomi said. "He sent me a picture of you."

"Damn it, Tate. You dumbass," Amber whispered. "He should've just left town. He should've left me here."

"Why would you say that?" Naomi asked, confused.

"Because if that asshole got his phone, then Tate is fucked. Tate's already dead."

Naomi felt weak all over again. "You don't . . . you don't know that."

"Yes, I do. Tate's dead. He killed him and it's all my fault."

Naomi heard footsteps again, but this time it sounded like they were retreating, like Amber was walking away.

"Wait! Wait! Maybe Tate could still be out there! Liam could've gotten his phone, but—"

Naomi stopped talking when she heard someone wail. It seemed to echo throughout the dark. The cries came from another corner of the room.

"For the love of God, will you *shut up*?" Amber shouted at the wailer. She groaned. "I swear this bitch is like clockwork."

Naomi turned toward the wails. "*Elly?* Elly, is that you?"

She didn't answer her. Her cries only grew louder. "I just want to go home! Why won't he let me go home?"

"Elly?" Naomi crawled to her. "Elly, it's me! It's me, Camryn."

But the cries didn't stop. "I want my moms!" Elly sobbed. "I don't wanna be here! Let me *out*! *Let me out!*"

"Elly!" Naomi said, holding out her hand. "You don't have to be scared. I'm right here."

"It's no use," Amber muttered. "She can't hear you."

"Yes, she can! She's just terrified," Naomi said, her own tears rising up. "It's gonna be okay. Someone's gonna find us!"

"No, they aren't," Amber said with a bland finality that infuriated her.

"Look," Naomi snapped, "I know this situation sucks, but you're not helping! We have to stick together if we're going to get through this, if we're going to get out of here!"

"You're cute." Amber let out a hollow laugh. "I was like you when I got dumped down here. Tried to fight my way out at first. Until he beat the shit out of me and chained me to the wall. Then I tried to beg my way out, but that didn't work either. He didn't care. He wants to see you in pain. He gets off on it."

Naomi's stomach sank.

"We're not leaving here. There's no way out. If you're stuck in here with us, girly, you might as well be dead."

48

"WHAT DO WE DO, DRE?"

Naomi's dad roughly swiped his hand over his face, looking shell-shocked. "I don't know. I'm still trying to understand what the hell I just heard. Khalil, can you play the message again, please?"

Khalil played the voicemail again.

They were all in the cabin's kitchen, hovered around the granite island. Khalil was perched on one of the kitchen stools, looking at Naomi's sister and brother, who were in the backyard while their parents listened to Naomi's voicemail for the third time. Maya had been given the task of keeping Blake—who was in one of the Adirondack chairs, playing his handheld video game—occupied.

Maya paced the cabin's deck, biting her nails. Their dog paced right along with her, whimpering softly.

Based on what he'd heard about her from Naomi, Khalil expected Maya to be camera ready and all over social media right now, talking breathlessly to her followers about how her sister had run away yet again. But Maya wasn't on her phone and hadn't been the entire time Khalil had been there.

"Sheriff Turner didn't tell us any of this," Naomi's dad said after the voicemail ended. "She *saw* Camryn last night. She picked her up. That woman was here a full hour, pretending to look around for evidence when she knew damn well that Camryn was wandering around the forest at three o'clock in the morning!"

"Not only that, I think the sheriff knows where Camryn is now or has an idea," Khalil said, gnawing his bottom lip anxiously, "but she's hiding it. I just don't know why."

"Could she have taken Camryn?" Naomi's mom asked. "Driven her somewhere?"

"Maybe, but the only person who can answer all those questions is Sheriff Turner. We need to talk to her," Naomi's dad insisted.

"Dre, are you saying we should accuse the sheriff of Sparksburg of *lying* to us?" Mrs. Stoakes raised her brows. "Of kidnapping Camryn?"

"Hell yeah!" He nodded. "I don't give a damn who she is. This is about our daughter, Dawn. This is a risk I'm willing to take. I'll call the sheriff right now. I want to see her ass in person—and I'll tell her as much! There's no time to waste." He reached for his own cell and picked up the business card she'd left behind.

"Khalil, can you forward us a copy of Camryn's voicemail?" Mrs. Stoakes asked.

"Sure. Of course," he said as Mr. Stoakes started to dial. "But can I be there when you talk to the sheriff again?"

She'd been the one to ask all the questions last time. He was ready to turn the tables. Maybe they could catch her in another lie to find out where Naomi was.

Her mom rested a hand on his forearm and squeezed. "I don't think that's a good idea. Your parents probably wouldn't want you to get involved in something like this. You've done more than enough to help us. You have no idea how much we appreciate it, but we'll take it over from here."

"I'm already involved, Mrs. Stoakes. I have to know what happened to her. I want to know if she's okay."

"Shit," Naomi's dad spat, closing his eyes and slamming down his cell. "She's not answering. The sheriff isn't answering her damn phone!"

"Naomi said in her message that the guy in the woods was parked in the trees on the opposite side of the road not too far from the exit to your cabin," Khalil said. "The tire tracks might still be out there in the mud." He shrugged. "Maybe we can see where they were headed if we can find them."

Mr. Stoakes nodded. "You know, that's not a bad idea."

"We are not trackers, Dre," Mrs. Stoakes groused. "What if we trample over evidence that police could use to find Camryn?"

"But we've gotta try, baby! We can't just wait around for the sheriff to tell us what's going on, especially now that we know she probably isn't on the up and up!"

"Then let's talk to the State Police," she insisted. "Go to them instead."

"The State Police already came here and looked around! Besides, what if they're in on it, too? They could have guys working with the sheriff."

"You don't know that!"

"No, but what I *do* know is—"

"My uncle is a tracker!" Khalil interrupted. The longer they went back and forth, the more time was lost. Every minute that went by lessened the chance that Naomi was still alive. They had to get moving. "Well, he's a hunter, but Uncle Otis tracks game all the time, and he knows the woods around here like the back of his hand. He grew up here. He still lives around here. He could help us."

Mr. and Mrs. Stoakes looked at one another.

"What do you think?" Mr. Stoakes asked his wife.

She sighed, looking at Khalil. "Be honest. Do you really think your uncle can track down Camryn?"

The truth was Khalil wasn't a hundred percent sure Uncle Otis could do it, but he knew if he told her that, Naomi's mom would shoot down his plan.

"Yes, Mrs. Stoakes," he said. "He can."

"Okay," she said, resigned. "Let's do it."

Her dad nodded. "Call your uncle, Khalil. I'm changing my clothes and will be ready to go in less than five minutes. Dawn, keep calling the sheriff and see if you can get her on the phone. Ask her if she knows where Naomi is, but don't tell her where we're going. I don't trust her, and don't want her to get in our way."

"I'm not calling," her mom said. "I'm going down there, Dre. I'm banging on her office door and confronting that bitch in front of all those deputies and the whole damn town. If she lies again, she's doing it in front of an audience."

"And I'll post it on Instagram live for all my followers," Maya said.

They turned to find Naomi's big sister standing in the opened glass door.

She shrugged. "Sorry, I was eavesdropping, but I really can help. I wanna help, Mom. The sheriff can't blow you off if she knows 20,000 people are watching, right?" Maya said. "They'll see what's happening here."

Dawn slowly smiled. "That is a great idea, honey."

As Naomi's dad rushed upstairs, Khalil called his uncle, who picked up on the second ring.

"Khalil, why are you calling me in the middle of the day at work?" Uncle Otis asked over the sound of drilling and sanding. It sounded like he was on-site. "Everything all right with your mama and daddy? With your brother?"

"They're fine, Uncle Otis," Khalil said. "But something else happened and it's bad. I need your help."

49

NOW THAT SHE HAD SOME OF HER STRENGTH BACK, Naomi wandered around in the dark, searching desperately for a door or a crack . . . *anything* that could be a means of escape. The room must be bigger than she'd thought because even though she heard the other girls, she didn't bump into either Amber or Elly despite running her hand along the walls and blindly reaching in front of her.

But the entire time, Naomi had a sense of someone hovering close to her. The presence would not go away.

Naomi wondered if it was the girl in the nightgown. Was she here with her now in this place, too? She wouldn't be surprised if she was—after all, the girl had led her here. Or had she tried to warn her away? Naomi remembered her appearing several times as she wandered through the forest, trying to find the main road. The girl had acted like she wanted to tell her something, even shaking her head at one point. Had the girl tried to caution her and help her avoid this fate?

"You're wasting your time," Amber taunted as Naomi stumbled around in the dark. "I told you, there's no way out of here."

"And *I* told you," Naomi replied, "that you're not help—"

Naomi yelped when she almost stumbled over a bucket, earning a hearty laugh from Amber.

"Be careful," Amber warned. "This place smells bad enough. You don't want to have to wade through shit, too, because you knocked over the poop pail."

After walking for several more feet, Naomi sank back to the floor in defeat. She leaned against the wall. It felt cool against her cheek, giving her a little solace in this place that was so stifling hot she could barely breathe.

She could only wait for their kidnapper to return. Without a watch, time seemed to stretch on forever. Aside from Elly's occasional sob or wail, the clink of metal from Amber's chains, and the sound of her own stomach grumbling, the darkness was quiet. Unnervingly so.

The quiet gave her time to think. She knew Dawn and Andre would be looking for her. She closed her eyes and grimaced at the agony she knew they were in, wondering where she'd gone. Maybe they thought she'd run away for good, that their last argument had been too much. She wanted to tell them that she hadn't deserted them. She knew they were only trying their best. She could see that now. If Naomi got out of here alive, maybe she could try harder to work with the Stoakes. To be a good big sis to Blake. To not fight so much with Maya. To not cause Dawn so much hurt because that was never her intention. If given another chance, Naomi would try her best to make things right.

Naomi sat up when she heard the throaty sound of a truck engine. Was that him? Had he come back?

She then heard the loud squeak of an old hinge and a door banged open, sending a shaft of light down into their dungeon through the floorboards above. Naomi held up her hand to shield her eyes.

She could finally orient herself to the space a little and see Elly. She was shocked to find that she was only ten or so feet in front of her. How had she missed her while wandering around in the dark?

The girl was huddled on the floor with her arms wrapped around her knees. She was gazing up at the ceiling with tears in her eyes as Liam thudded over the floorboards above them.

Elly was filthy, covered in dirt from her oversize T-shirt to her drawstring shorts. Her long dark hair was plastered to her head by sweat and mud. Dark circles were under her eyes. They stood out against her gaunt, pale face, which was covered with bruises and cuts. Naomi hoped she'd gotten them from the car accident and not from Liam.

"No, no, no, no, no," Elly whimpered.

His footsteps finally stopped and the shaft of light flickered.

Naomi's heart began to race. What was he going to do to them? To *her*?

"No, no, no! Nooo! Nooo!" Elly began to scream as he threw open a trapdoor overhead.

Naomi raced to Elly to comfort her and maybe even herself. She closed her eyes and wrapped her arms around the crying girl. But Naomi's eyes flashed open a second later when she felt nothing—her arms only latched on to air. Naomi stared down at her empty arms, dumbfounded.

Elly had disappeared.

"Elly!" she called out, feeling an expanding ache in her chest. She looked around wildly. "Elly! Where are you? Where'd you go?"

Now that the space was flooded with light, Naomi could finally see the cellar in its entirety. The concrete walls that were stained with mold. There were even worse stains on the earthen floor. The empty chains on one side of the room and the oversize paint bucket that had been used as a toilet.

But no one else was here. Not Elly. Not Amber. She was all alone.

"Hey there, little chickadee," Liam said as he walked down a rickety old folding ladder into the cellar. He grinned as he strolled toward her. He was wearing his uniform from Sunny Market, like he'd come directly from work. His hair that he usually tucked under a baseball cap now fell around his shoulders. Thanks to his height and stocky build, he looked like a giant in such a small space. "Who were you talking to?"

Naomi didn't answer him. She didn't know what to say.

Amber and Elly had been here. She'd argued with Amber and heard Elly's sobs. She'd smelled them and even thought she caught a glimpse of Amber a few times in the dark. But they weren't here. Like they never had been.

"Hey, you hear me ask you a question?" Liam pulled back his hand and slapped her hard across the face, knocking her off her knees.

Naomi screamed. She touched her cheek. It felt hot against her fingertips. Her eyes welled with tears.

"The next time I ask you something," he said, narrowing his eyes, "you better answer me. You understand?"

She nodded.

"Open your mouth! Tell me you understand," he ordered, bending down and drawing so close to her face that she could see the freckles on his nose and the inflamed pimple on his right cheek.

"Y-y-yes. Yes, I—I understand."

"Good." His grin was back. "Now, who were you talking to?"

"N-n-no one."

He tilted his head. "Didn't sound like no one."

"I thought . . . I thought s-s-someone else was h-here," she whispered, no longer able to keep the tears from spilling over.

"Really?" He chuckled. "You haven't been here long enough to lose your marbles, kid. Don't tell me you're cracking up already. I haven't even started to have any fun with you yet."

He reached out for her again, and Naomi flinched. She started trembling. Liam only laughed harder.

"But I'm on my lunch break. Just had enough time to check on you. Guess I'll save the rest for later. Gotta wait until this evening."

Naomi watched as he walked back up the ladder to the floor above.

"See you soon." He slammed the trapdoor closed, dropping her back into darkness.

50

KHALIL BRAKED IN THE DRIVEWAY IN FRONT OF Uncle Otis's front porch and hopped out. Naomi's dad did the same. A few July Fourth decorations were still on the property from the cookout more than a week ago.

Khalil couldn't believe how little time had passed; so much had happened since then.

He and Naomi's dad had already examined the roadway's shoulder near the Stoakeses' cabin. They'd found a few tire tracks. One even looked fresh, but they didn't want to do any more exploring without Uncle Otis.

As they walked toward the house, Uncle Otis stepped through the front door. He was carrying a duffel bag and was wearing his full hunting gear, but Khalil paused when he saw the bolt-action hunting rifle hanging from his uncle's shoulder.

"What's that for, Unc?" Khalil frowned.

"Oh, this?" Uncle Otis glanced over his shoulder at the rifle as he strolled down the stairs. "I don't go on any hunt without my rifle with me, boy. And from what you told me, I might need it."

Khalil swallowed, the gravity of what was at stake hitting him even harder. Naomi could be fighting for her life right now, and they might have to fight just as hard—maybe shoot someone—to save her. He glanced at Naomi's dad to see how he felt about all this. Khalil wasn't surprised by the concern etched across his face.

"Look," Naomi's dad said, taking a step toward Uncle Otis and holding up his hands, "Otis, is it? Otis, I appreciate your help with this, but I don't want anyone hurt or killed by friendly fire, especially my daughter."

"I'm always careful of my aim," Uncle Otis assured him. "And I don't shoot unless I have to. You don't want to go in there blind and empty-handed. If y'all still want my help, just know I'm bringing my rifle with me."

Naomi's dad lowered his hands, took a deep breath, and nodded. His ebony-hued face went from concerned to resigned. He pushed back his broad shoulders. "Fine, but I hope we don't have to use it."

Uncle Otis set his rifle and bag in his truck bed, then turned to face Khalil. "You sure your parents are okay with all this?"

"Unc," Khalil said impatiently, "I'm eighteen years old."

"That doesn't mean a damn thing, boy," Uncle Otis said with a headshake, adjusting the bill of his baseball cap. "I asked were they okay with this. Your mama ain't gonna have my ass later, thinking I dragged you into it, is she?"

"No, they're okay with it, Unc."

That wasn't completely true. He'd told his parents that he was at the Stoakeses' cabin, keeping vigil, offering any help he could in finding Naomi. But he hadn't told them he was going into the woods. They didn't know that his uncle was bringing a rifle and ammunition to track her down and maybe engage in a shoot-out with the person who had taken Naomi. Khalil doubted his mom or dad would approve of that.

Uncle Otis scratched his heavy beard, cocking a thick eyebrow as he studied Khalil's face. He sucked his teeth and shrugged. "All right, then," he said, thumping his hand against the truck door. "Let's get going."

"Otis!" called a familiar raspy voice. "Otis Crowley! Where the hell do you think you're goin'?"

Khalil and Uncle Otis both groaned.

They watched as Khalil's great-grandmother shoved open the screen door with her steel cane. "Otis!" she shouted again, stepping onto the porch.

Nana was in her housedress and bedroom slippers. A pink satin bonnet sat crookedly on her head.

"What's this I hear about you hunting for somebody?" Her gray brows furrowed. "And why are you taking one of my great-grandbabies with you?" she cried, her voice going up an octave.

Aunt Loretta, Otis's wife, came rushing out the door behind her. She looked exasperated. "I'm sorry, honey. I thought she was taking a nap."

"No, I wasn't takin' no damn nap!" Nana spat, looking insulted. She glared at Otis. "You ain't answer my question. Where are you going with that rifle? It ain't huntin' season."

Uncle Otis exhaled loudly. "I'm helping Khalil find his girlfriend, Nana. She ran away last night and they think something might have happened to her. No one knows where she is."

Nana's face crumpled. "Oh no. Oh Lord," she said in a stunned whisper. "You're talking about that girl whose family was staying at one of the cabins in Sparksburg, aren't you?"

Uncle Otis nodded. "Yes, Nana." He gestured to Naomi's dad. "This is her daddy. We're all going together."

She closed her eyes. Her shoulders sank as she nodded. "Loretta, bring me that chair over there," she said, pointing to a wicker chair near one of the front windows. "These old legs are tired of standin'. I've gotta sit down." She then waved over

Khalil, his uncle, and Naomi's dad. "Y'all come on up here. Stand in front of me. We've gotta do this first before you go."

"Do what, Nana?" Uncle Otis asked tiredly while Loretta did as she was ordered and brought the chair. Khalil's great-grandmother lowered herself onto the seat's stuffed cotton cushion and grunted with relief.

"We don't have time for this, Nana," Khalil insisted. "We've gotta go. Naomi could be—"

"Chile, you better make time," she said sternly. "Nobody listened to me when I said Black folks shouldn't live in that town. They shouldn't stay there. I said that place is wrong, and has been for a very long time. Now my own kin is going into the belly of the beast, and I'm not sending you there without a blessing. You hear me?"

Her tone let Khalil know there was no more room for argument, no matter how ridiculous this all felt. Even Naomi's dad gave in.

"Stand around me," she said, holding up her bare arms. "Grab hands. Khalil, you hold my hand, too. Otis, you do the same."

Khalil gritted his teeth in frustration. Anything could be happening to Naomi while they wasted time with some ridiculous ritual. He held Nana's gnarled hand and Mr. Stoakes's hand as well. They all formed a small circle on the front porch.

Nana bowed her head and closed her eyes. "Heavenly Father," she began, "we ask that you protect these men and this boy as they go on their search."

"Yes, Lord," Aunt Loretta whispered.

"May they find that girl and find her safe and in one piece," she went on.

Please let her be okay, Khalil thought.

"May those who mean her harm be bound from the evil they wish to inflict. May the anointed blood of Jesus and the spirits of the ancestors on the land guide them and keep them safe on their journey and their way home. Amen."

"Amen," they all murmured before letting go of each other's hands.

He turned so they could finally be on their way, but Nana wasn't finished. "Now bend down, boy," she ordered. Khalil leaned down so that he was eye level with her. She gently cradled his face.

"You're about the same age my cousin Jimmy was when he disappeared over there." She gazed at him, tracing his features with her milky-white eyes. "You even look like him. But our Jimmy didn't come home to us. You will, Khalil, won't you?"

"Yes, Nana," he whispered.

"May God keep you safe." She kissed his brow.

Khalil swore he felt a heat spread into his chest. He felt a little lightheaded.

"Go on, now," she said.

Nana gave similar blessings of protection and gave brow kisses to both Uncle Otis and Mr. Stoakes.

"I'll pray for your daughter," she told Naomi's father.

He nodded solemnly. "Thank you, ma'am."

The three men didn't speak as they headed to Uncle Otis's truck. Khalil wondered if they felt the heat surging through their chests, too. He kneaded it with his fist and took one last look over his shoulder at Nana, who still gazed at them.

"Be safe now!" she called out. "Protect each other!"

Khalil nodded before climbing into the truck's cab beside Naomi's dad. Less than a minute later, they drove away.

51

WHEN THE TEARS AND TREMBLING FINALLY CEASED, Naomi was brave enough to call into the dark.

She realized why Amber and Elly had vanished earlier when Liam threw open that trapdoor, and why she hadn't managed to touch them when she walked around the cellar.

They were ghosts, just like her burning girl. Liam had murdered them both.

We're not leaving here, Amber had said. *There's no way out. If you're stuck in here with us, girly, you might as well be dead.*

"Where are you?" Naomi asked the darkness, gazing around her. "He's gone now. It's just me again. You . . . you can come back. Amber? Elly?"

Silence answered her. Naomi waited, straining to hear any sound. She only heard scratching, then a squeak. Probably a mouse scurrying over the floorboards overhead. She waited again and heard the creaking of wood, but nothing else. Just quiet.

"You guys, please don't leave me down here," she begged. "You know what this is like."

She didn't hear anything at first, but then she thought she caught the faint sound of clinking metal as it dragged over the floor.

"Amber?" she called out, rising to her knees, straining to hear. "Amber, is that you?"

She heard a sniff, then a whimper. Naomi whipped around. Her eyes frantically searched the inky blackness for some form . . . some shape that could be the outline of a girl.

"Elly?" she said, crawling toward her cries. "*Elly?* It's me, Camryn! I'm so sorry. I tried to save you. I really did! I wish . . . I wish I had gotten here sooner. I'm so sorry. I—"

"I told you that she can't hear you, stupid," Amber suddenly hissed into Naomi's ear. "She can't hear any of us."

"Why . . . why can't she?" Naomi asked.

"Because she doesn't know she's dead. She just keeps crying and begging for him to leave her alone. It's like she's stuck in a loop—and it's *really* fucking annoying."

"How do we get her out of it?"

She turned in the direction of Amber's voice. She couldn't see her but she swore she could feel something coming off her. It was like static electricity or the bouncing molecules in the air before a lightning strike.

"How did you figure out you were dead?" Naomi asked as they listened to Elly's sobs.

"Can't really say. I'd been in and out before he killed me, floating between where you are and where I am now. I heard my mom calling me a few times and my grandma. I hadn't spoken to them in years. I didn't even know my mom was dead. By the time he strangled me, I was ready to die. I don't think your friend was ready though."

"When they called to you, what did they say?" Naomi asked.

"Huh?"

"When your mom and your grandma called to you, what did they say to you? What did they say that helped you be ready to die?"

Amber was quiet for a bit, as if she was thinking. "I can't . . . I can't remember for some reason. No, wait." She laughed. "My grandma said she had my favorite blueberry pie waiting for me with vanilla ice cream on top. And my mom called me by my nickname. It was the nickname only she used back when I was little. She said, 'Ladybug, it's okay. It's okay to let go now.' I saw a bright light and started to walk toward it. Then . . . then . . ." Her voice drifted off.

"Then what?"

"The light faded. I couldn't hear them anymore."

Naomi closed her eyes, trying to think of something that could help Elly end this torture. Something that could help snap her ghost out of reenacting her last moments. She crept forward, suddenly remembering something that she had heard Krissa say. It was a name she had used with Elly back at the Stoakeses' cabin the first day they met.

"Sweet pea," Naomi called out, trying to be heard over Elly's wails. "Sweet pea! Sweet pea, do you hear me?"

The sobs and wails abruptly stopped. Naomi heard a hiccuping sound, then a sharp intake of breath. "Who . . . who said that?" Elly answered.

"Holy shit," Amber whispered in awe. "It worked!"

"It's me. Camryn. Sweet pea . . . I mean Elly . . . that man can't hurt you. Not anymore. It's okay," Naomi assured her. "You're okay."

"No, I'm not okay," Elly said between sniffs. "Why am I here? Where are my moms?"

"You really can't remember how you got here?" Naomi asked. "You don't remember Liam kidnapping you? Do you remember the accident?"

"What . . . what accident?" Elly asked, sounding genuinely confused. "What are you talking about?"

"The car accident you had with your moms."

"We didn't have a car accident."

"Are you sure? They found your moms' car in a ravine. The police said they drove off the road somehow. Maybe he tailgated them and forced them to spin out. Is that what happened?"

"No. No, I don't think so." Elly went quiet again. "I don't remember being in a car. I—I remember eating dinner and going to bed early because I didn't feel well. I felt nauseous and really sleepy. But in the middle of the night, I heard a noise that woke me up. It sounded like it was coming from downstairs. I thought maybe it was one of my moms, but when I walked down the hall and looked downstairs, I saw . . . I saw it was him. It was him! He'd gotten into the cabin. I don't know how." She paused. "I—I started screaming and ran to my moms' room. I tried to wake them up. I shook them *so* hard. I yelled at them, but they wouldn't get up!"

Naomi remembered the toxicology tests showed that Krissa and Cheryl had both painkillers and sedatives in their system when they died. Was that the reason Elly couldn't wake them up? Was it why Elly had felt so nauseous and tired? Had Liam somehow managed to drug them?

"He made it upstairs," Elly went on. "I tried to run away from him, but I was so . . . so . . ." She whimpered. "He caught me and put this rag over my face. I blacked out and he brought me here. Then he . . ." She started crying again. "I asked him why he was doing this to me. Why was he hurting me?"

"Did he tell you why?" Amber asked.

Naomi was confused as well. Why had Liam targeted her, Amber, and Elly? Besides them not being from Sparksburg, there wasn't much else the girls had in common.

"He said my moms were sinners and that I was a child of sin. We all had to be punished. Then he started talking about his wife. About how she was perfect but she'd suffered. He kept ranting. I couldn't . . . I couldn't really understand him," Elly said. "He just wouldn't stop. I guess he killed me. But if I really am dead, then this should all be over, right? *Right?* Why am I still here?"

"That's the million-dollar question. Why the fuck are *any* of us still here?" Amber asked.

"My friend's great-grandmother said the spirits in Sparksburg . . . the ones that were murdered . . . who went missing here a long time ago are stuck. It's like they can't get home. They can't leave the land, so they haunt it. They haunt the woods. I guess you guys are stuck here, too."

"Oh, great," Amber murmured. "I'm doomed to haunt a cellar in the middle of nowhere because I had the bad luck to get murdered in the wrong zip code?" She laughed. "Well, I guess you've got bad luck too, girly, because you're gonna be stuck here with us when he kills you. Stuck here for all eternity."

"Unless she can get away," Elly said. "Just because we didn't doesn't mean Camryn can't."

"Or, she can kill *him* first," Amber suggested.

"What?" Naomi asked.

"You heard me," Amber said. Her voice hardened. "Kill him first and you can get out of here."

"But . . . but how could I kill him?" Naomi asked. "I don't have any weapons. I wouldn't even know what—"

"My chain. He left it here. You can strangle him with it."

"I don't . . . I don't know if I can do that," Naomi whispered. "He's so much bigger than me. Stronger. Amber, you said what happened to you when you fought back. How badly he beat you."

"So don't fight him. Just run," Elly said. "Maybe you can trip him on the stairs when he comes down next time. Hide in the dark. And when he falls to the ground—run like hell."

"And if that doesn't work? When he catches her, because he *will* catch her—then what?" Amber asked. *"Beg for his forgiveness?"*

"No," Naomi answered, feeling her heart sink, "if I can't run, then I go with your plan." She took a deep breath. "I'll have no choice."

52

KHALIL WATCHED AS HIS UNCLE OTIS LEANED DOWN. The older man braced his hands on his knees and squinted at the ground.

They had driven back to the road where Naomi had likely vanished and had been examining the shoulder for the past two and half hours. Uncle Otis had wandered over the gravel, mud, and brush on foot, not saying much, only shaking his head and muttering, "Nah, that ain't it," before continuing on his search.

Meanwhile, Naomi's dad was pacing in the dirt. He'd been hovering over Uncle Otis's shoulder earlier but retreated when Uncle Otis told him as nicely but as plainly as possible to back off.

Khalil could tell Naomi's dad was getting impatient. He kept glancing down at his watch and loudly sighing. The sighs were now turning into grumbles. Khalil wondered if Mr. Stoakes was starting to doubt Uncle Otis.

Uncle Otis paused once again. This time he didn't frown and shake his head. Instead he started to slowly nod and grunt, "Mmm-hmm. Mmm-hmm." Khalil and Naomi's dad walked toward him, trying to see what he was seeing.

"You finally spotted some tire tracks, Unc?" Khalil asked.

"Boy, there are nothing *but* tire tracks around here." Uncle Otis sucked his teeth. "But this here," he said, pointing down at the crusted-over mud, "are a man's shoe prints. And they're fresh. Had to have been made not too long ago." Uncle Otis pushed himself upright and gestured to the footprints. "Somebody was walking around here. Maybe it was the man who took your daughter."

"Okay. All right! Good. Great! Finally!" Mr. Stoakes clapped his hands and rubbed them together, looking relieved for the first time today. "So, uh, can you find a trail? Track him through the brush?"

"He ain't a deer." Uncle Otis adjusted the bill of his baseball cap. "He probably wasn't on foot the whole time either."

Mr. Stoakes's smile evaporated. That tense look was on his face again, in his body language. "Well then, what else should we be looking for? What do we do? How can I help move this along?"

"Move this along? Hey, man," Uncle Otis said, "I know you're worried about your daughter and all, but stuff like this, you can't rush."

"But we *do* have to rush," Naomi's dad argued, pacing again, "because time could be working against us. Not only will we lose the sun in a few hours, someone took my daughter, and they could be doing anything to her right now. He could be hurting her!"

"I get that, brotha," Uncle Otis said.

"No," Naomi's dad replied testily, "I don't think you do."

Khalil stared down at the footprints, at the direction they were heading. He walked a few steps and spotted another set of prints, though this time less pronounced. He kept walking until his uncle's and Mr. Stoakes's voices faded away. Then he saw something that made his breath catch in his throat. It made the blood sing in his ears. Khalil knelt down, reached out with a shaky hand, and picked it up.

One of the petals was gone, but he instantly recognized the flower. It was similar to the lily he'd given to Naomi on the hilltop on the last day he saw her.

What were the chances of the flower being here if Naomi hadn't been here as well?

He looked up to see if maybe there was a cluster of Turk's-cap lily stalks nearby. But he didn't see any more of the lilies anywhere—only several feet of shrubs that had been flattened by something heavy. They seemed to create a path in the trees.

"Look, I appreciate your help. I truly do, but maybe my wife was right," Khalil heard Mr. Stoakes say. "Maybe we should go to the State Police because it feels like we're going in circles out here."

"No, we ain't going in circles!" Uncle Otis said, almost shouting. "We've only been at it less than three hours and you're mad we haven't found your daughter yet. But I'mma tell you . . . all this huffin' and puffin' ain't making it go any faster!"

"Stop! Stop!" Khalil said, calling back to the men. "I found something." He held up the flower. The two men rushed to Khalil. "I gave Camryn this. I gave it to her the last day I saw her. There are no other flowers like this around here."

"Where'd you find it?" Naomi's father asked.

"Right here," Khalil said. "And there are shrubs and branches broken here, too. They're flattened out for yards and yards. Maybe a car or truck did it. Maybe it was the truck that—"

Mr. Stoakes didn't wait for Khalil to finish, he jogged in the direction that Khalil pointed and dove straight into the brush, going so far that Khalil and Uncle Otis could no longer see him. They only heard thumping feet, snapping twigs, and muttered curses at this distance.

"Hey! Hey!" Naomi's father shouted. "There's a road back here! A dirt road."

Khalil and Uncle Otis exchanged a look before rushing after Mr. Stoakes. When they reached the top of the slope, they saw him standing next to a mud path nestled among the trees. No one would see it unless they knew to look for it. Unless they knew it was there.

Uncle Otis nodded. “Okay, y’all, let’s head back to the truck. We’ll see where it leads.”

53

"SO ARE YOU GONNA INTRODUCE US TO YOUR friend?"

Naomi looked up at the question. It sounded like Amber had asked it.

She'd been sitting in the dark, silently making a plan for how she would get past Liam when he finally returned. She had considered tripping him as he walked down the stairs, like Elly had suggested. Or maybe she could catch him off guard, shove him so he'd take a bad spill, giving her enough time to make it up the stairs before he could stop her. But Naomi quickly dismissed that idea.

What if he grabbed her when she shoved him? What if he didn't fall and she only made him angrier and he decided to punish her even worse than he'd planned?

To be honest, by the time Amber had asked her the question, Naomi was relieved. She could finally take a break from second-guessing herself, from wandering through a maze of escape scenarios that all seemed to lead to dead ends.

"What do you mean? What friend?" Naomi asked.

"The girl in her pj's. The quiet chick who just hangs out in the corner over there," Amber said. "She didn't show up until you did."

"Oh," Naomi said, looking around in the dark.

“She’s . . . she’s been coming around since my first night here in Sparksburg. I think she was trying to lead me to you guys.”

“She told you we were here?” Elly asked.

“Not exactly.” Naomi thought for a bit. “She doesn’t speak. But I think she’s one of the missing around here from hundreds of years ago.”

“Why doesn’t she speak?” Elly asked.

“I’m not . . . I’m not sure.”

But that wasn’t true. She had suspected for a while now who the burning girl was.

“Are you Willa?” she called into the dark.

Willa, one of Khalil’s ancestors his great-grandmother had told her about. The formerly enslaved girl who had been separated from her brother and never seen again.

Naomi jumped. She swore she heard deep breathing against her ear. But she calmed when she realized who it was.

“You are Willa, aren’t you?” she asked, turning toward the noise.

She heard excited labored breaths and a keening sound.

“So why did Willa pick you?” Amber asked. “She could’ve visited anyone. Why you?”

Naomi thought for a moment.

“I guess because I was a missing girl, too. Like all of you. My parents call me Camryn, but my name’s also Naomi . . . Naomi Ward. I was kidnapped when I was ten months old and raised by the woman who took me. I called her mom. She was all that I knew. All that I trusted. But when I turned fifteen, she was arrested and I found out that she wasn’t really my mother. I couldn’t trust anything anymore.”

“Wow,” Amber murmured, “that’s fucked up.”

“Yeah, I know. I reunited with my family last year. But *years* had passed. They were practically strangers. They’d moved on and were living happy lives without me. My home wasn't with my mom anymore, but it didn't feel like I belonged with my real family either. I guess Willa . . . well, she saw that in me. That I'm just fucked up enough to understand her. She's lost and can't find her way back to where she thinks she should be. I am, too. But now . . ." Naomi brought her knees to her chest and wrapped her arms around them. She felt hot tears wet her cheeks. "Maybe, I can find my way someday, I guess, but down here it's so . . . so—"

"Bleak?" Amber said.

"Yeah. That's the right word."

She heard the revving of a truck engine. A few seconds later, the sound stopped.

Was Liam back already? It hadn't seemed like that much time had passed since the last time he'd come to the cellar, but it must have been hours.

Naomi tensed in the dark.

"Showtime," Amber said dryly.

"Where are the chains? Tell me where they are, Amber," Naomi whispered, now frantic.

"Over here," Amber said.

Naomi crawled across the cellar toward Amber's voice, feeling her way along the floor in search of them.

"Oh God. Oh God! No, no, no." Elly began to whimper.

"Don't you start up again," Amber snapped. "He can't hurt you, dumbass."

"But he can hurt *her*!" Elly screamed back.

"Come on, Camryn," Amber urged. "Hurry the fuck up! He'll be coming in soon. Did you find the chain?"

Naomi finally felt cold metal against her fingertips. "I got it! I got it!" she whispered.

She closed her hand around it and pulled, hearing the links clink against each other just as she heard a wooden door being thrown open. She quickly wrapped the chain around her wrist and arm and listened to his thudding footsteps above them. With the opening of the cellar door, a blinding bright light shone down into the space.

Naomi could see that, this time, the other girls didn't disappear. While Elly cowered in terror in one of the cellar corners, Amber and Willa drew closer to the light. Naomi could finally see Amber. She was exactly as Tate had described her, wearing the same halter top and shorts that she'd been wearing the day she'd been kidnapped. Her dirty-blond hair was pulled into a ponytail, revealing her makeup-smeared face.

"Are you ready?" she asked Naomi, meeting her gaze just as Liam's looming shadow appeared at the top of the ladder.

Naomi nodded and clenched her fist around the chain. Her muscles jittered in anticipation of what would happen next. But she knew this time she wouldn't be alone. The girls hadn't retreated into the shadows. They hadn't deserted her.

Just then they heard the rumble of another car engine. The sound caught Naomi and maybe even Liam off guard.

"Liam!" a familiar voice shouted. "Liam, I know you're in there. Come out, goddamn it!"

She heard Liam grouse loudly before taking a step back from the ladder and slamming the cellar door shut.

"What's happening?" Elly cried. "Where's he going?"

"Shh!" Amber admonished. "I'm trying to hear!"

Naomi was trying to listen, too. The voice she'd heard shouting was clearly Sheriff Turner's. But why was Sheriff Turner here?

Naomi heard shuffling footsteps, followed by ones that moved at a much faster pace, like they were running up or down stairs.

"What do you want, Alice?" Liam's muffled voice asked.

"Is she still down there?" Sheriff Turner replied. "Is she alive?"

"Not for long," he answered flippantly, making Naomi's stomach tighten. "Why?"

"Then I got here in enough time. Let her out. Let her go!"

Naomi blinked in shock.

"What?" Liam cried. "Why the hell would I do that?"

"Her parents have called me no less than twenty times. They even called the State Police. One of my deputies said her mom is down at city hall raising holy hell, refusing to leave. One of her kids is broadcasting the whole shitshow on social media as we speak."

"And?"

"And the mom keeps playing a recording of me talking to that kid the night she disappeared, Liam. They know I saw that girl! We're done, Liam. It's over!"

"No! No, I can salvage this. They can't connect you . . . either of us to the girl if there isn't a body, Alice! Let me handle this and—"

"And what? Kill *another* girl after that? Goddamn it, Liam, you told me Amber Nash was a one-off. A mistake!"

"Oh, don't bring up that whore! Mayor Bartz told you to take care of her, and I did it for you. I did you a favor."

"He didn't mean to take care of her *that* way and you know it! He meant to scare her off. Not kill her! I thought you just made one bad decision because of pain and grief . . . because it was so close to the anniversary of Jodie's death."

"Don't you talk about Jodie! Don't you dare bring her up!"

"But you keep doing it," she went on. "I told you people would start to notice these missing girls. I told you that it wasn't going to bring Jodie back! I know she died a horrible death on those ventilators."

"Shut up! Shut up! Shut up!"

"I was there, okay? It was slow and painful. I saw it, too. But you can't blame every outsider for what happened to her."

"She wouldn't be dead if it wasn't for one of them! They killed her, Alice!"

"Choking the life out of these girls doesn't solve a damn thing. It only serves to feed this hunger you have now. I tried to protect you, but I can't anymore! Do you understand? Now they're going to think I'm behind this. That *I* took the Stoakes girl, and I am *not* taking the fall for you."

"A recording doesn't prove anything."

"Release her, Liam. Turn yourself in. A kidnapping charge isn't as bad as first-degree murder. We might even get you a reduced sentence with an insanity plea."

"*Insanity plea?* But I'm not crazy!"

"Liam, I'm only going to say it one more time. Let me take you in, and I'll . . . I'll make sure that you—"

"No! No, I'm not going to jail! You hear me? I'm going down there and I'm finishing what I started!"

"Liam. Liam, I'm warning you!" Sheriff Turner shouted.

Naomi heard tussling, a hard thud that made her cringe, and the splintering of wood.

"What the fuck are they doing up there?" Amber asked.

"I think they're fighting," Naomi whispered.

She heard three pops that made her jump. Gunshots. The tussling sounds abruptly stopped. Everything above the cellar went eerily quiet.

"Did . . . did she shoot him?" Elly asked in a trembling voice.

"I don't know," Naomi whispered back, but she hoped to God that Sheriff Turner had.

Maybe now this nightmare would finally be over.

54

AFTER A MINUTE OR TWO, NAOMI HEARD SHUFFLING footsteps.

Her heart was pounding. She was breathing so fast and so hard that she might have just run a marathon. Her fist around the chain tightened to the point that her nails were digging into her palm. Naomi swore she might draw blood as she waited to see who would pull open the trapdoor overhead.

It was yanked open seconds later with such ferocity that she screamed. Naomi saw a trickle of blood drip onto the stairs, then she saw a boot and a jeans-clad leg.

Naomi realized with a sinking feeling that it wasn't Sheriff Turner who had come to rescue her. Liam had won the fight. Sheriff Turner was likely dead.

"She . . . she shot me," he slurred, holding his side as he took one lurching step down the ladder, then another.

Naomi could see more of him now. His upper leg and lower torso were soaked in blood. So was the hand braced against his left side—his poor attempt to stanch the bleeding from his bullet wound. But Naomi suspected that not all the blood was his own.

"Alice was . . . she was like a sister to me," he said as he took another step into the cellar. His pale face was blank and slicked with sweat. His eyes were wide. "And now she's dead," he went on, speaking as if someone else had shot her. Like he hadn't killed her himself.

When he reached the last stair, Naomi took several steps back.

"Do something!" Amber yelled. "Don't just stand there, Camryn! Fight him!"

"Run! Run, Camryn!" Elly cried.

But her plans for escape . . . all the fight faded out of her and was replaced with utter dread. There was something wrong with his face . . . his eyes. The features seemed to melt and change like a man transforming into something else. Like Dr. Jekyll turning into Mr. Hyde in real time. Even in the dim light, Naomi could see the blue of Liam's eyes becoming darker. They were turning . . . brown and then black. They were two black ink spots set against white with red-rimmed lids. He looked possessed.

"And I'm gonna die, too," he went on, "but not before you. She wanted me to let you go, but I can't. I can't and . . . *And my eye will not spare, nor will I have pity. I will punish you according to your ways, while your abominations are in your midst!*" He was shouting, holding up his bloody fist. *"Then you will know that I am the Lord, who strikes."* He lowered his hand. "I—I cannot allow you . . . you all to stay in our midst," he slurred while slowly shaking his head. "You are a blight who must be removed. Don't you understand?"

Naomi took another step back and bumped into something. She looked down and saw it was the bucket still filled almost halfway with excrement. She didn't hesitate. She picked up the bucket and hurled it at him. The liquid splashed Liam's shirt and face. He cried out in disgust.

Naomi took her chance and ran for the stairs. She made it three rungs up the ladder. She could see the floor above and the doorway leading outside before she felt a wet hand clamp around her leg and roughly tug her down. Her elbow connected with one of the steps and she shrieked in pain.

Liam pulled at her again—this time grabbing a fistful of her shirt, but Naomi whipped the chain at him, hitting him hard against the ear and cheek. He fell and landed on his back on the cellar floor.

Naomi started climbing again. She reached the floor above, seeing for the first time that she was in a dilapidated cabin. She raced to the open door, toward the dying afternoon light. When she reached the front porch, she almost stumbled over the pair of legs lying near the front door. She looked down and saw that it was Sheriff Turner. The woman's green eyes stared vacantly at the sky above. The left side of her skull was gone, like Liam had shot her at point-blank range. The contents were splattered across the cabin's wall and along the porch's floorboards.

If Naomi's stomach wasn't already emptied out, she would have vomited right there at the sight.

She forced herself to tear her eyes away from the woman's lifeless body and saw Liam's black Chevrolet Silverado and a Sparksburg sheriff's cruiser sitting several feet away. The cruiser's door yawned open and she could hear the crackle of a police radio inside. She ran to the vehicle and hopped inside. She unhooked the mic and screamed frantically into it.

"Help! Help! Liam killed Sheriff Turner! He shot her! Help me. He wants to kill me, too! He kidnapped me! I don't . . . I don't know where I am!"

"You get back here!" she heard someone shout, and looked up to find Liam standing in the cabin's doorway.

Naomi glanced down at the steering wheel, hoping that maybe the sheriff had left her keys in the ignition, but Sheriff Turner hadn't. Naomi considered running, taking her chances among the trees, but thought better of it. She slammed the door shut and locked it instead, watching as Liam wrenched away Sheriff Turner's baton from her dead body, extending it with a flick of the wrist. He came barreling down the stairs toward Naomi and the cruiser.

"Help!" she continued to shout into the radio. "Please, he's going to kill me!"

She screamed as Liam started to hit the glass over and over with the baton.

Naomi was right. His face *had* changed. It was no longer that of the man she remembered seeing at the grocer, but had morphed into someone else: the one she'd seen atop the bronze statue in the center of town. It was Reverend Charles Davis Meacham's face.

"And I will punish the world for their evil, and the wicked for their iniquity!" Liam yelled as a crack appeared on the window, then another. *"And I will cause the arrogancy of the proud to cease!"*

The window exploded, sending glass splattering everywhere. Naomi raised her hands to protect her face and eyes.

"And will lay low the haughtiness of the terrible," Liam said as he reached inside the now broken window, keeping his blackened eyes focused on her even as shards of glass cut into his forearm. He unlocked the door.

Naomi scrambled to the passenger side for some means of escape, but he was faster, wrenching the door open.

"Now," he said, "come and accept your punishment, chickadee."

Naomi squeezed her eyes shut.

She didn't see the rifle bullet, but she heard it.

She heard more shots and covered her head. She only opened her eyes when she heard Andre say, "Camryn, honey, it's Daddy. Are you okay?"

Liam was gone and Andre was hunched in front of the car door. Khalil stood behind him, peering over Andre's shoulder at her.

Naomi sobbed when she saw them, but this time with relief. She didn't think twice before scrambling across the seat and leaping into Andre's arms.

55

FOR THE THIRD TIME IN NAOMI'S LIFE, SHE WAS surrounded by a swarm of police officers, by flashing lights and cruisers.

Most of them had arrived at the crime scene within thirty minutes of her broadcast over the police radio and fifteen minutes after Andre's 911 call. Both Sheriff Turner's and Liam's bodies were already in body bags and being carted away. While the EMTs examined and cleaned and bandaged her cuts, Naomi told the State Police investigators everything that had happened, from her meeting Sheriff Turner on the road in the wee hours of the morning to the fight she'd overheard between the officer and Liam and the rifle shot that saved Naomi's life.

All the while she kept trying to make eye contact with Khalil. Her father told her that Khalil had listened to the voicemail and put the pieces together about her kidnapping. She thought that Khalil had given up on her, that he'd forgotten about her. Instead, he'd been the one to guide Naomi's father and his Uncle Otis here. She wanted to thank him. She wanted to wrap him in a bear hug and kiss him senseless, but it didn't look like she would have the chance. He and his uncle were also being questioned by police.

Besides, like her, Khalil probably was eager to get to his family. Because it was an active crime scene, Dawn and his parents were being told to stay away by police. She'd heard that half the town had come to see what had happened and were being held back a hundred yards by officers and police barriers.

"So he kept you alone down there in the cellar?" the police officer asked, gesturing to the broken-down cabin that was now being roped off with yellow police tape.

Naomi could see two crime scene technicians examining the gruesome stains on the cabin's wooden planks. The stains left behind by Sheriff Turner. She cringed before focusing on the officer's badge and his gray uniform.

"Yes," Naomi said slowly.

The cop noticed her hesitation. "Camryn, was anyone else down there? Was anyone else involved in this?"

"You can tell him, honey," Andre urged, squeezing her shoulder. "They can't hurt you now."

"He . . . he killed other girls," she whispered to the officer as Andre held her. "Elly Jamison and . . . and Amber Nash. He killed them down there."

The cop frowned. "Elly Jamison and Amber Nash were down there with you? You saw him kill them?"

She pursed her lips and slowly shook her head. "No. I didn't . . . I didn't see it."

"Then how do you know he killed them? We haven't found Amber or Elly anywhere on the property. Did he confess it to you?"

She couldn't tell him about the ghosts, about the girls whose tortured souls were still stuck in the darkness, who seemed chained to that cellar. She'd made it out. They'd rallied around her and helped her do it. Now she wanted desperately for the other girls to do the same, at least in the afterlife.

"Camryn, how do you know Liam killed those other girls?"

The officer huffed with impatience. "You've got to give me somethin'. Did you see evidence that the girls had been there? Did you . . . did you see their bodies?"

She suddenly felt hair prickle on the back of her neck and on her arms. Naomi looked up and spotted Willa standing several feet away. As police officers, technicians, and emergency personnel walked around the crime scene or talked in huddles, Willa stood serenely in the midst of it all, silhouetted by the setting sun. Naomi watched as the girl slowly raised her arm, turned, and pointed into the distance.

"Are they over there?" Naomi whispered to her, gradually rising to her feet.

Willa nodded.

"What did you say, honey?" Andre asked. Naomi removed the thermal blanket from around her shoulders. It hadn't been able to alleviate the chill she'd felt for the past hour anyway. She began to walk in Willa's direction.

"Where is she going?" the cop asked.

"To Amber and Elly," Naomi answered, almost in a daze. She kept her eyes focused on Willa. "To their bodies."

Willa began to walk toward a group of trees not far away from the cabin. Naomi followed her, weaving her way through the sea of bodies and uniforms.

When she reached the line of trees, she turned back to Andre and the officer. "Over here," Naomi said, inclining her head before pushing aside branches and shrubs.

Willa walked several more yards, then stopped. She pointed to the ground in front of her. When Naomi drew near, she saw the mound of dirt haphazardly hidden under a pile of branches. It was about three feet wide and nearly five feet long. She never would have spotted it at a distance, but up close, it was obvious that this had been recently dug.

"They're here," Naomi said, gesturing at the mound. "He buried them here."

So she'd found Amber and Elly after all, though not in the state she'd hoped. At least this way they were no longer lost and hopefully now, with their bodies recovered, Amber and Elly could be free of this place. They were no longer missing girls.

The officer rushed forward, then turned and cupped his hands around his mouth. "Hey! Hey! We need a CSI team over here!" He looked at Naomi and her dad. "I'm going to need you two to step back. Don't touch anything. All right? We don't want any evidence disturbed. Okay?"

But Naomi wasn't listening. She was focused on Willa again, who beckoned her to follow.

Were there more girls? Had Liam buried someone else here?

"Where is she going now?" the cop asked Andre, who shrugged as Naomi followed Willa deeper into the forest.

"Your guess is as good as mine," Andre said.

Naomi didn't know where she was going either, but she trusted Willa. She followed her until they reached an open field nestled serenely among a stand of trees. It was overgrown with weeds and shrubs that came up to her elbows in some spots, but it seemed oddly placed out here, like the land had been cleared long ago to build something and then was forgotten.

The light was almost gone now, fading fast behind the horizon, but Willa seemed to give off her own glow, growing brighter by the minute. Naomi watched as Willa abruptly stopped and fell to her knees on a moss-covered spot near one of the oak trees. She placed her palm flat against the ground and looked up at Naomi with tears in her eyes, motioning for her to do the same.

Naomi knelt beside her and placed her hand on the ground on the same spot, overlapping her fingers with Willa's. When she did, she felt a static shock that lasted only a second or two.

She took a sharp intake of breath and yanked her hand away, but in those mere seconds she saw a movie reel of memories. Willa's memories.

She saw her as a squealing toddler, getting chased by her brother, William, as their mother looked on, smiling while scrubbing clothes on a washboard. She saw a five-year-old Willa laughing at a story her father told her and her brother at bedtime. His handsome face was illuminated by a kerosene lamp as he made shadow figures on their cabin wall to illustrate his tales. She saw Willa dancing at a church picnic when she was ten years old, wearing a brown dress and with her hair in braided pigtails held in place by sage-green ribbons.

Then Naomi saw darker memories. One was of Willa's father hanging from a tree. His limp body, bloody and swollen. She saw Willa's mother being dragged into the forest by a group of men with torches. Naomi saw Willa crying for her brother the day they were separated forever. She reached for him, even as she was shoved along by Mrs. McDougall, who took her to her new home. And finally, the day Willa was buried. Her body had been burned by Mr. McDougall before being dumped into a pit already filled with others who had also vanished from their loved ones. The town's inhabitants used the pit as a mass burial site.

When Naomi pulled her hand away, she had tears in her eyes, too. "They're here!" she cried. "They're all here!"

"Who? More of Liam's victims?" the police officer asked.

"No," she said, shaking her head. She wiped tears away with the heels of her hands. "They're *older*. They've been here a lot longer." She looked around the field. "They buried them all out here. They're all over this place."

"Who buried them, honey?" Andre asked.

"The town. They're stuck, Dad. We need to help them get out!"

He squinted down at her. "What?"

"Are you listening? They need to get out!" she shouted, pulling at the grass. "They need to get out! Dig them up! We have to help them!"

"Camryn," Andre said softly, falling next to her. "Camryn, stop, baby."

"No! No!" she yelled.

She started ripping into the moist soil with her bare hands, seizing fistfuls, trying to reach those long buried, who were now nothing but bones and muddled memories. She'd dig them up herself if she had to.

Naomi only stopped when she felt gentle hands on her shoulders. She whipped around, prepared to shove whoever it was away, but it was Khalil. It was his unwavering eyes that she met. His uncle was standing behind him.

"Willa's in there, Khalil," she choked. "She's . . . she's the one that your great-grandmother told me about. She's in there with all the rest of them. And no one's listening!"

He nodded. "I hear you. I believe they're down there. If cops don't dig them up, we'll dig them up together. I'll do it with you," Khalil said. "We'll come back here. I promise."

"I will, too," Andre said.

Uncle Otis shrugged. "I got shovels back at the house. I can help."

Naomi finally let the soil slip between her fingers. "Thank you. Thank you."

She closed her eyes and sank against Khalil, feeling like a burden that had been solely hers had finally been lifted from her shoulders.

When she opened her eyes again and slowly stood, she saw that Willa was gone.

56

NAOMI AND ANDRE STEPPED OUT OF THE POLICE cruiser a couple of hours later. Fear and panic had finally given way to sheer exhaustion. Andre practically had to hold her upright as she staggered across the gravel driveway.

Naomi looked up at the cabin's front porch just as Dawn whipped open the front door, haloed by the lights in the great room. Maya and Blake stood anxiously behind her.

"Hey, guys," Naomi said weakly.

Bear came barreling through the doorway first. The dog ran down the porch stairs, barking and panting excitedly. He hopped onto his hind legs and circled her and Andre, making Naomi crack her first smile of the day. She reached out to pet him and he eagerly licked her hand.

"All right, Bear," Andre said with a chuckle. "Calm down, boy. We know you're happy to see her. Let her get through the door first though."

Maya was the second person to reach them. When she did, she enveloped Naomi in a viselike hug. "We thought you were dead," she sobbed, catching Naomi by surprise. "I was so scared!"

For a moment, Naomi wondered if her older sister was putting on an act for the sake of their parents. Or maybe she'd managed to sneak in a selfie stick and was live streaming this for all her followers, earning hearts and thumbs-up emojis. But when Naomi pulled away, she could see there were real tears in Maya's eyes, and there was no phone in sight.

"I'm so sorry, Camryn," Maya said between hiccups and sniffs. "I didn't mean that . . . that stuff I said yesterday. If that's what made you run away. I didn't mean it. I'm sorry!"

"It's . . . okay," Naomi said. "I didn't say very nice things either."

Blake stayed silent but hugged her waist fiercely.

The only person who didn't rush toward her was Dawn. She stood in the cabin doorway with her hand clenched around the handle. Her lips were pursed. "It's late, guys. Let's get Camryn and Dad inside. Get you two fed and washed." She said it like they'd just come back from a long hike, not like Naomi hadn't left her room in the middle of the night and been kidnapped.

"I'm . . . I'm not really hungry," Naomi said sheepishly, confused by how Dawn was behaving.

"That's understandable." Dawn nodded. "A shower and bed, then. We'll worry about the rest in the morning."

"O-okay," Naomi said.

She'd thought if anyone would be emotional right now, it would be Dawn. After all, Sheriff Turner said Dawn had "raised holy hell" at the Sheriff's Office, playing Naomi's voicemail over and over again, refusing to leave until she spoke with someone who could help find her daughter.

Was Dawn angry at her? Had the last words Naomi said to her and all the events of the day pushed her too far? Or maybe she was exhausted as well with no more tears left to cry.

While the rest of the family stayed downstairs, Naomi walked to the floor above. Bear shadowed her the entire way. When she went into the bathroom to take her shower, he tried to follow her there, too, so he could keep her in his sight. She had to reassure him with a pet and soft words that she would be fine without him. She emerged from the bathroom later to find him waiting for her, nodding off on the hardwood.

When Naomi walked into her bedroom, she found pj's waiting for her and a freshly made bed.

Naomi walked across her room, toward the curtains covering the glass doors. She hesitated before drawing them back, half expecting to find Willa waiting for her in the field. But she wasn't there. There was only grass, a few wildflowers, and moonlight.

"Cam," Dawn said. "I know you said you weren't hungry, but I brought this up for you just in case."

At the sight of the small plate of crackers and cheese slices that Dawn placed on her bed, Naomi's stomach growled.

"Thanks," she whispered, reaching for the plate. She sat down on the bed and began to nibble a few crackers.

"How are you feeling?" Dawn asked, stepping around Bear and sitting down on the bed beside her.

"Like I've been hit by a truck," she said, biting into a slice of cheese.

"I could imagine. You went through . . . a lot today." Dawn searched Naomi's face. "Your dad told me everything that happened. He told me that you helped the police find Amber Nash and Elly."

"I did, but by then they were already dead," Naomi murmured.

"I know, honey." Dawn placed a hand on her shoulder. "But at least they were found. The people who cared about them can know what happened to them, and trust me, knowing is painful but it's *much* better than not knowing at all."

She had a point. Naomi nodded.

"Did . . . did the girl lead you there?"

Naomi stilled.

"I mean the one you kept seeing outside your window,"

Dawn explained. "Dad said . . . he said before you found the place where the girls were buried, you were talking to someone. It was like you were . . . you were following someone. Was it her?"

Naomi nodded. "Her name's Willa." She gnawed her lower lip. "She's a ghost, Mom. Willa led me to Amber and Elly. I thought they were still alive down there, because they talked to me. They kept me company when I felt so alone and scared. But I figured out they were dead, too." She watched Dawn's face, seeing hints of disbelief. "Look, I know it sounds crazy but—"

"It's not crazy, honey." Dawn squeezed her shoulder. "Don't say that. After everything that's happened . . . after what your dad said he witnessed today, I'm not making any more judgments. Okay? He didn't just see you looking at someone. He said . . . he said when you touched the ground, you glowed. It was like you touched something out there." Her eyes flicked toward the balcony doors before returning to Naomi. "Do you still see her? Is she out there right now?"

Naomi shook her head. "No, she's gone. I don't think I'm going to see her again—or the others. I guess she has no reason to visit me anymore now that I did what she needed me to do." She shrugged. "I'm happy Willa finally has some peace. I hope they all have it now, but . . . and I know it sounds weird, but I'm kinda sad to see her go. To see them *all* go. It was like I was part of a missing-girls club. Now I'm back to being by myself: the messed-up girl that I am. I'm sorry I keep putting you guys through this."

Dawn lowered her eyes.

"You know, I've replayed that day you were kidnapped over and over again. I think about what I could've done differently. How I could've saved us from all this. I should've put both you and Maya in the cart, instead of just you. I should have brought

Maya's favorite stuffed toy with her instead of keeping it back in the car. She wouldn't have had that tantrum and run off. I think about how I should've given up on the idea of going shopping that day when I saw you guys were in a fussy mood.

"I've thought of all these scenarios and how different things would have been. But the truth is, there is nothing I could've done. Because what happened, as hard as it is for me to accept it, was meant to happen. You are *exactly* who you were meant to be. You are smart and so open that a spirit came to visit you because she knew you would listen . . . Naomi." Dawn's eyes went bright with tears as she held her face. "Dad and I will call you that, if that's what you want. We don't want to change you, honey. We just want you to be who you are. We just want you to be happy, Naomi."

Naomi wrapped her arms around Dawn and squeezed her tight.

"Thanks, Mom," she said.

"And do me a favor. Don't ever stop calling me that," Dawn said wiping the tears from her eyes.

That wouldn't be a problem. Saying *Mom* and *Dad* was a lot easier now. They had searched for her. Fought and raised holy hell for her. And despite everything she'd put them through, they still loved her. They'd earned those titles.

"Well, I'll let you get some rest." She stood, taking Naomi's now empty plate. "Shout if you need anything. I'll be downstairs." She patted her hip. "Come on, Bear. Come with me."

"Mom?" Naomi said as Bear rose to his feet.

"Yes, honey?"

"Can you . . . can you stay in here with me? Just for a little bit. At least until I fall asleep?"

Dawn nodded. "Of course, baby."

Naomi sank beneath the covers, still wearing her robe, too

fatigued to even put on her pajamas. Dawn lay beside her and held her close. Naomi rested her head against her chest and closed her eyes. It didn't take long for her mind to go quiet as she listened to the soft thud of Dawn's heartbeat and eventually drifted to sleep.

EPILOGUE

Two years later . . .

NAOMI STARED AT THE TREES, CRAGGY ROCK FACE, and stretches of open road outside her window as the car zipped down the highway.

Once again, she was on a road trip into the Appalachian Mountains with the Stoakeses, and once again, she wasn't quite sure what awaited her at the end of the journey. But this time, she didn't have Blake jabbing his elbows into her rib cage. Nor was she rolling her eyes as Maya made yet another video for social media, documenting their adventures.

Naomi's brother was currently at summer camp back in Maryland, hiking and paddleboating with his friends. Her sister was finishing up her summer internship at a publicity agency in Manhattan. Naomi had their parents and the SUV's back seat all to herself. To illustrate that point, she stretched out her legs over the leather interior, taking advantage of the extra space.

"Do you need me to turn down the air-conditioning?" Andre asked from the front seat, giving her a quick glance over his shoulder. "I know it's not as hot here as it was back home."

"No, I'm fine, Dad. Thanks."

Overhead, Naomi spotted a series of signs, showing that they would soon be approaching a tollbooth. A few minutes later, Andre slowed to a stop, falling in line behind a silver car. Andre lowered his window and held out a few dollar bills. A white-haired older woman in the tollbooth barely looked at him as she took the money, but then her eyes widened behind her bifocal lenses.

"Hey! I know you guys!" she drawled, pointing at the trio. "You're famous, ain't you? I saw you on TV!" She leaned in closer, tilting her head to peer at Naomi in the back seat. "You're the girl who got kidnapped twice."

Naomi resisted the urge to sigh. Being spotted happened less and less nowadays, but there were still those rare occasions like this one. She nodded. "Yeah, that's me," she said flatly.

"Geez!" The older woman shook her head. "You've got the worst luck, huh?"

Naomi had heard this several times as well. She'd even heard that she must be cursed.

Actually, I think I'm pretty lucky, she wanted to say, but didn't.

How many people had been abducted twice—and lived to tell the tale? But why bother arguing? Life was too short. So she gave the woman a polite smile as the toll gate rose.

"Well, uh, y'all have a nice day!" the woman called out awkwardly, returning her smile as Andre drove off.

As Naomi returned to looking at the mountains, she thought about that summer in Sparksburg.

Sometimes, at odd moments or in her dreams, she would get random flashbacks, images and sensations that were so real she felt as if she'd been dropped back into her past. She'd remember the first time she saw Willa standing beneath her balcony, gazing up at her, and the smells and the sounds she heard while locked up in Liam's pitch-black cellar. She could remember the mind-numbing horror she felt seeing Sheriff Turner's dead body. But when those sensations overwhelmed her, Naomi would call up a vision of Khalil smiling as he gave her the lily on the hilltop, when he asked her to be his girlfriend. She would remember falling asleep in Dawn's arms, exhausted but relieved, knowing that she'd finally helped free the souls who were trapped in that bloodstained land.

She knew she couldn't run from those memories. She refused to run from Sparksburg and the Shenandoah Valley, too. She'd returned to the mountains in Virginia a few times since that summer, getting updates on the Virginia State Police's investigation into the murders.

After questioning Liam's father, Nelson, detectives figured out how Liam had managed to drug the Jamisons: It was through the Sunny Market's food delivery service. Liam made it look like they were being sent a complimentary order from the market and spiked their wine and food with old painkillers that had belonged to his wife, Jodie, and a personal prescription of sedatives he'd been given to help him sleep. Naomi supposed Liam had been planning for all of them to be asleep when he broke into their cabin that night, but Elly wasn't.

And along with Elly's and Amber's bodies, police eventually found Tate's a month later in the Shenandoah National Park at one of the campsites. They were never able to determine for sure if Liam had killed him, too, but it was likely.

Naomi found it strange that Liam had no criminal record before all the murders. No history of assaults. Barely even a speeding ticket. It was like he became another person overnight.

She'd told Dawn about Willa's, Amber's, and Elly's ghosts, but she didn't tell her about what had happened with Liam, even after all this time. She never told how Liam had seemed like something or *someone* had taken him over. Naomi couldn't excuse his actions or what she was sure he had intended to do. But she wondered if Liam had been spurred on by a devil on his shoulder. Reverend Meacham was not a good man—bloodthirsty and hate-filled—and she bet he was an even worse spirit.

Besides the investigation, Naomi had a few other reasons to return to the Valley. She'd visited only a month ago with Khalil for Uncle Otis's annual cookout, thanking his uncle once again for saving her life. And she'd been back to Sparksburg for the ceremony commemorating the mass grave Willa had led her to as a historical landmark. An archaeological team from the University of Virginia and Hampton University had been examining it for more than a year now, removing skeletons and trying their best to identify the bodies of the folks buried there. Dawn told Naomi that she should be very proud of finding the site, but she was just happy that the victims were found. They weren't lost anymore. And, to be honest, standing there in that clearing during the ceremony, Naomi did not feel as lost either.

Naomi's phone buzzed. She picked it up from the seat beside her and saw a message on-screen from Khalil. They'd spent all yesterday together, hoping to catch a few more snatches of couple time before they had to head back to their respective dorms at the start of the semester.

Are you there yet? he asked.

Almost, she typed back.

As soon as she typed those words, the scenery outside her window began to change. The rows of trees disappeared as the road narrowed to one lane. Finally, she spotted a large gray sign on the shoulder that said U.S. DEPARTMENT OF JUSTICE, BUREAU OF PRISONS FPC ALDERSON, WV.

Andre and Dawn, who had been bantering playfully in the front seat, suddenly went quiet. A silence fell over her as well. Only the drone of AC and music on the car stereo filled the void.

As they continued down the road, they passed a series of brick buildings with white trim and porticos, eerily reminding Naomi of her own college campus. She didn't know what she'd expected of the prison where her mother was now serving the remaining seventeen years of her sentence, but it wasn't this. She saw a few women in sweatshirts and khakis trimming bushes near the porch stairs and realized they were prisoners.

Andre pulled into one of the open parking spaces and turned off the engine. No one moved or said a word for several minutes.

"Thank you guys for doing this . . . for driving me here, I mean," Naomi finally said.

She could have easily done this trip on her own. Naomi had her license now and could have driven herself to Alderson. But in many ways, she was relieved her parents had offered to come with her without her even asking.

"Of course we would, honey," Dawn said.

"We've got your back, kid," Andre echoed.

"You know me doing this doesn't mean I love you guys any less, right?" she whispered, feeling tears prick her eyes. "Because I love you guys. So, *so* much."

They'd lost her and found her more than once, and accepted and embraced her for the complicated girl that she was. How could she *not* love them?

"I don't want to hurt you guys, but I *have* to do this. At least to say goodbye to her. I never got that chance to say goodbye, and now I know how important that is . . . to have closure."

The ghosts in Sparksburg had taught her that.

Her parents nodded. "We know, honey," Dawn said, though Naomi could hear a crack in her voice.

Knowing that Dawn was stoically holding back tears made her own tears spill over.

"All right," Andre said, clapping his hands. "Let's do this."

They climbed out of the car and Naomi squinted at the brightness of the sun. She stared at the door leading to the prison's visitors' entrance and took a slow, deep breath.

"We'll wait for you here," Dawn said with a sniff, giving Naomi a quick hug. Naomi turned to Andre, who hugged her, too.

She began to walk away. As she neared the sidewalk, she hesitated. She faced her parents again for reassurance. For comfort. Dawn gave a wave and a smile. Andre gave her a thumbs-up.

"You got this!" he called to her.

She blew them a kiss, turned, and tugged open the prison door.

AUTHOR'S NOTE

Sundown Girls is a work that is a mix of fact and fiction. I borrowed liberally from the past and present to help create the world that my characters inhabit in the novel.

First, I should note that Sparksburg, Virginia, is a fictional town. However, the name is inspired by a real town—Lynchburg, Virginia, which is near the Blue Ridge Mountains and is named after the abolitionist John Lynch. The Lynchburg area is where part of my father's side of the family has lived for generations. (In fact, quite a few still live there.)

The history of the fictional town of Sparksburg, Virginia, was inspired by the real history of "sundown towns" in America. These were municipalities or neighborhoods that barred non-white people from living there through codified discrimination, intimidation, or both. Much like the origin story I created for Sparksburg in my novel, the founding of several real sundown towns involved the forced removal of non-white populations to create "whites-only" havens.

Decatur, Indiana . . . Romeoville, Illinois . . . Harrison, Arkansas . . . Oregon City, Oregon . . . all were once sundown towns. And the stories of these former sundown towns all seemed to follow a pattern of Black populations that were terrorized (often with the approval and participation of local leaders and police forces); driven from their homes through threats, arson, and/or murder; and never permitted to return. For the novel, I pulled inspiration from historical events in many of these towns and from places that may not have officially become sundown towns, but witnessed similar terrors.

One example is the Wilmington Massacre of 1898 in Wilmington, North Carolina, which was a once predominantly Black community that included many Black professionals—from the health inspector to the county coroner to even the town's newspaper owner and editor. Seeing this wealth and autonomy of the community did not sit well with some local white political and business leaders who created the "White Supremacy Campaign," which included intimidating Black voters at the election polls. When Black men in Wilmington ignored their threats and voted anyway, white mobs attacked them and went on an arson and killing spree in town. Families fled for their lives, hiding in the woods and the Black cemetery for days. A few residents who were willing to come back were allowed to collect some of their things but not to reclaim their property, forever changing the face of Wilmington thereafter.

Another famous example of the forced removal of a Black community lies under the waters of Lake Lanier in Forsyth County, Georgia. The man-made lake is known as a scenic tourist getaway and rumored to be cursed because of its tragic past. The land was once the site of a thriving Black community called Oscarville. In the fall of 1912, several Black men in Oscarville were accused of assaulting a white woman. One of the men was lynched by a mob that kidnapped him from the county jail where he was awaiting trial. The Black residents of Oscarville received threats. Several houses and churches were raided and burned. The community fled—some outright abandoning their homes, fearing further harm. The land was eventually taken over by Forsyth County's white residents, who used it as farmland. The building of the nearby Buford Dam in 1947 would lead to the creation of Lake Lanier but not erase the memories of what happened on those 38,000 acres thirty years before.

The most infamous example of the wholesale removal of Black residents is probably the Tulsa Race Massacre of 1921. The Black inhabitants of the Greenwood neighborhood of Tulsa, Oklahoma, aka "Black Wall Street," were attacked by white mobs when word spread that a local Black shoe shiner had allegedly assaulted a white woman and was arrested. It led to gunfights in the streets, murder, and the burning of homes and businesses. Eyewitnesses said that private planes were used to drop firebombs on Greenwood.

According to the 2001 Tulsa Reparations Coalition, the number of deaths ranged from 39 to 800 people. In addition, more than 10,000 Black residents were left homeless, and the neighborhood lost the modern equivalent of nearly $40 million in property value. But unlike the other Black neighborhoods and towns decimated by terror, Greenwood was able to rebuild in the 1940s. It later fell to urban renewal.

Black populations weren't the only ones banned from sundown towns. Again, this phenomenon impacted all non-white communities. Denver and Seattle, which are liberal and diverse metropolises today, were once sundown towns that banned Chinese residents from living there. The old gazebo bell on Main Street that used to ring to let all of Sparksburg know that Black people had to leave town at sunset or face dire consequences was inspired by a piercing siren in Minden, Nevada, a former sundown town, that would alert Native Americans from nearby tribal communities to get out of Minden before dark. In June 2021, Nevada banned all use of sirens, alarms, and bells that were historically associated with sundown ordinances. Despite that, Minden only stopped using its siren in 2023 after much heated debate.

I suppose the most unnerving part of my research for the novel was finding out just how many of these towns existed (literally hundreds) and that there was once a sundown town in my own backyard: Silver Spring, Maryland, which I decided to make the Stoakes family's hometown. It's a place that I have not only frequented, but always felt welcomed. So, I was shocked to learn the town had banned Black residents until the 1970s, considering the vibrant, multicultural community it is today.

It just goes to show that this dark history is lurking everywhere, and much closer than you'd think.

CITED WORKS

Biddle, Daniel R. "The Wilmington Massacre of 1898." Equal Justice Initiative, November 10, 2024. http://eji.org/news/wilmington-massacre-of-1898/. Accessed July 11, 2025.

Ellsworth, Scott. "Tulsa Race Massacre." *The Encyclopedia of Oklahoma History and Culture*, Oklahoma Historical Society. http://www.okhistory.org/publications/enc/entry?entry=TU013. Accessed July 11, 2025.

Loewen, James W. S*undown Towns: A Hidden Dimension of American Racism.* The New Press, 2018.

Metz, Sam. "Former Nevada 'Sundown Town' Stands by Siren Amid Racial Reckoning." *The Denver Post*, July 26, 2021. http://www.denverpost.com/2021/07/26/nevada-sundown-town-siren-racial-reckoning/. Accessed July 11, 2025.

Nasheed, Jameelah. "Lake Lanier: The History of a Black Town, Enduring Racism, and Mysterious Deaths." *Teen Vogue*, August 18, 2023. http://www.teenvogue.com/story/lake-lanier-deaths-history-black-town. Accessed July 11, 2025.

Rotenstein, David. S. "Silver Spring, Maryland Has Whitewashed Its Past." History News Network, October 15, 2016. http://www.hnn.us/article/silver-spring-maryland-has-whitewashed-its-past. Accessed July 11, 2025.

ACKNOWLEDGMENTS

WRITING A BOOK is never an easy process, but this book came with its own unique challenges that still make me marvel at the lovely final product that managed to be whittled into shape by the end. Thanks to those who guided me (and counseled me) through the whole thing.

Thanks to my agent, Barbara Poelle, for being my advocate for more than a decade now. Who knew that a mutual Twitter follow could turn into one of my most rewarding relationships I've ever had.

Thanks to Stacey Barney, my editor at Nancy Paulsen Books, for believing in *Sundown Girls* and its message. I wasn't always sure about the process (LOL), but I trusted that I was in good hands. Your insight and talent as an editor made this book even better.

Thanks to my hubs, Andrew, and my daughter, Chloe, for your support and patience.

Thanks to my mom and dad for being my earliest cheerleaders.

And thanks to the many, many readers that have read and embraced my work. I'm always in awe of the love you guys have shown me and my books. You make me proud to be a storyteller.